**A handmade happy-ever-after!**

# the
# Knitting
## diaries

Three heart-warming stories by bestselling authors
Debbie Macomber, Susan Mallery and
Christina Skye, where the path to true
love is stitched from yarn…

**Debbie Macomber** is a number one *New York Times* bestselling author. Her recent books include *44 Cranberry Point, 50 Harbor Street, 6 Rainier Drive* and *Hannah's List*. She has become a leading voice in women's fiction worldwide and her work has appeared on every major bestseller list. There are more than a hundred million copies of her books in print. For more information on Debbie and her books, visit www. DebbieMacomber.com.

*New York Times* bestselling author **Susan Mallery** has entertained millions of readers with her witty and emotional stories about women and the relationships that move them. *Publishers Weekly* calls Susan's prose 'luscious and provocative' and *Booklist* says, 'Novels don't get much better than Mallery's expert blend of emotional nuance, humour and superb storytelling.' While Susan appreciates the critical praise, she is most honoured by the enthusiastic readers who write to tell her that her books made them laugh, made them cry and made the world a happier place to live. Susan lives in Seattle with her husband and her tiny but intrepid toy poodle. She's there for the coffee, not the weather. Visit Susan on the web at www. susanmallery.com.

**Christina Skye** is the *New York Times* bestselling author of thirty-two books. She is a pushover for Harris tweed, Scottish cashmere, Chinese dumplings, French *macarons* and dark chocolate. Not necessarily in that order.

A classically trained China scholar with over two million books in print, she has appeared on various national television programmes, including *ABC Worldwide News, Travel News Network, The Travel Show with Arthur Frommer, Geraldo, Voice of America, Looking East,* and *Good Morning, Arizona*.

She generally has her knitting right beside her while she works. But don't expect speed. 'The sheer pleasure of colours and texture running through my fingers helps me concentrate on the mystery of characters coming alive before my eyes. Knitting pulls me to a quiet place where a story unfolds at its deepest level. It's my best writing tool.' Test-drive her knitting patterns at her website, where she explores the writer's path, the joys of knitting and details about all her upcoming books.

# the Knitting diaries

## Debbie Macomber

SUSAN MALLERY  CHRISTINA SKYE

Mills & Boon, an imprint of Harlequin (UK) Limited,
Eton House, 18-24 Paradise Road, Richmond, Surrey TW9 1SR

THE KNITTING DIARIES © Harlequin Enterprises II B.V./S.à.r.l. 2011

*The Twenty-First Wish* © Debbie Macomber 2011
*Coming Unravelled* © Susan Macias Redmond 2011
*Return to Summer Island* © Christina Skye 2011

ISBN: 978 0 263 90202 0

027-0912

Printed and bound by
CPI Group (UK) Ltd, Croydon, CR0 4YY

# The Twenty-First Wish

## DEBBIE MACOMBER

To
Candi Jensen
in gratitude for San Francisco yarn crawls,
wine on your back porch
and best of all
your friendship

Dear Friends,

The summer I turned twelve was the first time I picked up a pair of knitting needles. My mother wasn't a knitter and I pestered her all summer because I so badly wanted to learn. Mom finally broke down and took me to a yarn store, where those wonderful ladies patiently taught me. The first thing I made was a purple vest for my mother—as a thank-you because she found a way for me to knit.

I believe I inherited my love of craft from my Grandmother Adler, my father's mother, who died before I could have any memories of her. My older cousins have told me stories about Grandma sitting in her rocking chair, sound asleep and snoring while still crocheting. Yup, Grandma Adler was my kind of woman. Several of the pieces she crocheted have been passed down to us cousins and they are cherished treasures.

From the time I learned to knit until this very day, I've always had a project going. My writing career took a sharp turn upward after *The Shop on Blossom Street* was published. Combining my passions of knitting and writing was clearly what resonated so strongly with my readers. Knitting was and is an authentic part of my life.

When knitters get together, surprising things can happen, especially if those knitters also happen to be authors. The idea for this anthology came from Christina Skye, who is highly skilled as both a knitter and a writer. We were on a yarn crawl in San Francisco, driving from yarn store to yarn store with our friend Candi Jensen, when Christina casually said, 'We should think about writing a knitting anthology together.' We took the idea to our publisher and from that point forward it was a go. Susan Mallery is a new knitter, but she added some great ideas, so here we are.

I hope you enjoy *The Twenty-First Wish* and this return visit with characters from Blossom Street.

As always I love hearing from my readers. You can reach me at my website at www.DebbieMacomber.com or at PO Box 1458, Port Orchard, WA 98366, USA.
OK, needles ready…

*Debbie Macomber*

PS You might recognise Candi Jensen's name. She's the talented producer of the Emmy-nominated PBS series *Knit and Crochet Today* and one incredible knitter *and* crocheter.

## Courtney's Wedding Purse

**MATERIALS:**

100% Cashmere 2 ply. Jade Sapphire Exotic Fibers
100 yds color ivory.
Needles—U.S. 2, single point.
Beads (TOHO recommended)—Approximately
330 #08 silver-lined crystal, 14 #06 silver-lined
crystal, 2 accent crystals, 2 crystal hearts (to decorate
the ends of the I-cord). Optional lining for bag.

String 330 #08 Beads

Cast on 214 stitches.

Row 1. Working from wrong side:

TO BEAD ONE WORKING FROM WRONG
SIDE—Knit 1, slip next stitch as if to purl, slide
bead up next to needle, continue knitting.

* Knit 1—bead 1, repeat from * to last 2 stitches,
knit 2.

Row 2. * Knit 1—purl 4, repeat from * to end of row.

Row 3. * Knit 4—purl 1, repeat from * to end of row.

Row 4. Right side facing; knit 1—purl 2—place
bead—purl 2, to end of row.

TO PLACE BEAD BETWEEN STITCHES—
Purl next stitch, slide bead up to needle, purl next
stitch, continue knitting.

Row 5. Repeat row 3.

Row 6. * Knit 1—purl 2 tog—purl 2 tog, repeat from * to end of row.

Row 7. * Knit 2 tog—purl 1, repeat from * to end of row.

TO BEAD 1—Bring yarn to front of work, slip next stitch as if to purl, place bead next to stitch, bring yarn to back of work, leaving bead sitting in front of slipped stitch.

Row 8. Right side facing; Knit 2—bead 1, to last stitch, knit 1.

Row 9. Purl.

Row 10. Knit 1 * Yarn over (wrap 2 times), knit 2 tog. Continue from * to last stitch, knit 1.

Row 11. Purl 1—Purl into wrap, continue to last stitch, knit 1.

Row 12. Knit.

TO BEAD 1—Bring yarn to back of work, slip next stitch as if to purl, place bead next to needle, bring yarn forward, purl next stitch.

Row 13. Wrong side facing; Purl 1—bead 1, continue to last stitch. Purl 1.

Row 14. Knit.

Row 15. Purl.

Row 16. Knit 2 * bead 1—knit 5, continue from * to last 6 stitches, knit 6.

Rows 17, 19, 21, 23. Purl.

Row 18. Knit.

Row 20. Knit 5—bead 1, to last 3 stitches, knit 3.

Row 22. Knit.

REPEAT ROWS 16–23, until piece measures 4 inches from eyelet.

Knit 1—bead 1, to last stitch. Knit 1. Purl next row.

Knit 2—bead 1, to last 2 stitches. Knit 2. Purl next row.

Knit 1—bead 1, to last stitch. Knit 1. Purl next row.

**BASE:**

Row 1. Right side facing; Purl.

Row 2. Knit.

Row 3. Knit 7—Knit 2 tog, continue to end of row.

Rows 4, 6, 8, 10, 12, 14, 16: Knit.

Row 5. Knit 6—Knit 2 tog, continue to end of row.

Row 7. Knit 5—Knit 2 tog, continue to end of row.

Row 9. Knit 4—Knit 2 tog, continue to end of row.

Row 11. Knit 3—Knit 2 tog, continue to end of row.

Row 13. Knit 2—Knit 2 tog, continue to end of row.

Row 15. Knit 1—Knit 2 tog, continue to end of row.

Row 17. Knit 2 tog 6 times.

Cut yarn and pull through last 6 stitches.

## FINISHING:

Sew up base and side seams.

Knit 2 lengths of I-cord approximately 13 inches long.

Weave I-cord through eyelet. Double pull.

Trim ends of I-cord with 7 of the #06 beads, 1 accent crystal, 1 crystal heart.

Optional: Line bag.

# *One*

April 22

Today I sign the papers on our new house! I'm excited and exhausted and feel completely out of my element. I have so much still to do. I should've been finishing up the packing or cleaning the apartment before the movers arrived. But no. Instead, I sat down and began to knit. What was I thinking? Actually, knitting was *exactly* what I needed to do. Knitting always calms me, and at this point my nerves are frayed. I haven't moved in years and I'd forgotten how stressful it can be. Usually, I'm organized and in control, but today I'm not (even if I look as though I am). On the inside—and I don't mind admitting this—I'm a mess.

Mostly, I'm worried about Ellen. My ten-year-old has already had so much upheaval in her life. She feels secure in our tiny apartment. And it *is* tiny. It was just right for one small dog and me, but I never intended to stay here so long. When I moved into this space above the bookstore it was with the hope—the expectation—that Robert and I would reconcile. But the unthinkable happened and I lost my husband to a heart attack. After his funeral I remained here because making it from one day to the next was all I could deal with.

Then Ellen came into my life and it was obvious that two people and a dog, no matter how small, couldn't live comfortably in this minuscule space, although we managed for more than a year. I did make an earlier offer on a house but that didn't work out.

After bouncing from foster home to foster home, Ellen had ended up with her grandmother, who died when she was eight. So Ellen needed stability. She'd endured enough without having a move forced upon her so soon after the adoption.

In retrospect, I'm grateful that first house deal fell through, since it would've happened too fast for Ellen—although I was disappointed at the time. Even now, Ellen feels uneasy about leaving Blossom Street, although I've reassured her that we aren't *really* leaving. Blossom Street Books is still here and so is the apartment. The only thing that'll be different is that at the end of the workday, instead of walking up the stairs, we'll drive home.

Sitting in the office of the Seattle title company, Anne Marie Roche signed her name at the bottom of the last document. She leaned back and felt the tension ease from between her shoulder blades. As of this moment she was the proud owner of her own home. Today was the culmination of several months of effort. She smiled at the two sellers who sat across the table from her; they looked equally happy.

"Is the house ours now?" Ellen whispered as she tugged at the sleeve of Anne Marie's jacket.

"It is," she whispered back.

A few years ago Anne Marie had merely been going through the motions. Robert, her husband, had died, and she'd found herself a widow at the age of forty. She had no one in her life who loved her, no one she could love. All right, she had friends and family and she had her dog, Baxter, a Yorkie—admittedly a special dog—but Anne Marie needed *more,* wanted more. She'd craved the intense, focused, mutual love of a spouse, or a child of her own. Then she'd met Ellen through a volunteer program and they'd grown close. When Ellen's grandmother, Dolores, who'd been raising the girl, became seriously ill, Anne Marie had stepped in—at Dolores's urging. She'd taken over as the girl's foster mother and, after Dolores's death, adopted her. Dolores must have known she was reaching the end of her life, and when she saw how attached Ellen and Anne Marie were, she'd been able to die in peace, confident in the knowledge that her granddaughter would be safe and, above all, loved.

"You can cross finding a house off your list of twenty wishes," Ellen said, referring to the list Anne Marie had compiled with a group of widowed friends the year she'd met Ellen.

The child's straight brown hair brushed her shoulders, with a tiny red bow clipped at each temple. Her eyes were wide with expectation—and a little fear. Anne Marie hoped Ellen would quickly adjust to her new home and neighborhood, although Ellen kept insisting she liked her old one just fine.

"We want you to be as happy in this home as we've

been," Mr. Johnson, the previous owner, said. With a great deal of ceremony he and his wife handed the house key to Anne Marie. The Johnsons, an older couple who'd lived there for more than twenty years, planned to move to Arizona to spend their retirement near friends.

"I'm sure we will," Anne Marie said. She'd looked at a number of places and this was the first one that felt right, with its large backyard and spacious rooms. Ellen would be able to go to the school she currently attended, which Anne Marie considered a bonus.

She would do whatever she could to ensure that the transition would be a smooth one for her daughter. Ellen had made friends on Blossom Street, people she visited almost every day, and she could continue doing that. Her favorite stop was A Good Yarn, Lydia Goetz's store. Both Anne Marie and Ellen had learned to knit, thanks to Lydia.

"You *promise* I'll like the new house as much as Blossom Street?" Ellen asked with a skeptical frown.

"You're going to love having a big bedroom."

"I like my old bedroom," she said, lowering her head.

"Yes, but you'll like this one just as much." This was a conversation they'd had a number of times already. "And Baxter's going to enjoy racing around that big backyard, chasing butterflies."

The hint of a smile touched Ellen's face, and Anne Marie put her arm around the girl's shoulders. "Everything's going to be fine," she said. "You'll see."

Ellen nodded uncertainly.

Now that the paperwork had been completed, Anne Marie thanked the title agent, who'd been so helpful.

With the house keys safely inside her purse, she stood and reached for Ellen's hand. "Mel's taking us out for a celebratory lunch," she said on their way out the door.

"What's *celebratory* mean?"

"It means we have something to celebrate, and that's our brand-new home." New to them at any rate. She raised her voice to show how pleased she was that this day had finally arrived.

"What about Dad?"

"We'll see him later." Over the past few months, Anne Marie's relationship with Tim Carlsen had become… complicated. He was Ellen's biological father and hadn't known he had a daughter until after Anne Marie had adopted her. Tim had connected with Ellen through a long and indirect process. Anne Marie had reluctantly— very reluctantly—granted him permission to visit Ellen. Thankfully, Tim, who'd acknowledged his problems with drug and alcohol abuse, was now clean and sober. He'd turned his life around several years before, unlike Ellen's biological mother, who was still incarcerated. She'd surrendered her parental rights, which had made it possible for Anne Marie to adopt the child. It was only after Anne Marie saw how much Tim loved his daughter that she'd softened toward him. All too soon, a rosy, and completely unrealistic, picture had formed in her mind—the three of them together, as one happy family.

Then Tim had dropped his bombshell and that dream had been blown to smithereens. He was engaged to Vanessa, a woman he'd met at his AA meetings. Anne Marie had felt incredibly foolish even entertaining the notion of the two of them as a couple.

Shortly afterward she'd met Mel through her friend

Barbie. He was a widower, the same age Robert would have been—close to twenty years older than Anne Marie. Mel was a comfortable person, easy to be with, unthreatening and undemanding. He got along well with Ellen, too. They'd been dating for a few months, and while it wasn't a steamy romance or an exciting one, she was content.

Mel's attention had helped soothe her ego after the letdown she'd experienced with Tim. The ironic part was that shortly after she'd started seeing Mel, Tim and Vanessa had parted ways. After her disappointment with Tim, Anne Marie wasn't willing to make her heart vulnerable to him again. She'd made that clear and he'd accepted her decision. She let him see Ellen, however. Her daughter loved being part of her father's life and looked forward to spending time with him.

"Where's Mel taking us to celebrate?" Ellen asked as they rode the elevator down to the ground floor. There was a light drizzle outside, not unusual for April in Seattle. It wasn't heavy enough to warrant an umbrella, but damp enough to curl Anne Marie's naturally wavy hair.

"We're meeting him in Chinatown," Anne Marie answered.

"We're having Chinese?"

This was Ellen's all-time-favorite food. "Can I order chow mein with crispy noodles?" she asked.

"I'm sure you can." How thoughtful of Mel to remember Ellen's preference for Chinese cuisine. He really was a good man; she doubted there was anything he wouldn't do for her if she asked.

"What about almond fried chicken with extra gravy?"

"You'll need to discuss that with Mel." Once out on

the sidewalk, Anne Marie took Ellen's hand again, and with their heads bowed against the cold and the wind, they hurried toward the restaurant.

Mel was already there and had obtained a booth. A large pot of tea with three small ceramic cups rested in the center of the table. Anne Marie was grateful Mel had thought to order it.

He stood as they approached and leaned forward to kiss Anne Marie's cheek.

"Hello, Pumpkin," he said to Ellen.

"Hi, Punky," she returned with a giggle. Where Ellen had come up with that name for Mel, Anne Marie had no idea. Maybe her version of "pumpkin"? In any event, Anne Marie appreciated their relaxed, friendly relationship.

When the waitress arrived, they ordered far more food than they'd ever manage to eat.

While they waited for their lunch, Mel made conversation with Ellen. "This is perfect weather for Baxter to wear that sweater you knit him," he said.

Ellen had made her own list of twenty wishes, and learning to knit was one of them. Fortunately, Lydia's yarn shop was only a couple of doors down from the bookstore, and Lydia had encouraged Ellen's first efforts. With practice, Ellen had improved to the point that she was able to complete a sweater for Baxter.

"After lunch, would you like to show Mel the house?" Anne Marie prompted. She wanted Ellen to feel good about this move. Ellen had gone with Anne Marie to view various houses and had found something wrong with each one. It finally dawned on Anne Marie that Ellen simply didn't want to leave Blossom Street, which she should've realized from the start. The little girl wouldn't say so directly but she came up with convenient excuses to reject every home they'd seen—until this one. If Anne Marie had been more experienced as a parent she might have caught on earlier. But Ellen's resistance was the main reason she'd put off the search after the first deal fell through.

"Do you want to see the house?" Ellen asked Mel, sounding hesitant.

"I'd enjoy that, especially if you'd give me a personal tour."

Ellen glanced at Anne Marie.

"Mel would like you to show him around," Anne Marie explained.

"I can do that," Ellen said, revealing her first enthusiasm for their new home. "I know every room. Did Mom tell you I have a big closet of my own and my bedroom faces the backyard, so I can look out my window and watch Baxter? He likes to chase birds and butterflies and bugs. I won't have to take him for walks anymore because there's a fence…. I can just open the door and let him go out."

"True, but it's still a good idea to keep an eye on him," Anne Marie reminded her. "*And* to take him for walks."

Ellen nodded.

"I'll bet there are lots of kids your age in the new neighborhood," Mel said.

Anne Marie hoped that was the case, although she hadn't seen any.

Ellen toyed with her fork and plate, moving the fork around the plate's circumference. "I like my old neighborhood best," she muttered.

"But it's a retail one," Mel said.

Ellen looked quizzically at Anne Marie.

"He means there are shops on Blossom Street instead of houses."

"I *like* shops. I have friends there. Susannah lets me help her with the flowers in Susannah's Garden. Last week I stood out front of her store and gave away pink carnations. Baxter was with me."

"That was fun, wasn't it?"

Ellen nodded again. "And Alix sometimes brings me leftover croissants from the French Café across the street."

Laughing, Anne Marie brought her head close to Mel's and added, "That doesn't happen often because they sell out of croissants almost every day."

"I like them warm so the jelly gets runny on them," Ellen said. "Mom puts them in the microwave for me in the morning."

"I'll have to try that," Mel told her. "Sounds good."

"Lydia and Margaret are my friends, too." Ellen continued to list her favorite people on Blossom Street.

"Lydia owns A Good Yarn," Anne Marie pointed out to Mel.

"Yeah, I remember," he said.

"Lydia and Mom taught me to knit, and we knit every day, don't we, Mom?"

Before Anne Marie could respond, their food arrived. The conversation lagged as they passed around the serving plates. Mel asked for chopsticks, but Anne Marie and Ellen used forks—although Ellen proclaimed that she wanted to try chopsticks *next* time. She was just too hungry today.

"You have lots of friends, don't you?" Mel asked Ellen.

Mouth full, the girl nodded eagerly.

"But they're all adults. Do you have any friends from school on Blossom Street?"

After a short pause, Ellen said, "Cody and Casey, but they're older and they go to a different school than me."

Anne Marie could see that Mel was trying to help Ellen see all the possibilities that awaited her in her new home. She thanked him with a smile, and he clasped her hand beneath the table.

Half an hour later, when they couldn't eat another bite, Mel asked for the bill. Carrying their leftovers, Anne Marie and Ellen walked to the parking garage for their car. Mel drove to the house on his own.

Anne Marie and Ellen got there before him and after parking in the driveway, Anne Marie unlocked the front door, conscious that this was the first of many times. The inside looked different now that it was empty of furniture. The Johnsons had left the house meticulously clean, the floors scrubbed and polished and the walls freshly painted and unmarked.

Mel showed up soon afterward. "What a lovely house," he commented, stepping inside. He paused in the doorway to survey the hall and the living room.

"Come," Ellen said, grabbing his hand and tugging him toward the hallway. "My bedroom's this way."

"What about your mom's?" he asked, looking back at Anne Marie over his shoulder.

She nearly burst out laughing.

"Mom's across the hall from me," Ellen told him.

"*Directly* across the hall," Anne Marie said pointedly. Although they'd been dating for several months, their relationship hadn't gotten physical—not beyond kissing, anyway—although Anne Marie sensed that Mel was interested in taking it further.

While Ellen showed him the bedrooms and the other areas of the house, she put the leftover Chinese food in the otherwise empty refrigerator. The official move was the next day—Saturday morning. The movers would take care of the furniture, while friends and family had volunteered to bring over the boxes. Anne Marie hoped to get Ellen settled before the end of the school year, which would give her a chance to make friends in her neighborhood this summer.

She heard Ellen and Mel clattering down the hallway, their footsteps echoing.

"Do you want to see the kitchen?" Ellen was asking Mel.

"Of course. Will you cook me dinner one night?"

"I don't cook that good without Mom helping me."

"I bet she'd do it if you asked."

"Do you like macaroni and cheese?" Ellen asked. "I can make that in the microwave. It comes in a box."

"Ah…" Mel met Anne Marie's look as he entered the kitchen.

"I think Mel would be thrilled with whatever you cooked," she inserted smoothly, smothering a laugh when Mel rolled his eyes.

"I'll eat anything you decide to serve me," Mel agreed.

"Okay." Ellen nodded seriously. "A boy in my class brought chocolate-covered ants to school last week."

"Chocolate-covered ants?" Mel repeated.

"I didn't eat any," Ellen said, then explained, "There weren't enough for everyone."

"That's a shame," Mel said with obvious insincerity, although Ellen didn't seem to notice.

Ellen was about to say something else when the door-bell chimed.

Anne Marie shrugged, answering Mel's unspoken question. "I'm not expecting anyone," she said. It seemed a bit early for the neighbors to be introducing themselves. However, this could be a visit from a political candidate, as an election was coming up soon.

Ellen beat her to the door and threw it open. Even before Anne Marie could see who'd come calling, her daughter announced, "It's Dad!"

Anne Marie cast Mel an apologetic look. "Hello, Tim," she said cordially, standing behind Ellen.

"Hello." He smiled at his daughter. "How's my girl?"

"Good." Ellen beamed happily, always excited about seeing her father.

Tim gazed at Anne Marie, as if seeking confirmation that everything really was fine. His smile had a curious effect on her, which she did her best to ignore. She stood in the doorway, blocking his entry. "What can I do for you?" she asked politely, praying Mel would stay in the kitchen until Tim left.

His timing was bad. Mel already had a problem with Tim's coming around as much as he did, and Anne Marie didn't want him to think Tim stopped by whenever he felt like it. That wasn't the case; he generally made arrangements well in advance. Thank goodness, because she tried to keep the two men apart as much as possible.

"I can only stay for a few minutes," Tim said. "I came over to drop off a small housewarming gift."

"Oh." Anne Marie felt properly chastised—and a little embarrassed.

"Can I come in?" he asked.

"Oh—of course." She stepped aside to let him in as Ellen held the screen door, not hiding her delight.

# *Two*

April 22

Mom says I'll get used to my new house, but I won't. I keep telling her I like it right here on Blossom Street. Lydia said I'd have a big room all to myself and a closet, and that I'll make new friends. But I like my old friends. I don't want new ones. Baxter doesn't want to move, either. I told my dad I'd rather stay here and he said I might not like the new house now but I will later. He said I'd still have my friends on Blossom Street. Mom said that, too.… I'm not sure she really wants to move, either, because she's been knitting a lot and she knits real slow when she's worried about something. She doesn't think I pay attention but I do.

Tim decided he shouldn't have come to the house—not yet. Ellen had said Anne Marie was signing the final papers that day, so it was probably too soon. In their visit the previous weekend, he'd spent a lot of time reassuring his daughter that the move would be a good thing. He wondered how successful he'd been.

More than anything, Tim wanted to help Ellen make a comfortable transition to her new neighborhood. He'd picked up a plant for the yard, which he'd set on the porch. But the housewarming gift was just an excuse, and Anne Marie had seen through it right away.

Anne Marie.

He'd blown it with her, handled the situation between them poorly. His AA sponsor had repeatedly emphasized the importance of honesty, but Tim had been afraid that if he told Anne Marie he was engaged to Vanessa, she wouldn't let him see Ellen. Because his daughter meant everything to him, Tim had been afraid to take that risk. He'd have had to be blind not to see that Anne Marie was falling for him but he hadn't acknowledged it. Instead, he'd delayed telling her the truth, which was a passive— and dishonest—way of encouraging her.

Knowing her better now, Tim understood that Anne Marie would never have used the fact that he was involved with someone else as a pretext for keeping his daughter away from him. The irony was that his engagement hadn't lasted very long once Ellen—and Anne Marie—became part of his life.

Tim could hardly bear to think of his troubled past, his wasted years. Thank God for his family's support. It'd been an act of tough love for his parents to step back and allow him to self-destruct. As a parent himself, he knew that couldn't have been easy. But when he'd finally hit bottom, his family had been there, waiting. His mother and father were the first ones to offer him guidance and practical help.

They'd gotten him into a rehab center and from that moment on he hadn't looked back. He'd been sober ten years now. It was while he was trying to make restitution to the people he'd hurt that he learned he might have a child.

The discovery had shocked him, thrown him into a tailspin. That day was the closest he'd come in all those years to taking a drink.

Just after he'd entered rehab, Candy, the woman he'd been living with, had attempted to contact him. He'd ignored her phone calls once he became aware of them. He wasn't permitted to receive any outside calls while in rehab; the only reason he even knew she'd tried to reach him was the multiple messages she'd left on his cell phone. When he got his cell back, he deleted each one without listening. Candy belonged to his old life and he was starting fresh.

Later, she'd written him, but Tim wanted nothing to do with her, so he'd tossed out the letter, unopened and unread.

Not once did he suspect she might be pregnant.

Nine years later…he'd sought out Candy's mother to repay the money they'd stolen from her in order to buy booze and drugs. Back then, all Candy and Tim could think about was the next hit, the next drink. Time melded together, hours, days, weeks. Often he didn't know or care where he was or who he was with, as long as he could get drunk or high.

After rehab, Tim had wanted to repay the old woman and apologize. If he was ever going to become the man he hoped to be, that meant restitution. So he went to see Candy's mother. What he found was the house empty and listed for sale. The next-door neighbor told him Dolores had recently passed away.

Then she'd added that the granddaughter Dolores

had been raising had gone to live with a woman called Anne Marie.

A granddaughter, aged nine.

A chill had gone through Tim at those words. The timing was too coincidental to discount. That very minute he'd known. This granddaughter, this little girl, was *his* little girl.

His daughter.

Tim hadn't slept that night or the following one. Thankfully, the neighbor knew Anne Marie's full name, and after a couple of days to sort out his feelings and consider his options, he'd contacted her at the bookstore.

At first Anne Marie assumed Tim wanted to take Ellen away from her. The thought had actually crossed his mind. Ellen was his flesh and blood, so he should be the one to raise her. But he'd consulted an attorney and discovered he had no legal rights where Ellen was concerned.

Candy had signed away her parental rights, and the grandmother had stepped in. More shocking yet, Tim learned he wasn't even named on the birth certificate. After the old lady's death, Ellen became a ward of the state; when Anne Marie adopted her, he lost any chance of raising her, although a blood test proved that she was indeed his child.

It'd taken weeks of gently, carefully, proving himself to Anne Marie before she allowed him into their lives. The funny, wonderful part was that Ellen seemed to recognize almost from the first that he was her father. In fact, before he could tell her, she asked him outright.

He'd been so tongue-tied he hadn't been able to answer.

"I knew it," she'd said, and smiled happily. He'd nearly

dissolved into tears. So much for being manly and in control of his emotions.

That night Ellen showed him her list of twenty wishes. She explained that Anne Marie and her widowed friends had each made a list, so she had, too. One of her wishes was to meet her father, and now she had. She'd thrown her arms around his neck, hugging him tight.

From then on, Tim's relationship with Vanessa had gone steadily downhill. He realized it must've been hard on her to see him develop a relationship, no matter how innocent, with another woman. His sponsor had advised him to tell Anne Marie about Vanessa. He'd tried a couple of times and then, coward that he was, kept his trap shut. He *couldn't* lose Ellen. By then he was completely captivated by his daughter and refused to take the risk.

Then Vanessa had gotten drunk. After three years of sobriety, this awkward situation with Anne Marie had proved to be too much for her. Vanessa's second slip followed shortly thereafter, when Ellen broke her arm. Tim could see where this was going. Vanessa couldn't deal with such a complex relationship. That second slip was compounded by a third.

Tim broke off the relationship entirely, and frankly, he was glad he'd done it. Once he'd made that decision, he made another. He wanted to get involved with Anne Marie—only he was too late. By then she'd started dating Mel and was no longer interested in him.

He couldn't blame her.

Tim had met Mel a number of times and clearly the older man considered him competition. If that was the case, Tim didn't see it. Anne Marie was always polite but distant; whatever chance he'd had with her was over.

"You brought us a gift?" Ellen asked, looking eagerly around.

"Ellen." Anne Marie chastised her softly.

"It's a plant," Tim said. "On the porch."

"Thank you."

He heard the reserve in Anne Marie's voice. He stuck his hands in his pockets and was about to make his excuses and leave when Ellen asked, "Do you want to see the house? I gave Mel a tour. I can give you one, too."

Tim looked at Anne Marie, seeking her approval before he agreed. She nodded slightly.

"I'd like that very much."

His daughter closed the screen door behind him.

He trailed her into the living room and stopped when he saw Mel standing there, arms crossed. The other man didn't need to say anything to convey the fact that he wasn't keen on Tim's presence at the house.

"Hello, Mel," he said. He offered his hand, and Mel accepted.

"Good to see you again," Tim said, although that was an exaggeration.

"You, too." Mel's returning comment lacked sincerity, at least in Tim's opinion.

"This way, Daddy," Ellen said, grabbing his hand. "I want to show you my bedroom."

Tim followed his daughter to one of the closed doors. Ellen opened it and spread her arms wide. "See how big my room is?"

He stood with his hands on his hips. "Where do you want your bed?" he asked, relieved that she seemed more enthusiastic about the house.

"By the window."

Clearly she'd given the matter some thought.

"Then I can stand on it and watch Baxter play in the yard."

"Good idea."

"And my dresser will go over here." She bounded to the far side of the room to show him.

"Where are you going to put all your books?" The ten-year-old had more books than any kid he knew, which made sense since Anne Marie owned a bookstore.

"Mom's buying me my own bookcase and I want to keep it over there." She pointed at the wall across from the window.

Ellen was a bright child who loved to read; he was pleased she enjoyed books as much as he did. Tim had been a voracious reader from the time he was old enough to hold one in his hands. That wasn't the only interest he shared with his daughter and Anne Marie. They all seemed to love playing board games and being around the water, to name two.

He and Ellen spoke for a few more minutes and Tim knew he should leave. As it was, he'd trespassed on Mel's time with her and Anne Marie.

"So when's the big moving day?" he asked once he'd joined the others.

"Tomorrow," Anne Marie said.

"Need help?"

"Not really."

He doubted she'd be interested in any assistance from him but had wanted to ask, just in case.

"A big truck is coming for the furniture," Ellen said, "but all our friends from Blossom Street are helping us move the boxes."

"I've got muscles." Tim bent his elbow and flexed his biceps. "See? I can lift boxes, too. Many hands make for a lighter load," he said, misquoting a saying he didn't quite remember. "Or something like that."

"Can Dad help us move?" Ellen asked excitedly.

"I don't think so, Pumpkin," Mel answered.

Tim recognized the other man's mistake even before Mel did. Mel apparently hadn't realized that Anne Marie didn't like anyone else speaking for her.

Which was no doubt why she'd changed her mind about allowing him to be involved.

"The more helpers we have, the less work," she said.

"*I'll* be here," Mel said, as if that would make all the difference.

Anne Marie ignored his remark. "If you're available, Tim, Ellen and I gladly accept your offer," she said. "Thank you."

"Just tell me what time and I'll be there." He resisted the urge to gloat. It would be poor sportsmanship, so he didn't, but he certainly felt like it.

Mel narrowed his eyes. "What might be more helpful is if you took Ellen for the day," he suggested. "She'll get in the way—"

"I want to be with my friends," Ellen protested, interrupting him.

"I want Ellen with me," Anne Marie said emphatically.

"What about Baxter?" Mel asked, a bit irritated now. "Surely you don't want the dog underfoot? Maybe Tim could take him."

"I've already arranged for someone to look after Baxter." Anne Marie obviously wasn't pleased with the way Mel had taken control. Tim hadn't known her long but he was well aware of her capable nature—and her independence.

"I should've known you'd be on top of things," Mel said, apparently trying to make amends, although his compliment sounded grudging.

An awkward silence stretched between them. Ready to leave, Tim reached inside his pants pocket for his car keys. "I'd better get back to the office before my dad wonders where I am." Tim worked as a broker at his father's insurance agency.

"Yes, good idea," Mel said.

"Mel," Anne Marie whispered.

Taking the hint, Mel stepped forward. "It's time I left, as well."

Anne Marie and Ellen walked them both to the door. "Thank you for lunch, Mel. That was a special treat."

"Thank you," Ellen echoed.

"Would you like to take the leftovers home?" Anne Marie asked.

"No, you and Ellen keep them." Then, with a sideways look at Tim, Mel announced, "Ellen's favorite is chicken chow mein with crispy noodles."

So that was how it was going to be. Mel was telling Tim he knew more about his daughter than Tim did. Tim felt his anger rise, but before he could respond, he inhaled a deep, calming breath and let the comment pass.

"Thank you, Tim, for the rhododendron," Anne Marie said next. "I'll plant it right away."

"I'll plant it for you," Mel said.

Apparently, Mel was a slow learner, Tim thought. By now he should know better than to leap in and answer for Anne Marie.

He could predict her response.

"No, thank you, Mel. I'll do it." Anne Marie cast them both a warning look.

"Bye, Daddy. Bye, Punky," Ellen said.

Mel's face lit up triumphantly. He turned and started toward his car. Tim had parked behind him.

"She calls me Punky," he said as they headed down the driveway together.

"Punky," Tim repeated, suppressing a laugh. "Where did she come up with that?"

Mel shrugged. "I don't know. I didn't ask."

Not to be outdone, Tim said, "Ellen has a special name for me, too."

"Oh?" Mel didn't look as though he believed him.

"She calls me Daddy."

With that, Tim opened his car door, slipped inside and drove off.

# *Three*

## April 23

Moving day. I'm so thankful for all the friends who offered to help. I've been talking to Ellen about this move for weeks, describing it in positive terms. Yesterday evening, when I tucked her into bed at the apartment for the last time, I compared the move to starting a new knitting project. Even though it can be exciting and fun, it's a little scary, too. There's a lot of work involved and sometimes you make mistakes, but when you're finished you have something that didn't exist before. Something beautiful. This was an analogy Ellen could understand. We've both completed our current knitting projects, so we'll begin new ones. The timing's perfect. A new house. A new neighborhood for Ellen to explore. And a new knitting project.

"Ellen," Anne Marie called, walking from room to room in their small apartment. "Where are you?"

"Here, Mom." Ellen emerged from her bedroom, dragging her backpack.

Anne Marie knew Ellen had placed her most precious items inside the backpack instead of entrusting them to a box for someone else to transport. She had her knitting and her list of twenty wishes, along with a framed photograph of her grandmother and a book of poems Tim had given her. From the obvious weight of the knapsack, she'd stuffed other things in it, as well. Anne Marie hadn't checked; she was busy enough doing her own last-minute packing.

"Tim's here," Anne Marie told her. Of all the friends who'd offered to help, he was the first to arrive.

After knocking once, he'd let himself into the apartment. "How are my girls this morning?" he asked cheerfully. He held a take-out coffee in one hand and wore blue jeans and a sweatshirt with the Mariners logo on the front. Both Tim and Ellen enjoyed baseball and declared themselves to be diehard Mariners fans.

"Girls?" Anne Marie repeated, one eyebrow cocked.

"How's my *girl?*" he corrected, and seemed rather amused with himself.

"Daddy!" Ellen raced to her father as if she hadn't seen him in at least a month rather than the day before.

After setting his coffee on the kitchen counter, Tim caught Ellen and lifted her up for a hug.

Anne Marie looked away. She was happy Ellen had found her father and grateful for the affectionate relationship between them. Still, moments like this were hard to watch for reasons she couldn't—or didn't want to—identify. Finding him had been one of the girl's wishes, which had prompted Anne Marie to allow the former addict into their lives. She could tell he genuinely loved the child.

"I brought my truck," Tim said when he'd put Ellen back on the floor. "I can start taking down boxes if you like."

"Can I ride over to the new house with you?" Ellen asked.

"That's up to your mom."

Anne Marie appreciated the fact that he'd acquiesced to her authority. "Fine by me. The others will be here any minute."

She had plenty of volunteers—so many she'd had to turn some down. Her stepchildren, Melissa and Brandon, and Melissa's husband, Michael, had offered, too. But they lived quite far away these days and she didn't want to inconvenience them.

In her usual organized fashion, Anne Marie had carefully planned the move. She'd decided her friends would transport the boxes before the hired movers showed up. Whatever didn't fit in Tim's truck would go in their individual cars. With Lydia's husband and family helping, Winter and Pierre from the French Café, plus Tim and his truck, Anne Marie thought it would only take one trip. They'd have lunch while the movers hauled the furniture from the apartment to the house, and after the truck had left, her small crew of friends would place the boxes in the appropriate rooms.

Tim sipped his coffee. "Where's…?" He didn't finish his question.

"Mel is stopping by after lunch. He had an appointment with a couple of out-of-town clients this morning." Mel owned a thriving architectural firm and often met with clients on weekends.

She held her breath, waiting for some derogatory retort from Tim, which never came. She was relieved he'd kept his opinion to himself. Honestly, those two men could be as bad as junkyard dogs, so intent on challenging each other. Anne Marie sometimes felt like a scrap of food they were competing for. Her one hope was that Ellen didn't sense the undercurrents between Mel and Tim. If she did, she hadn't said anything.

"Alix has Baxter for the day," Ellen explained to her father, obviously missing her adored dog.

"That's good, don't you think?" Tim asked.

Ellen shrugged. "I guess."

"He might get lost or stepped on by someone if he was here. And you know Alix will take great care of him."

"Alix and Jordan promised to bring him to the house this afternoon," Anne Marie said. "Then Baxter can help you unpack your bedroom."

Ellen nodded, but it was plain to see that she wasn't happy to have Baxter with someone else, even someone she knew and trusted.

Within ten minutes, the Goetz family arrived. Brad, Cody and Casey ran energetically up the stairs; Lydia hadn't been able to leave the store, as Saturday was one of her busiest times. Soon, with Anne Marie doling out instructions, they hauled boxes down to Tim's truck. Pierre and Winter followed five minutes later.

"Winter won't be lifting anything," Pierre said.

*"Pierre,"* she muttered under her breath, looking slightly embarrassed.

Her husband replied in French. Anne Marie had been to France and had taken a few lessons, but he spoke far too quickly for her to understand. The one word that leaped out, though, was *bébé*.

"You're pregnant?" Anne Marie clapped her hands in delight. "That's fantastic!"

Winter smiled. "We just found out last week."

His expression proud, Pierre slipped his arm around his wife's waist. "We're due in early December," he said. "Just in time for Christmas," he added with a grin.

"Congratulations!"

Winter elbowed her husband. "We weren't going to say anything until after the first trimester, but apparently Pierre forgot about our agreement."

Again he replied in French, and whatever he said made Winter laugh and hug him. "I should've known it would be too hard for him to keep quiet. He said he can't resist telling everyone because he's so excited."

"As he should be."

"Since Pierre doesn't want me to lift anything, I'll volunteer to prepare lunch."

Anne Marie had planned to purchase pizza or chicken wings, but she certainly wasn't turning down Winter's offer. "That would be wonderful."

"Okay, let me go back to the café and get started. Sandwiches okay?"

"Your sandwiches? Better than okay!"

Soon after Winter had left, Lillie and Hector came up the stairs. Anne Marie had met Lillie and her daughter, Barbie, through the reading group she'd held at the bookstore. They were both widows and had compiled their own lists of twenty wishes. Shortly afterward, Lillie had met Hector. They were dissimilar in superficial ways but alike in the ways that mattered and had fallen in love. Anne Marie assumed they'd eventually get married.

"We're here to help," Lillie said, "even though we're not on the official duty roster." She wore a man-size faded blue shirt with the sleeves rolled up past her elbows and jeans with white tennis shoes. Nevertheless, she looked as elegant as she always did. "Oh, Barbie and Mark send you their best," she added. Barbie, who owned an upscale dress shop, had recently married Mark Bassett, the man she'd met around the same time Lillie and Hector had begun their relationship.

"Shall we begin?" Pierre said. "*Allons-y*. Or in English, let's go."

Anne Marie wanted to do her share of the physical work, but she was needed to supervise and direct traffic. With so many people helping it didn't take long for everything to be loaded. Winter had coffee and pastries delivered from the café and during their break, Ellen sat next to Tim, keeping her backpack close to her side.

Since they had a quiet moment, Anne Marie asked Tim, "Would you mind looking after Ellen next weekend?"

"Sure. I don't have anything planned."

"Mel is taking Mom to see *Jersey Boys* at the 5th Avenue Theater," Ellen informed him.

"Oh." His gaze held Anne Marie's. "I'll be happy to stay with Ellen."

"Thank you. I—"

Her cell phone chirped and she glanced quickly at call display. Seeing that it was Mel, she walked over to the kitchen sink, turning her back to Tim and the others.

"Hi," she said in a low voice.

"Hi. How's everything going?"

"Great. We're on a break. The boxes are all loaded and ready to go, and once the van shows up I'm out of here."

"Listen, it looks like this meeting might go longer than I realized. I can't tell you how bad I feel about letting you down."

"Mel, please, we've got lots of people. You aren't letting me down. There's no reason to apologize. I understand."

"I'll come as soon as I can."

"Yes, but take all the time you need with your clients."

"Okay." His voice was regretful. "I'll see you later, then." When she shut off her phone she could feel Tim's eyes on her. She didn't explain the call; it simply wasn't his business.

Once they'd all headed over to the house and the moving van arrived, the rest of the morning passed in a blur of activity. While the two professional movers carried the furniture inside and set it in the various rooms according to Anne Marie's instructions, Winter came over with lunch. The small work party sat on blankets spread out on the lawn and enjoyed their soup and sandwiches—croissants with tuna, smoked salmon and turkey fillings.

Tim brought Anne Marie a small container of cream of mushroom soup, which she refused. "No, thanks. Don't have time." She continued to direct the movers.

"Save it for later."

"Okay." She was hungry but she had more important things to deal with.

When the movers were finished, her friends unloaded the boxes, piling them in their designated rooms.

"Can Baxter come home now?" Ellen asked when they were done for the day.

Anne Marie phoned Alix and Jordan, who drove to the house with their infant son—and the dog—half an hour later.

"Baxter!" Ellen crouched down and held out her arms. The Yorkie didn't need any encouragement; he ran toward Ellen at top speed, leaped into her waiting arms and licked her face frantically.

Soon the only volunteer left was Tim. Alix and Jordan went home. Brad had to take Cody to baseball practice and Casey wanted to be dropped off to spend time with Lydia's mother at the assisted-living complex. The girl had grown close to her adoptive grandmother, which Anne Marie knew would benefit them both. Hector and Lillie had plans with his family that afternoon and Pierre had to go to work. Anne Marie thanked them all. She'd been blessed with generous friends. Exceptional friends.

Ellen had gone to her room; Tim lingered. "Anything you need me to do?" he asked.

She shook her head. She'd prefer it if Tim wasn't around when Mel arrived.

"Baxter!" Ellen suddenly yelled. Looking upset, she dashed out of her bedroom. "Where's Baxter?"

"I thought you put him outside," Tim said.

"I did, but he isn't in the backyard!"

"You didn't let him inside, did you?" Tim asked Anne Marie.

"No. He must be in the yard," she said. "There isn't anywhere else." He was probably asleep under the apple tree and Ellen hadn't noticed.

The three of them hurried into the yard.

Baxter was nowhere to be seen.

Tim walked along the fence and squatted down to examine it, concentrating on the side that led to the alley. He raised his head and waved at Anne Marie.

She ran over. "What?" she asked fearfully, her heart pounding as she crossed her arms over her chest. She knew what he was about to tell her.

"Looks like he dug a hole under the fence."

"Baxter!" Ellen wailed. "We *have* to find Baxter."

Tim tried to soothe her plaintive cries as he hugged his daughter tight. "We will, sweetheart," he murmured. "Don't you worry, we'll find him."

# *Four*

April 23

Baxter's missing! We have to find him. I want my Baxter.

"We have to go after him!" Tim could hear the panic in Anne Marie's voice. Ellen had run back outside, clutching the dog's leash.

"He couldn't have gotten far," Tim said. "You two go search for him and I'll stay here in case he comes back."

Anne Marie seemed uncertain. Normally she liked to be in charge but she'd gone pale and was obviously as upset as Ellen.

"Go," he urged. "He's got to be close by. He's probably confused and can't find his way back."

His own thoughts were tumbling over each other. Someone could easily take a dog as cute and friendly as Baxter. Or maybe he'd tried to return to the familiar territory of Blossom Street; Tim had heard of such things.

Ellen herself felt that Blossom Street would always be her real home. The apartment represented safety and security to her and she couldn't yet imagine feeling that way anywhere else.

"Come with me," Anne Marie said, decisive now as she reached for Ellen's hand. "We'll find Baxter."

"Of course you will," Tim confirmed, hoping his words lent them both confidence.

"He's wearing the green sweater I knit him," she whispered. "And his collar."

Anne Marie nodded. "Yes! And he has all his tags."

"That'll make it easier to locate him," Tim said. "People won't forget seeing a cute dog wearing a green hand-knit sweater—plus he's got ID. Just you wait. He'll be home in no time."

While Anne Marie and Ellen scoured the neighborhood, Tim went inside the house. Baxter might have gone into one of the still-empty rooms and fallen asleep.

He did a thorough walk-through of the house, checking every closet and behind every door.

No Baxter.

He returned to the backyard and once again walked all the way around. Still no Baxter. When he examined the hole beneath the fence, he found a piece of green fuzz. So, as he'd guessed, Baxter had slipped through that hole. He got a board from the garage and immediately blocked the escape route.

When he'd finished, Tim started pacing. He regretted now that he hadn't gone with Anne Marie and Ellen. He couldn't tolerate this anxiety, and his fears, for Ellen in particular, tormented him.

When his cell phone rang, he grabbed it so fast it nearly sprang out of his hands. Some quick juggling saved it from falling onto the lawn. "Hello," he said loudly, certain it must be Anne Marie with news.

"You sound mighty eager to hear from me." Mel, and his tone was sardonic.

Tim's shoulders sagged with disappointment. "What do you want?" he asked, not bothering to disguise his dislike of the other man. Actually, Mel was all right, and in other circumstances they'd probably get along fine. But, in his opinion, the fiftysomething architect was too old for Anne Marie. Then again, she seemed to prefer older men; her husband, Robert, had been about the same age. This could all be a lost cause, he reminded himself, feeling even more discouraged.

"I called to talk to you," Mel told him.

"How'd you get my number?" Tim demanded.

"Why are *you* in such a bad mood?"

Tim sighed; he was taking his frustration out on Mel. "Okay, I apologize. What's the problem?"

"No problem, and in answer to your question—"

"What question?"

"How I got your phone number."

"Yeah?"

"From Anne Marie."

Anne Marie? That didn't make sense.

"A few weeks ago her battery was dead, and Ellen was with you, so she borrowed my phone. Your number's on my call log."

"Okay." He remembered the occasion, since Mel's number had come up on *his* phone. "This isn't a good time," he said. "I'll tell Anne Marie you called." Maybe. Mel considered Tim competition, as well he should. And vice versa... Tim had ruined his chances with Anne Marie, but he was working hard to win her back, although that was difficult with Mel in the picture.

"Is she around?" Mel asked, disregarding Tim's comment.

"No," he said curtly. "Baxter's missing."

Mel exhaled audibly. "Oh, great. I suppose Anne Marie and Ellen are in a real panic."

"They're looking for him now. I'm waiting at the house in case Baxter comes back here."

"So you're still there. I thought you would be," he said cynically, "especially since I got delayed."

"Listen, I really don't have time for this. Like I told you, Baxter's lost and Anne Marie and Ellen are out looking for him."

"When did the dog go missing?"

Tim glanced at his watch. "Thirty minutes ago, maybe forty." It felt much longer.

"Who let him get out?" Mel asked in an accusatory voice, as if Tim was personally responsible for what had happened.

"No one," he snapped, allowing his irritation to show. "Baxter either dug a hole under the fence or found it there."

"Shouldn't someone have been keeping a closer eye on him?"

"Yes, probably, but the deed is done. There's no point in looking for someone to blame."

"Poor Ellen," Mel said kindly.

Anne Marie wouldn't take the loss of her pet lightly, either. Increasingly on edge, all Tim wanted was to get off the phone. "What can I do for you?" he asked brusquely. "I don't want to tie up the line in case Anne Marie needs to get hold of me." And why was Mel calling him in the first place?

"It's about Anne Marie," Mel said, his voice serious.

"What about her?" Tim could almost feel what was coming.

"She's dating me, not you. Do you understand?"

"Oh, I understand, all right." Tim didn't even try to keep the derision out of his voice.

"I know she had feelings for you at one time, but that's over. I'm in the picture now."

"And you're telling me this why?" What went on between him and Anne Marie was none of Mel's business, nor was her relationship with Mel any of his.

Tim started to pace the lawn once more, the phone still pressed to his ear.

"I don't like the fact that you hang around Anne Marie and Ellen so much."

"Fine, whatever. But you need to understand something, too, Mel. Ellen is my daughter and I have every intention of being part of her life. Nothing you say or do is going to change that."

"I have no objection to you being part of Ellen's life."

"Big of you." This time his words dripped with sarcasm.

Mel disregarded his slight. "I just felt it was a good idea for the two of us to clear the air."

"The air is already clear," Tim said. He clenched his fist at his side. "The only reason I see Anne Marie is because of Ellen. If it wasn't for my daughter, I wouldn't be anywhere near her." In fact, if it wasn't for Ellen, he wouldn't even know Anne Marie.

Just as he turned the corner of the house, he came to an abrupt halt as he almost walked straight into Anne Marie. One glance at her face, and he knew she'd heard every word of his last statement.

"I have to go." Not bothering to explain further, he snapped his cell phone shut.

"Daddy! We found Baxter!" Ellen dashed toward him, clutching Baxter's leash, the dog at her heels.

Tim had been too unnerved to even notice them. Anne Marie held his gaze, her eyes narrowed and filled with—was that pain? He opened his mouth to speak and realized that anything he said now would only make matters worse.

"Daddy, guess what?"

"What?" he asked, without looking in his daughter's direction. His focus was on Anne Marie as she blinked rapidly, then turned and walked into the house.

"I met a girl named April and she lives down the street. I met her at the flower shop. Baxter was with her."

Tim started toward the house, wanting to at least *try* to talk to Anne Marie.

"April's my age, too."

"That's nice, sweetheart."

Ellen grabbed his shirt. "That's not all."

"You mean there's more?" Obviously excited, Ellen smiled up at him. Although his heart was racing with dread, he gave the girl his full attention.

"She has a dog, too."

"Named Baxter?"

"No, silly! Her name is Iris and she's a Yorkie, just like Baxter."

"You have a new friend and so does Baxter," he said, pleased for his daughter and worried about Anne Marie at the same time.

"April wants me to teach her how to knit."

"That's great. I need to talk to your mother now, all right?"

"Okay. April's going to ask her mother if she can come over and help me finish unpacking my bedroom. She likes books, too."

Tim hugged his daughter, grateful that she'd found a new friend. He hurried toward the house, leaping up the front steps. "Anne Marie?" he called when he didn't see her.

She came into the hallway, her arms crossed. "You don't need to explain. You made it fairly evident that your only interest is in Ellen, and I accept that."

Tim shook his head. "Not true."

"Who was that, anyway? Vanessa?"

"I haven't seen Vanessa in months. We're finished. It was Mel."

Her eyes widened in shock. "Why? Was he looking for you—or me?"

"I told him I'd pass on the message that he phoned," Tim said, skirting the truth but not lying, either. Not exactly.

Tim struggled to find a way to tell Anne Marie that he cared for her as well as Ellen. He wanted to confess how foolish he'd been not to recognize his own feelings. Now that he had, it seemed too late.

"Tim, listen, it's okay," she said. "Ellen loves you and you love her. I won't stand between you. Our daughter is all that matters, and what goes on between the two of us isn't important. Now, if you'll excuse me, I need to unpack."

"Can I help?" He didn't want to leave. In fact, he was willing to do just about anything to stay.

"No." She marched to the door and held it open for him. "Thank you for everything you did today. I appreciate it, but I want you to go now."

He nodded. Without further argument, he walked to the door—and then hesitated. "Can we talk about this?"

"No." Her denial was flat.

He nodded again, although he wished he could explain that hurting her was the last thing he wanted to do. Every time he was with Anne Marie, he realized how important she was to him. He'd learned a lot about life in his AA meetings, a lot about himself, too. He knew better, but he'd let his pride take over. Mel had gotten to him and he'd lashed back—with unintended consequences. Serious consequences.

He had the distinct feeling that he'd just ruined whatever chance he might still have had with Anne Marie.

# Five

April 25

My friend Lydia Goetz once told me there are two kinds of knitters in the world. Those who find tangled yarn a challenge and will spend hours restoring it and those who'd rather throw out the whole thing than deal with the mess. I haven't quite decided which type I am. What I will say is that I feel like my life's a tangled mess but instead of knotted yarn it's my emotions. I thought I was over Tim. Completely over him. I assumed nothing he said would have the power to hurt me. I was wrong. When I heard him say the only reason he had anything to do with me was because of Ellen I actually stopped breathing. I was incapable of drawing in air—it hurt that much. It still hurts, and that angers me even more. I have emotionally removed myself from him.

Monday afternoon, Anne Marie walked back from the French Café where she'd had lunch. As she crossed the street she saw that Lydia was inside A Good Yarn. The shop was technically closed on Mondays, but Lydia was often there catching up on paperwork.

What she needed, Anne Marie told herself, was a talk with a good friend, and there was no better friend than Lydia Goetz.

Walking all the way through the bookstore, she came out in the alley behind the yarn shop. She knocked at the back door and a moment later, Lydia unlocked it, smiling when she saw Anne Marie.

"Do you have time for a cup of tea?" Anne Marie realized she sounded wistful.

Lydia's shoulders relaxed. "I was just thinking that. Come on in."

Anne Marie followed her through the back of the store where boxes of yarn waited to be unpacked.

"How did the move go?" Lydia asked.

"So smoothly I could hardly believe it. I really appreciate Brad's and the kids' help."

"They loved it, especially Casey. She's been moved from one family to the next all her life and never had more than a suitcase. She found it…interesting that two people could accumulate so much stuff."

Anne Marie groaned. "That's not the end of it, either. I have an entire storage unit that still needs to be emptied." The move to the apartment three years earlier was only meant to be temporary.

While she was married to Robert, Anne Marie had left over a disagreement regarding children. She'd wanted a family and, as the father of a grown son and daughter, he hadn't. When neither of them was willing to budge, they'd separated. To be fair to Robert, Anne Marie had agreed to no kids when she'd married him. Over the years, however, her feelings had changed.

Unfortunately, Robert had remained adamant. No children. When they'd reached that impasse, she'd moved into the small apartment above the bookstore—her way of letting her husband know she was serious. She wanted a family. Children of her own.

Then Robert had a heart attack and was gone, and with him, her dream of bearing a child. It was while she'd been dealing with her grief that she'd met several other widows; one Valentine's night, they'd made those lists of twenty wishes.

As one of her wishes—to do something for someone else—she'd volunteered at the local grade school and been paired with Ellen. Although she was doing well academically, Ellen had been extremely shy. Anne Marie became her "lunch buddy," and that was how everything began, how both their lives had been transformed.

Lydia filled the kettle and plugged it in, then reached for her knitting. "Well, I'm glad it all went well."

"Tim was a big help, too," Anne Marie commented, mesmerized by the way her friend knit, gracefully weaving the yarn around the needles, creating what appeared to be a child's sweater, one knit in the round from the top down.

"I heard Tim was there, but Mel didn't show up."

"He was with clients," Anne Marie explained, wondering what her friend knew.

"Casey likes Tim. She said his red truck was cool."

Anne Marie remembered how eager Casey had been to ride with Tim and Ellen on the way to the house. Tim had agreed, which thrilled Ellen, who admired the older girl.

"We had a scare Saturday afternoon when Baxter went missing," she said, "but it actually worked out well."

Lydia looked up in alarm. "Missing? You got him back, right?"

The kettle whistled and she set aside her knitting.

As she took two mugs from the cupboard and poured hot water over the tea bags, Anne Marie clarified her remark. "Ellen and I were out looking for Baxter and, yes, we did get him back—thank goodness. We also came across a flower shop and a bakery."

Lydia brought the tea to the small table, along with sugar and milk. "It sounds just like Blossom Street."

Anne Marie thanked her for the tea, added milk, then sat back. "Well, not *exactly* like Blossom Street, but close enough for Ellen to realize her new neighborhood isn't so different from her old one. She made a new friend, too— the girl who actually found Baxter—and, as it happens, April has a dog. Another Yorkie."

"You couldn't have arranged that more perfectly if you'd tried," Lydia said with a smile.

"I know." Anne Marie stared down at her tea. "Anything new on Blossom Street?" Ellen wasn't the only one who was going to miss living here. She'd still be working here, but—despite what she'd told Ellen—it wasn't quite the same.

"I saw Bethanne Hamlin on Saturday—and she had news."

"Oh? What?" Anne Marie sipped her tea. Bethanne frequented the yarn shop and was a good friend of both Lydia and Anne Marie. She ran a highly successful party business that she'd started shortly after her divorce and often visited the bookstore.

"Bethanne told me that Andrew and Courtney Pulanski are engaged."

"That's wonderful! When's the wedding?"

"Mid-July."

Anne Marie had never met Courtney, although she'd heard plenty about her. Bethanne's son, Andrew, and Courtney had been dating for several years; they'd met in their senior year of high school, after Bethanne and Courtney had taken one of Lydia's knitting classes.

"Bethanne's knitting Courtney a pair of beaded finger-less gloves for the wedding. I special-ordered the yarn," Lydia told her. "Cashmere."

"She's such an accomplished knitter," Anne Marie added. "I'm sure the gloves will become a family heir-loom."

"Me, too," Lydia said.

Anne Marie put down her cup. She searched for a way to broach the subject that had been weighing on her mind all weekend. She'd unpacked boxes late into the night on Saturday and fallen into bed exhausted. Tired though she was, she'd been unable to sleep.

All thanks to Tim Carlsen.

"Did anything else happen on Saturday?" Lydia asked after a moment of silence.

"You could say that."

"Between you and Tim?"

Anne Marie's head shot up. "How'd you know that?"

Lydia shrugged, her smile sympathetic. "Call it a lucky guess."

Anne Marie exhaled slowly and picked up her tea, needing something to do with her hands. "I overheard a conversation he was having on his cell. As it turned out, he was talking to Mel, although he never really said why—other than to pass on the message that Mel called." She paused. "At first I thought it might've been Vanessa."

"The woman he was engaged to?"

Anne Marie nodded. "He told Mel the only reason he had anything to do with me was because of Ellen."

"Ouch." Lydia winced, not even attempting to minimize the hurt his words had inflicted.

Anne Marie looked away rather than reveal how upset she was.

"Why would he say this to Mel?"

"All I can think is that Mel phoned to clear the air. When I talked to him later, he didn't mention it. But he and Tim are constantly goading each other. It's ridiculous."

"So Mel decided to set matters straight?"

"Apparently."

"And I assume Tim was basically assuring him he had no interest in you," Lydia said.

"That seems to be the case."

"And that upsets you?"

More than Anne Marie ever dreamed it would.

"You still care about him, don't you?"

"No." Her denial was quick and emphatic. "How could I after everything he's said and done?"

"How could you?" Lydia repeated, then leaned forward and pressed Anne Marie's hand. "Well, first of all, the two of you have a strong bond in Ellen. She means the world to you both."

"True."

"He's hardworking, funny, sincere and darn good-looking."

All of that was accurate enough, especially the good-looking part. Tim was an attractive man; it wasn't as if Anne Marie hadn't noticed. When they'd first started seeing each other—while he'd been engaged to Vanessa and she hadn't known it—they'd had such fun together. He'd been wonderful to her and to Ellen. They'd gone on several outings, the three of them, and she'd grown close to Tim. He was easy to talk to, and before she realized what was happening, she'd fallen for him and fallen hard. She'd never let him know that, although he'd probably guessed.

The one and only time Tim had asked Anne Marie out to dinner without Ellen had been to tell her about his relationship with Vanessa.

The news had shaken her badly. When she'd had the opportunity to meet the woman who was going to become Ellen's stepmother, it had gone poorly. Vanessa, who'd taken an instant dislike to Anne Marie, had made her as uncomfortable as possible.

When Tim had announced that his relationship with Vanessa was over, it was too late. Anne Marie couldn't— wouldn't—trust him again. She wasn't willing to give him a second chance. She'd assumed that she'd completely recovered from her infatuation with Ellen's father. And then she'd overheard Tim talking to Mel.… His revelation had distressed her more than she would've expected.

Okay, she'd admit that her relationship with Mel wasn't passionate, but it was comfortable and pleasant. He was a widower, and they had a great deal in common.

"Is Tim dating anyone else now?" Lydia asked, breaking into Anne Marie's musings.

"Pardon?" she asked, looking up, mesmerized again by the graceful movements of Lydia's hands. As a distraction she took a sip of her tea.

"Tim? Is he seeing someone else now that Vanessa's out of the picture?"

"I don't think so." But she hadn't known when he was involved with Vanessa and he was even less likely to discuss his dating life with her now.

"What does your gut tell you?" Lydia asked.

"That it was a mistake to let Ellen see him."

Lydia stared at her long and hard. "You don't mean that."

Anne Marie sighed. "No, I don't. Ellen's become a different child since she met Tim and learned he's her father." The painfully shy, reticent little girl had blossomed before Anne Marie's eyes. Tim's love had a lot to do with that transformation. Ellen's eyes lit up every time she saw her father.

"In my opinion—and this *is* just my opinion—you need to acknowledge that you still have feelings for him."

Anne Marie opened her mouth to ardently object—and then hesitated. If nothing else, the incident on Saturday proved how much she continued to care about Tim, despite all her efforts not to. For months she'd buried her feelings for him, not realizing how ineffective those attempts had been.

"I'm dating Mel now." *Mel* was her future, not Tim.

"Mel," Lydia murmured.

"Yes, Mel. He's generous and…and kind and sweet." She knew she was trying too hard to convince Lydia.

"Yes," Lydia agreed softly. Holding Anne Marie's gaze, she said, "But he isn't Tim Carlsen."

"Tim couldn't care less about me. By his own admission, the only reason he has anything to do with me is Ellen." Her voice cracked and she struggled to hold on to her composure.

Lydia glanced up from her knitting and, again, leaned forward to press her hand over Anne Marie's. "Don't be so sure. I've seen the way he looks at you."

# *Six*

April 26

Something's wrong with Mom. I don't think she likes the new house and I think she misses the apartment. I thought I'd hate living away from Blossom Street, but I don't. April isn't in my class, but we go to the same school. I didn't know that. She said I could sit with her on the bus and I promised to teach her to knit. Mom gave me a pair of needles and some yarn and I'm going to show April. I told her it feels awkward at first but it won't take long to figure it out. She thought it was great that I knit Baxter's green sweater. She wants to knit one for Iris and I told her she could, but she should start with something easier. She's going to knit a pot holder for her mom. I knit one for my mom and she really likes it.

"Can April stay for dinner?" Ellen asked Anne Marie the minute they walked in the door Monday night. Her daughter and her new friend had played at April's house after school that afternoon. The two girls had been inseparable since they'd met on Saturday.

Anne Marie was delighted Ellen had made a friend so quickly. Even better, they attended the same school, although they had different teachers. They'd become instant friends, the way kids did at that age.

"Ah…" Anne Marie had no idea what to prepare. "Sure, April can have dinner here, as long as it's all right with her mom and dad."

"It is," Ellen told her. "We already asked."

Anne Marie did a thorough search of her kitchen cupboards. She'd gone to the store and stocked their shelves, and she could cook any number of dishes—but she couldn't decide on even one. That showed how depressed she was; she wasn't capable of making such a simple decision. Of course there was always the old standby. "How about macaroni and cheese?'"

"We had that for lunch," Ellen called back.

Well, the freezer was her next option. She was about to check it when her cell phone buzzed. Sorting through the packages of frozen food, she answered it.

"Hello."

"What are you two doing for dinner?" Mel asked.

"I don't know yet. Why?"

"I thought I'd stop by and take you and Ellen out to eat."

"Thanks, but I don't think that'll work. Ellen invited her new friend over."

"She has a new friend already?"

"She does. April lives down the street. She found Baxter on Saturday, which is when we met her."

"Why don't I bring dinner?"

This was an offer too good to refuse. "Sounds great. What do you have in mind?"

Mel chuckled. "How about if I pick up one of those roasted chickens with all the fixings?"

"Thanks!" Mel was so thoughtful—and he'd just solved the problem of tonight's dinner.

"I figured you must be exhausted after last weekend."

"I am." The move had taken more out of Anne Marie than she'd realized. That, and what she'd learned about Tim's feelings toward her.

As soon as she'd closed her cell, she walked down the hall to Ellen's room, where the girls were playing with Baxter and Iris. "Mel's coming by with dinner. He's bringing chicken. Would you two set the table?"

Ellen and April exchanged a glance. "Who's Mel?" April asked.

"He's my mother's boyfriend," Ellen replied.

"I thought Tim was your mother's boyfriend," April said, cocking her head.

"He used to be but he isn't anymore. It's…complicated."

"Yeah, grown-ups can get that way," April said sagely.

Smiling, Anne Marie returned to the kitchen.

By the time Mel arrived with dinner, the table was set. They all sat down together with Baxter and Iris settled underneath, content after their own meals.

"Anyone miss me on Blossom Street?" Ellen asked Anne Marie. She reached for a chicken leg; April took the second one.

"Lydia sends her love. Oh, and Bethanne was in the yarn store on Saturday and guess what? Andrew and Courtney got engaged."

Ellen's eyes brightened and she waved the chicken leg. "Can I be in their wedding? I want to be the flower girl!"

"That's not something you ask," Anne Marie explained. "You wait to be invited. But Courtney has several nieces and nephews your age."

Ellen put the chicken leg back on her plate and sighed with disappointment. "I *love* weddings."

"I know you do."

"I was in a wedding once," April said. "But I was only three and I don't remember it. My mom has pictures, though. I was supposed to sprinkle rose petals down the church aisle but I ate them instead."

Anne Marie and Mel laughed.

"Let's play weddings after dinner!" April said excitedly. "We can be wedding planners like on TV."

"Okay!"

Conversation flowed smoothly during the rest of the meal. They talked about television shows and upcoming movies, and Anne Marie appreciated Mel's lack of condescension, his good-humored patience with the girls. Afterward, they asked to be excused and tore back into Ellen's bedroom, while Mel and Anne Marie lingered over coffee.

"Thank you for bringing dinner," Anne Marie said.

"I wasn't here to help with the move like I'd planned. It's the least I could do."

"Mel, I understood. You had a business meeting."

"I know, but I felt bad about letting you down and then there was all that angst over Baxter. I should've been here instead of—"

He didn't need to complete the sentence; she knew he meant Tim. Rather than pursue the subject she let it drop.

Her conversation with Lydia had stayed in her mind all afternoon. Anne Marie didn't *want* to have feelings for Tim. Mel was good with Ellen, so considerate and caring, and she needed to concentrate on her relationship with him.

He helped her clear the table and was about to kiss her when Ellen dashed into the kitchen. "Hurry!" she cried.

"Hurry?" Anne Marie repeated, noting the disappointed look in Mel's eyes. "Why?"

"Come and see," Ellen said urgently.

"See what?"

"The wedding. Come on!" She wore a white sundress and a lace-trimmed pillowcase as her veil.

Anne Marie dried her hands on the dish towel and followed her daughter down the hall. Mel came, too. Standing in the doorway of Ellen's bedroom, she leaned against the door frame, Mel beside her.

"These are the church pews," April said, gesturing at the books laid across the carpet in two even rows, with a center aisle wide enough for Ellen to walk down.

"Who's the groom?" Anne Marie asked

"We haven't decided yet," Ellen said. "Baxter's going to be the best man, though." The girls had affixed a black ribbon to the dog's neck to resemble a bow tie. However, he didn't look pleased with his role.

"What part does Iris play?" Anne Marie asked April.

"She's the maid of honor."

"Of course. I should've guessed."

"We need someone who can sing the wedding march," Ellen said. "We're wedding planners so we have to arrange it. April and I don't know the words. All we know is 'Here comes the bride.'"

Anne Marie was about to tell them she couldn't sing it, either, when the doorbell rang.

"That must be April's mom," Anne Marie said. But even before she opened the front door she knew it wasn't. Her intuition told her it was Tim.

The way Mel felt about him would make this awkward. Mel, nothing! Her *own* feelings were as tangled as any yarn she'd ever snarled. She didn't want to face him, not yet. She hadn't had time to absorb what she'd learned or the hurt he'd caused her. Still, her heart seemed to speed up as soon as she saw him and she was instantly annoyed with herself.

"Hello again," she said without any warmth, standing on the other side of the screen door, which she kept closed, aware of how rude she was acting, yet unable to stop.

"Hi." He held the handlebars of Ellen's bike. "I brought this back. It had a flat tire."

Anne Marie continued to leave the screen door shut. "I didn't know you'd taken it."

"I promised to repair it for Ellen."

Mel came up behind her, placing a possessive hand on her shoulder.

Ellen joined them, wearing her white dress but having discarded her "veil." "My bike's fixed already?" she squealed. "Thank you, Daddy!"

"I did it this afternoon," he said, smiling at his daughter. "Where would you like me to put it?"

"In the garage," Anne Marie told him.

"Come and see the wedding," Ellen said. "April and I are wedding planners. Baxter's the best man but he keeps running off. We couldn't decide who should be the groom. Will you, Daddy?'"

"Ah, sure," he said, but Anne Marie sensed his hesitation.

She opened the screen door, walked down the steps and over to the garage, which was located behind the house. Mel went with her; she could feel his disapproval every step of the way. No one spoke, which made this all the more disconcerting.

"Will you tell Ellen I'll play groom some other time?" Tim asked once he'd finished securing Ellen's bicycle.

Anne Marie crossed her arms against the evening chill. Thankfully, Tim realized she didn't want him there.

"That would probably be best," she murmured.

"I agree," Mel added.

Anne Marie could have done without his comment but didn't bother to object. At least he wasn't contradicting her opinion or her request.

Tim had started to leave when the back door flew open and Ellen came out. "We're ready," she shouted. "April and I are going to hum the song 'cause we don't know the words." She dashed toward Tim and grabbed his hand.

Tim threw Anne Marie an apologetic glance as he walked slowly toward the house.

"I've been meaning to talk to you about Tim," Mel said, not hiding his irritation.

"About what, exactly?"

"Well, for one thing, he turns up far too often. Do the two you have a parenting plan?"

"Not...really." At this point their agreement was pretty loose.

"That might be something to consider," Mel said. "Tim seems to think he can come by anytime he pleases. For obvious reasons, that's not a good idea."

Anne Marie turned back to the house. She didn't ask

what those obvious reasons were, but she had to admit Mel was probably right. However, she wasn't in any mood to hear it. If she limited Tim's access to Ellen, he'd assume she was punishing him because he wasn't interested in her. "Can we talk about this later?"

Not waiting for his reply, she hurried inside. The instant she did, she was greeted by the sound of the girls giggling delightedly. Unable to resist, she had to look for herself.

Sure enough, Tim had taken on the role of the groom. He wore Ellen's black velvet hair bow clipped to the top button of his shirt.

"We need a preacher," Ellen said. "Mel, will you be the preacher?"

Mel shook his head. "Trust me, Ellen, I wouldn't make a good preacher." The ten-year-old's face fell with disappointment.

"What about your mom?" April suggested.

"She can't," Ellen insisted. "Mom's the bride."

"Oh, right."

Anne Marie opened her mouth to protest but no one noticed. Wasn't *Ellen* the bride? *She* most definitely wasn't willing to pretend to be Tim's bride. "Hold on, you two—"

"I'll be the preacher," Ellen volunteered, ignoring Anne Marie.

"You'll need a Bible."

"Got it." Ellen stood on tiptoe to get her children's Bible from the top bookshelf.

"Can girls be preachers?" April sounded unsure of this.

"Girls can be anything they want," Anne Marie assured her firmly. Despite her discomfort, she couldn't let a comment like that pass unanswered.

"Even a firefighter?"

"Even a firefighter," Anne Marie said.

Now that she'd resolved that issue, Anne Marie seemed to lose control of the situation. She was handed a plastic flower and the pillowcase was pinned to her hair as a makeshift veil. As the two girls hummed "Here Comes the Bride," Anne Marie carefully marched down the aisle between the rows of books. Holding her Bible, Ellen went to stand in front of Tim. Mel remained in the background, looking disgruntled and ill at ease.

When Anne Marie reached Tim's side, he tucked her arm in the crook of his, staring straight ahead. The best man had returned but clearly hadn't understood his role. He stretched out on the floor, knocking over several "pews." Iris, the maid of honor, peered out from under Ellen's bed.

With great ceremony, Ellen opened the Bible. In formal tones she began, "Dearly beloved, we are gathered together this evening in the presence of God and these witnesses to join together—"

April leaned close to Ellen. "What's *beloved* mean?" she asked.

"You can't ask questions during the wedding," Ellen told her friend.

"Okay. Sorry." But April didn't sound contrite.

Anne Marie quickly whispered the definition as Ellen frowned.

The ceremony took only a few minutes and by the time they'd finished Anne Marie and Tim both found themselves grinning. Ellen's performance—complete with sweeping gestures—was worthy of an acting award.

Anne Marie had gradually relaxed enough to enjoy the charade.

The only person who didn't appear the least bit entertained was Mel. He stood out in the hallway, wearing a frown.

Shortly after the "vows" were exchanged, Tim kissed Anne Marie on the cheek, then pulled out his wallet.

"What's the money for?" Ellen asked when he removed a dollar bill.

"The groom always pays the preacher."

Ellen raised her hand to stop him. "Give the money to the poor."

"I'm poor," April said, and held out her palm.

"No, you aren't," Ellen retorted. "Wedding planners make *lots* of money."

"I guess you should put your money away," Anne Marie said with a shrug.

Grinning, Tim did as she suggested. When he glanced up he apparently caught sight of Mel. "I'd better go." He bent down to hug Ellen farewell.

"You need to thank your father," Anne Marie said.

Ellen wrapped her arms around Tim's neck. "Thank you again for fixing my bike and for being the groom and for everything," she said in a breathless voice.

"You're welcome, sweetheart."

"Can we go bike riding again soon?"

"Sure. I'll set a time with your mother."

When Anne Marie escorted him to the front door, Tim held her look for a moment, then raised his eyes to meet Mel's, who stood directly behind her. "Does next Saturday work for you? I can pick Ellen up around ten."

"We have plans for Saturday," Mel inserted without allowing Anne Marie the opportunity to respond.

She ignored him. "Saturday morning will be fine, Tim. I'll have Ellen ready by ten."

His expression uncertain, Tim nodded. "Okay. See you then."

"Bye," she said, closing the door. Neither man had addressed the other again. She took a deep breath to compose herself, then turned deliberately to Mel. "What was that about?" she snapped.

Mel didn't pretend not to know what she meant. "I've told you. I don't like the idea of Tim spending so much time with you and Ellen. Besides, we did discuss going for brunch."

She was in no state to deal with his insecurities and frankly she was a little unsettled by the make-believe wedding. "I think you might be making an assumption regarding our relationship, Mel. We're good friends—"

"Friends?" he repeated, breaking in. "We've been dating exclusively for the past six months. Correction, *I've* been dating *you* exclusively. And yet Tim is still in your life."

"Ellen's his daughter!"

"That doesn't mean *you* have to be involved with him."

Anne Marie expelled her breath and walked into the kitchen. They had to lower their voices, otherwise the girls might hear. "I don't want to argue about Tim."

"I don't either, but I need to find out where I stand with you. Just tell me flat-out—am I wasting my time here? I know you cared about Tim at one point."

"That's over," she said immediately. "I told you before."

"Is it, Anne Marie?"

"Yes…" But she didn't sound nearly as emphatic as she wanted to.

"I think that tells me everything I need to know."

Anne Marie felt terrible.

Calling goodbye to the girls, Mel started toward the front door. She stopped him. "Don't go," she whispered, her hand on his forearm.

He hesitated.

"Please."

Mel exhaled slowly as though undecided.

Anne Marie slid her arms around his middle and hugged him close. Mel was solid and warm, and she knew exactly where *she* stood with *him*. Tim was like shifting sand, not to be trusted. Eventually her heart would align itself with Mel's.

# *Seven*

April 27

I've made a decision. I'm going to ignore my feelings for Tim and concentrate on Mel. Once I do
that, my heart will follow. Ever since last Saturday
I've been miserable. Well, no more. I refuse to get
emotionally involved with Tim again. He's good
for Ellen and she loves him. I can't and won't keep
him away from his daughter. However, I think Mel
might be right. We need to establish a parenting
plan. We need an agreement between us. Now that
I've settled that in my own mind, I want to start a
new knitting project. I'd like to make something
for Courtney's wedding. I'm sure Lydia will have
a few ideas.

Wednesday afternoon Tim phoned Anne Marie at the
bookstore. "I hope I didn't cause a problem between you
and Mel when I came by the other night," he said.

"Why would that be a problem?" she asked, unwilling to mention her argument with Mel. "It wasn't a big

deal, and Ellen loved the fact that you went along with her wedding-planner fantasy."

"I've often wondered what it would be like to be married. I just never expected to have a dog as my best man."

Despite herself Anne Marie laughed. "As I recall, he fell asleep during the ceremony. Some best man he turned out to be."

"You don't have any room to talk. Your maid of honor wouldn't come out from under the bed."

"True."

After a brief silence, Tim said, "Is Ellen there?"

"She met up with Casey Goetz after school, but she's due at the bookstore soon. Any particular reason you're asking?"

"Would you mind if I took her to Lake Wisdom? My parents recently bought a cabin there, and since it's such a sunny afternoon, I thought she might enjoy a boat ride."

The weather was unseasonably warm for April, and Anne Marie knew Ellen would love an outing like that. "I'm sure she'd be thrilled." They discussed the fact that Ellen would need a life vest if she went out on the water, then chatted amicably for a few more minutes.

"I'll pick her up at the store in half an hour."

"Okay."

Anne Marie glanced at her watch; it was now three-thirty.

As usual, Tim arrived precisely when he'd said he would. He had on jeans and a light jacket and wore a Mariners baseball cap. It was hard not to stare, to appreciate how handsome he was, but Anne Marie resisted.

"You ready, Ellen?" he asked.

She bounced off her chair, slammed her book shut and nodded. "Can Mom come, too?"

"I wish she would," Tim said.

Anne Marie automatically shook her head. "I'd like to, but I need to be here."

Teresa, who worked with her, was quick to weigh in with her opinion. Too quick. "We've had a slow afternoon." She looked at Tim and explained, "It's generally slow the first sunny day of spring. Besides," she added, turning to Anne Marie, "I thought you were supposed to take Wednesdays off." Anne Marie tried to give herself a midweek break but she'd gotten out of the habit.

"You'd be welcome," Tim said, encouraging her.

"*Please* come, Mom." Ellen folded her hands in a prayerful gesture. "You *always* have to work. I want you to go to the lake with us."

Anne Marie wanted to enjoy the sunshine, too, but she hesitated. She hadn't talked to Mel since Monday night, and while they'd parted on good terms they'd each felt unsettled by their disagreement. If he were to learn she'd gone to the lake with Tim, he'd be justifiably upset.

Tim opened his eyes wide and folded his hands like Ellen's. With both of them gazing at her in supplication, she couldn't refuse. Her one hope was that Mel wouldn't find out about this. "Oh, all right," she said, giving in.

Ellen hooted and jumped up and down, clapping.

"I'll have to stop at the house and change clothes," Anne Marie told them. "I can't very well go out on the water wearing this." She motioned at her white pants and pink jacket.

"We have time," Tim said with a boyish grin.

Once she'd driven home, changed her clothes and packed a few things for Ellen, it was close to four-thirty.

"I need to be back before seven," she said as she slid into the front seat next to Tim. That wasn't strictly true, but she had an evening of paperwork planned. And imposing a time limit gave her at least the illusion of control.

"You will be," he promised as he started the engine.

The drive to the lake took another thirty minutes. He turned off the main road to a secluded one, then eventually drove down a dirt track that led to the water's edge. A rustic log cabin was nestled among tall fir trees. She saw two wooden rockers on the front porch; they looked comfortably worn, as though many conversations had taken place there over the years, many sunsets watched. The pristine lake was glass-smooth with the sun reflecting on the surface of the water, which was a deep greenish blue. Another cabin could be seen on the other side.

"Oh, Tim, this is lovely," Anne Marie said. "It's so peaceful."

"Mom and Dad have wanted a summer place like this for years and they finally found exactly what they were looking for."

"Can we go out in the boat now?" Ellen asked. After strapping on her vest, she raced down to the dock.

"Wait for us," Anne Marie called.

A boat ride had sounded like a simple thing when Tim first mentioned it. Anne Marie couldn't remember the last time she'd been in one—or one that small, anyway. Tied to the dock, the rowboat bobbed gently on the lake. Anne Marie wasn't sure how she was supposed to climb in and out.

"I'll help you," Tim said, as though reading her mind. "You have nothing to fear—I was a Cub Scout."

"Not a Boy Scout?"

"No, I didn't pass the test."

"Oh, great."

He chuckled. "I'm a natural on the water. I've been doing this for years."

"So you say."

"It's all right, Mom," Ellen said, clasping Anne Marie's hand. "I can swim—I'll save you."

Tim got in first, then helped Ellen lower herself into the boat. Anne Marie went last. She sat on the edge of the dock and gingerly eased herself in, sighing with relief once she was safely seated.

"Ready?" he asked.

"Yeah!" Ellen shouted. "Let's go!"

It soon became apparent that Tim was as comfortable on the water as he'd claimed. He rowed with regular, even strokes, and the boat seemed to glide effortlessly across the lake.

"See that cabin over there?" he asked, pointing to the one Anne Marie had noticed earlier.

"I see it," Ellen told him, shading her eyes from the sun.

"There's a story about the people who used to live in these two cabins, ours and that one."

"Oh?" He had a twinkle in his eyes, and Anne Marie was convinced he was about to make up some wild tale.

"Years ago, these cabins were owned by rival families. The Krugers and the Livermores."

"Krugers and Livermores?" Anne Marie repeated. "Like the Montagues and Capulets? Or the Hatfields and McCoys?"

"Something like that."

"What's *rival* mean?" Ellen asked

"They competed with each other," Tim explained.

"Were they friends?"

"Rivals can be friends, but in this case they weren't."

"You mean like Mel and you?" She looked from Tim to Anne Marie.

"Sort of," Anne Marie said, saddened that her daughter was aware of the antagonism between Mel and her father.

"If one family bought a boat, then the other family did, as well," Tim went on as if he hadn't heard Ellen's last statement. "The two husbands were employed by rival companies, so when one family purchased a cabin on this side of the lake, the second family bought land and built a larger cabin on the other side."

"Is ours bigger?" Ellen asked.

"We have the smaller house," Tim said.

"Oh." Ellen seemed disappointed.

"As it happened, both families had teenage children. The Krugers had a daughter named Dani and the Livermores had a son, Scott, who was the same age as Dani."

"I feel a romance brewing," Anne Marie said.

"You're right." Tim directed the comment to her. "Dani and Scott were both out on the water one afternoon when Dani's canoe tipped over."

"This story isn't going to have an unhappy ending, is it?" Anne Marie asked.

"No way," Tim said, pulling rhythmically on the oars. "This is a romance, remember?"

"Mo-om, let Dad tell the story."

"Okay, okay, continue." Anne Marie gestured toward Tim.

"Seeing that Dani was in distress, Scott paddled over and rescued her."

"And the Kruger family was so grateful the rivalry ended," Anne Marie concluded.

"Nope. The Kruger family blamed Scott for causing Dani to fall out of the canoe."

"Didn't Dani defend him?" Anne Marie asked.

"She tried, but her family refused to listen. The Krugers disliked the Livermores so much that if there was any kind of mishap, the Livermores were automatically to blame."

"That's ridiculous," she muttered.

"I agree."

Ellen patted Anne Marie's knee. "Shh, I want to find out what happened."

"Would you like the short version or the long one?"

"Short version," Anne Marie insisted. "Definitely the short version."

"Okay," Tim said. "They lived happily ever after."

"Who did?" Ellen demanded. "I want the long version 'cause I don't know who married who."

Anne Marie groaned and glanced up at the sky. "Tim, honestly. All right, give us the long version."

"That night," he began, "Dani snuck out of the house and got in the canoe and paddled over to Scott's place. She woke him up and apologized for the way her family had reacted. They should've been grateful and they weren't. Dani wanted him to know she appreciated what he'd done."

"Did she kiss him?" Ellen asked excitedly.

"Not that night, but then they started meeting every night in the middle of the lake. They'd sit under the moonlight and talk."

"They did fall in love, though, right?"

"It wouldn't be a romance if they didn't. Except neither of their families wanted them to be together."

"Did they get married?"

"They did eventually—and guess what?"

"What?" Ellen echoed.

"The Krugers and the Livermores became the best of friends. Dani and Scott now have three children. Let me see." Tim squinted into the distance. "I believe their oldest daughter is around your age."

"That *is* a romantic story," Anne Marie said, mainly grateful that no one had drowned in the middle of the lake during a midnight tryst.

They spent an hour on the water, the most pleasant, peaceful hour Anne Marie could remember in a long while.

"I'd better get you back to shore if I'm going to have you home before seven," he said. He sounded as reluctant as Anne Marie was to leave the tranquility of this special afternoon.

"Oh, yeah—I should be back by seven." Only she didn't want to leave. The temptation to stay on the lake was almost overwhelming. The sun felt warm on her shoulders; she'd finally begun to relax. Ellen yawned and rested her head against Anne Marie's leg. "Maybe we could stay a bit longer...."

"You're sure?" Tim asked, slipping the oar into the smooth water.

Anne Marie nodded. Eyes closed, she raised her face to the sun, reveling in the warmth of late afternoon. The birds chirped, the water rippled, and she could feel a light breeze on her face. She didn't immediately realize they'd stopped moving. When she opened her eyes, she saw Tim sitting there motionless, both oars suspended above the water.

"Is everything okay?" she asked.

"No."

He sounded uncharacteristically serious, and she tried to lighten the situation—whatever it was—with humor.

"Don't tell me there's a monster in this lake that's going to come out of the water and swallow us whole."

"Not to my knowledge."

"Then what's wrong?"

"Nothing." He set the oars in the water again and headed toward the cabin as if he were taking part in a race. Their speed was in stark contrast to the easy, tranquil quality of their earlier ride.

Once they'd reached shore, Tim secured the boat and hopped onto the dock. He helped Ellen up and then Anne Marie. "It's time I got you back," he said curtly.

Anne Marie had no idea what was going on. Taking her cue from him, she settled Ellen in the backseat while he stowed their belongings in the trunk. The inside of the car was warm and cozy, and Ellen closed her eyes, dozing off within minutes. Anne Marie got into the car; so did Tim. He braced his hands against the steering wheel.

"Tim," she whispered, not wanting to disturb Ellen. "What's wrong?"

"You don't want to know."

She placed her hand on his knee, preventing him from starting the engine. "Actually, I do."

"Really?" He turned and looked at her, his eyes holding hers.

Anne Marie wasn't sure who moved first. But the next thing she knew, Tim had his arms around her and his lips were on hers.

This wasn't a soft exploratory kiss—it was hot and hungry, moist and openmouthed, as if they were intent on absorbing each other completely. The kiss went on and on until Anne Marie broke away, breathless.

"Ellen," she whispered for fear her daughter would wake and find them like this.

"I tried to warn you…" Tim whispered back. His shoulders heaved and he clutched the steering wheel with both hands.

Anne Marie leaned against the back of the seat and closed her eyes, making a determined effort to catch her breath. "Wow," she gasped, hardly aware she'd spoken.

Tim snickered softly. "You can say that again." He was silent for the next few minutes. "Now what?" he finally asked.

Anne Marie blinked. "What do you mean?"

"The way I see it, we have two choices."

"Only two?"

He didn't respond to the question. "We can overlook what just happened…" he began.

"Or?"

"Or we can explore it further."

"Ellen's in the backseat."

"I didn't mean this minute." His gaze bore into hers. "You're the one who has to decide what you want, Anne Marie. The decision is yours."

It suddenly occurred to her what that kiss was all about. And it wasn't because he was attracted to her. He'd said as much. Anne Marie closed her eyes once more and pushed aside the exciting sensations that cascaded through her. His touch was thrilling—wonderful—but she couldn't trust him. He'd taught her painful lessons in the past and she'd be a fool to ignore them.

"You didn't need to do that, you know," she said stiffly.

He frowned. "What are you talking about?"

"You kissed me just now because you're afraid of what I might do."

"Might do?"

"Don't worry, Tim. I'll never block your access to Ellen. She's your daughter and she loves you. But I also know that if it wasn't for Ellen you wouldn't have anything to do with me. And I'm fine with that."

"Anne Marie, listen—"

"No, please, I don't want to hear your excuses. Mel suggested the two of us set up a parenting plan and I think that's a good idea. You don't need to flatter me with attention and kisses, Tim. We understand each other without playing games."

His frown darkened. "You honestly believe that's what the kiss was about?"

She didn't say anything.

He waited for a moment, then started the engine. "Your silence is answer enough."

He was angry and upset with her. Perhaps it was best this way.

In fact, she knew it was.

# *Eight*

April 27

I saw Mom and Tim kissing this afternoon! They
didn't know I wasn't really asleep. They kissed real
hard and I was hoping maybe they might want to get
married for real. April and I could be their wedding
planners! But then something happened, only I don't
know what because Mom and Tim both got quiet. I
tried to listen, but I couldn't understand what they
were talking about.

When we got home, Mom said she's going to knit
something for a bride named Courtney, who's marrying the son of her friend Bethanne. Mom's going
to talk to Lydia, and I want to come along. I want to
knit something for a bride, too, except I want Mom
to be the bride, just like April and I planned.

When Anne Marie and Ellen returned from Lake
Wisdom, there was a message on her home phone, which
had been installed Tuesday, and on her cell.

A message from Mel.

Anne Marie listened to both with more than a twinge

of guilt. While she'd been necking like a teenager with Tim in his car, Mel, the man she was dating, had tried to reach her.

She waited until Ellen was down for the night before she called him back. "Hi," she said. She knew it sounded tentative—and guilty. She had to resist the urge to apologize for kissing Tim.

Mel instantly picked up on her agitation. "Are you okay?" he asked.

"Yes… So what's up?"

"Actually, I phoned for two reasons," he said.

"Oh?" She paced the kitchen as she held the phone against her ear.

"First, to apologize for the other night. I overreacted with Tim."

"It's all right, really," she rushed to tell him. Even discussing Tim casually was dangerous. "I understand. It was unfortunate, but it's over and best forgotten."

"I guess I'm jealous," Mel continued, oblivious to everything she'd said. "There were a dozen better ways to handle the situation. I behaved badly. I hope you'll excuse my little temper tantrum."

"Mel, it's over," she said again. "Forgotten." Now, if she could forget Tim's kisses just as easily.

"You're far more forgiving and generous than I deserve."

If he didn't stop soon, she was going to burst into tears and confess that she'd spent the afternoon with Tim and had succumbed to his charms, of which there were many.

"Secondly, I called to remind you about Friday night."

"Friday?" Her memory had gone completely blank—no

doubt understandable in the current situation. She stopped pacing, frowning as she tried to remember.

"We have tickets to see *Jersey Boys*."

"Oh, right!" Anne Marie had been ecstatic at the opportunity. Her husband, Robert, had loved the Four Seasons, and she knew many of their songs by heart.

"You mean you *had* forgotten?"

"Oh…momentarily." Tim had agreed to watch Ellen, which meant she'd be seeing him again soon…in front of Mel. This was guaranteed to be uncomfortable. "But I'm looking forward to it."

His voice lowered seductively, tenderly. "And I'm looking forward to spending time with you."

Another bolt of guilt struck her. Mel was a gentleman and a romantic, and she was an idiot to let Tim anywhere close to her heart.

"Everything's okay between us, then," Mel went on to say.

"Oh, yes, everything's just fine." She resumed her pacing.

"Good." How relieved he sounded.

"I'm glad you called me back," he said next. "I was beginning to worry."

"Why would you worry?"

"It's after ten."

Anne Marie couldn't very well admit why she hadn't been home earlier.

"Teresa at the bookstore told me you'd gone out for the afternoon," Mel said.

"Yes, Ellen and I…spent time together." Thank goodness Teresa hadn't told him everything.

"That's great. Ellen's a terrific kid."

"She is," Anne Marie said, and felt the pressing urge to get off the phone before she slipped up.

It took another five minutes to extricate herself from the conversation. She tried not to be obvious about wanting to end the call and hoped she'd succeeded. Her pacing continued even after she'd hung up.

Stupid, stupid, stupid! What was she thinking, letting Tim and Ellen talk her into going to the lake—and so soon after her resolve to remove him from her thoughts! She was courting temptation and she knew it. Oh, she hadn't realized they'd end up kissing again or that…that she'd feel his allure—again. She shook her head. She was smarter than this.

Her relationship with Tim had, from the very beginning, been problematic. She'd had to frequently remind herself that he was a recovering alcoholic and drug addict. He'd been sober and clean for a long time, but that didn't change the basic fact: he had all the personality traits of an alcoholic, even if he didn't drink.

Before she'd allowed Tim into their lives, Anne Marie had done extensive research on alcohol and drug addiction. She felt it was necessary to know what they were facing before she agreed to let Tim see his daughter.

Legally, he had no right to Ellen and Anne Marie believed it was her duty, her moral obligation, to protect Ellen from any psychological harm he might inadvertently inflict.

She went to bed that night feeling confused, angry with herself…and intent on counteracting any damage she'd done to her relationship with Mel.

The next day, as she'd feared, Tim contacted her. He showed up at the bookstore, but the minute he walked in she pretended to be busy.

He approached the service counter and greeted her with a smile that could have melted a glacier. "How's it going?" he asked.

She looked up, and returned his greeting with a tight smile, despite her determination not to display the slightest hint of emotion. "Very well, thanks."

"Do you have time for a lunch break?" he asked. "We don't need to go far. I checked, and the soup at the French Café is spicy black bean, which Ellen told me is one of your favorites."

It didn't matter what Winter was serving, Anne Marie wasn't going to have lunch with him. "Sorry, I can't leave the shop, but thanks, anyway."

Out of the corner of her eye she saw that Teresa was about to say it was perfectly fine; she'd watch the store. Anne Marie sent her a warning glare, and Teresa instantly shut her mouth.

To distract Tim, Anne Marie came out from behind the counter and placed a book on its shelf. "Oh, and did you remember you offered to look after Ellen on Friday night?"

"Tomorrow?"

"Yes. Mel's taking me to *Jersey Boys*."

He was silent for a moment. "It must've slipped my mind, but it shouldn't be a problem."

"If it is, I can ask April's mother.... That might work even better now that I think of it. I'd like to set up a babysitting exchange with her."

"I said I'd do it," Tim said. His mouth thinned. "We'll get dinner and go to a movie."

"Okay, then." She walked over to another shelf, dismayed when Tim followed her.

"I thought we should discuss this parenting plan you mentioned."

"Yes, but now isn't the best time to do that."

"Well, whenever it's convenient. Just let me know." Still, he lingered. "So, everything's fine between you and Mel?"

"Oh, yes," she said, glancing over her shoulder as she spoke. Then, since she'd practically melted in his arms less than twenty-four hours earlier, she felt the need to add, "I hope you'll look past what happened at the lake because I'd like to forget the entire incident."

"If that's what you want."

"I do." She turned to face him, and he boldly met her eyes.

"Unfortunately, I'm not finding it that easy." He paused, his silence heavy with meaning. "Those kisses were pretty...revealing, Anne Marie."

She laughed off his comment and lowered her voice. "Okay, so I'm human. You're hot and so are your kisses— I'll admit it. But when I realized what it was all about, I came to my senses."

"You really believe I'd manipulate you like that?" He stiffened and his shoulders arched back, as though he was flinching from a physical attack.

"I...believe you love Ellen and will do whatever it takes to ensure that she stays in your life," she said evenly, moving about the store, straightening a book here, adjusting a poster there.

Tim trailed behind her.

"It happened before, Tim. What else am I to think?" Then, hoping to lighten the conversation, she murmured, "Don't get me wrong, our kiss was...nice." She shrugged carelessly. "I find your company enjoyable. Who wouldn't?"

"But you'd rather spend time with Mel?"

She wasn't sure she could pull this off much longer. "Let's put it this way. Mel and I have been dating for months. We get along beautifully and he's good to Ellen."

Tim shoved his hands in his pockets. "You get along with me, too, and I'm crazy about Ellen."

"This is obviously some kind of competition between you and Mel."

He glared at her, eyes narrowed and lips tensed. Anne Marie could see that it was taking all the self-control he possessed not to explode in anger. "This all goes back to not telling you about Vanessa, doesn't it?"

Anne Marie felt the heat of embarrassment invade her face. Even her ears started to burn. "Yes, I suppose it does."

"Shakespeare sure got it right," he muttered.

"Shakespeare got a lot of things right. Which particular one are you referring to?"

"Hell has no fury like a woman scorned."

Anne Marie blinked. "First," she snapped, unable to resist correcting him, "that wasn't Shakespeare. It was William Congreve, a Restoration playwright. And second…if this is what you want to think, then you're free to do so."

"I'm not going to argue with you, Anne Marie. So you remember your literary references better than I do. Congratulations. Kudos to you. But say what you like—we both know what happened at the lake was real. Real for me and real for you. If you want to tell yourself I have some twisted ulterior motive, then go ahead."

Clenching her fists, she blurted out, "I made a fool of myself over you." She glanced anxiously at Teresa, who was at the other side of the store, although still within hearing distance.

"And you love turning the tables on me now."

"No." She wanted that to be perfectly clear.

He shook his head. "I've never lied to you. Never," he said emphatically.

"Fine, if that's what *you* want to tell yourself. However, I feel that a lie of omission is still a lie." She couldn't help it; her arms began to flail about and her voice rose. "You let me build up this romantic fantasy and then after months—yes, *months*—you conveniently remember to mention that you're engaged." This whole scene was mortifying, but her anger and sense of betrayal overcame her embarrassment.

"What was I supposed to do?"

"What were you supposed to do?" she mimicked in singsong fashion. "Well, telling the truth comes to mind. Couldn't you see that I was…attracted to you?"

"Yes. Anne Marie, I saw it and I agonized over it. Listen…" Tim walked away from her, then returned. "I realized how you felt—but I was afraid that if I said anything, you wouldn't let me see Ellen."

"You don't have a very high opinion of me, do you?"

"I didn't know you. My daughter, a daughter I'd only just found out about, had been taken away from me. I was left without any legal recourse. I had one opportunity to win you over and I—"

"Are you telling me you deliberately led me on?" This was too much!

"No! Now you're purposely distorting everything I say."

The frustration they were both feeling was almost more than either of them could take. Tim had raised his voice to match hers.

"It might be best if we had this conversation some other time," she said quietly, afraid their argument was keeping customers at bay. Several people had entered the store, but hadn't yet ventured beyond the displays near the front.

"Good idea." He whirled around and stormed out.

When Tim had left, Anne Marie began to shake. She placed her hands on the nearest bookshelf and slowly exhaled. She took several deep breaths, trying to control her emotions.

Teresa approached her. "Are you okay?" she asked tentatively.

"No."

"I'm sorry."

Anne Marie nodded. She simply couldn't respond to Teresa's sympathy, afraid she might burst into tears.

"Do you know who you remind me of?" Teresa asked.

"No." Furthermore, Anne Marie didn't care.

"My husband and me. That's the way we fight, too, but then we always make up afterward. You and Tim will reconcile and it'll be really good when you do. Mark my words."

Anne Marie was too upset to even think in terms of reconciliation. Not knowing what to expect, she made contingency plans for Ellen for Friday night. April's mother was available to fill in, if necessary.

As it turned out, Anne Marie didn't need her. Tim arrived soon after she and Ellen got home.

Ellen let him in, with Baxter dancing excitedly around them both.

"How're you doing, sweetheart?" he asked his daughter. "Hi, Baxter."

He hugged Ellen, then straightened when he saw Anne Marie. Holding her gaze, he intentionally resumed speaking to his daughter. "I understand we have a date tonight."

"A date?" Ellen said, sounding pleased.

"I'm taking you out for dinner and a movie."

"Do I get popcorn, too?"

"As much as you want."

Ellen grinned at Anne Marie. "Don't worry, Mom. I'll eat my vegetables at dinner."

"Good girl." Anne Marie felt bad about her argument with Tim earlier and took a hesitant step into the room. Mel would be here any minute, however, and with Ellen still standing in the hallway, she couldn't talk to Tim about what had happened. And really, what was there to say? All she knew was that the lump in her throat had stayed with her all afternoon.

"When will you have Ellen back?" she asked.

His eyes refused to meet hers. "Nine, nine-thirty. Depends on how late the movie ends and traffic afterward."

"Okay… I don't expect to be home before ten-thirty or eleven."

He nodded. "Ready to go, Ellen?"

"Yes!" She ran to grab her sweater—one Lydia had knit for her with a Yorkie on the back.

Tim opened the screen door.

"Have fun, you two," Anne Marie said. She scooped the dog into her arms and raised one hand in farewell.

"You, too." Tim paused, looking at her. "I mean that," he said, his voice low enough so only she could hear.

He seemed to be saying he regretted their argument as much as she did. Anne Marie wanted to believe that. Her lip quivered and she bit it hard, unwilling to give way to tears. "Thank you," she whispered.

He nodded and then, head down, walked out the door.

Mel appeared soon after Ellen and Tim had left. He kissed Anne Marie's cheek, then slid his arms around her, saying, "I adore Ellen, but it's been too long since it was just the two of us." His peck on the cheek had surprised her. She'd anticipated a real kiss, had actually hoped for one. She wanted to have strong feelings for Mel.

"Yes," she agreed. "It's been ages." She rested her head on his shoulder. She felt content in his embrace. Comforted. Unfortunately, there were none of the sparks she'd experienced with Tim, none of the heady rush of emotion. Mel was gentle, kind, honest. He would never mislead anyone.

In a word, Mel was *safe*. Anne Marie needed safe and so did Ellen.

The production of *Jersey Boys* proved to be everything Anne Marie had read and more. The music brought back memories of Robert, of dancing and laughing with the husband she'd loved, but unlike a few years ago, those memories offered more happiness than sorrow and deepened her enjoyment of the play. The story itself was the classic American tale of opportunity and success and the cost of fame.

"Thank you," she said when he'd driven her home, "for a lovely, lovely evening." Mel's arm was around her shoulders.

A sense of dread settled over her, dissipating her pleasure and her serenity, when she saw Tim's car parked out front. She felt Mel stiffen.

"I'd forgotten Tim had Ellen for the night," he said.

Anne Marie merely nodded, and Mel, apparently, had nothing more to say on the subject of Tim.

He escorted Anne Marie to the front door, but to her disappointment didn't seem eager to stay. "Coffee?" she suggested, hoping he'd accept...yet hoping he wouldn't.

"No, but I'll see you in."

Anne Marie wasn't fooled. Mel didn't want to abandon her to Tim and frankly she was just as glad. If she was alone with Tim they might start talking again. They might kiss again, and if they did, she'd be lost....

Tim came to the door, almost as if he'd been waiting for her, longing for her return. He smiled—until he saw Mel. He looked away, immediately removing his jacket from the hall closet.

"Welcome home," he said as he pushed his arms through the sleeves.

"Thank you. How did everything go with Ellen?"

"We had a great time." Tim nodded once in Mel's direction. "Good to see you, Mel."

"You, too, Tim."

Both men were being polite in the extreme.

Without another word, Tim let himself out, closing the door quietly behind him.

# *Nine*

April 29

None of my plans for dealing with Tim have panned out. In fact, everything seems to have backfired. I resolved to put him completely out of my mind, but all I do is think about him…and about the possibility of him, Ellen and me together. I know how foolish that is, but I can't make myself stop. It's definitely time to pay Lydia a visit and start a new project. If ever I needed a distraction, it's now. I wonder if doctors realize how therapeutic yarn can be.…

Not surprisingly, Anne Marie spent a sleepless night. On Saturday she was scheduled to work half a day at the bookstore. Ellen accompanied her, planning to visit her friends along Blossom Street—Lydia and Alix and Susannah and others—with Baxter in tow.

As they drove into town that morning, Anne Marie lost count of the number of references Ellen made to her evening with Tim, especially the Thai dinner they ate in a booth where they had to take off their shoes. The movie afterward had been the latest 3-D animation and Ellen described the plot to her no less than five times.

"Lydia said we should stop by A Good Yarn when you're finished working." Ellen hurried into the bookstore just before noon, Baxter bouncing beside her. "We can go there, can't we?"

"Yes, I was planning to." Anne Marie hoped to have another chat with her friend; Saturdays were often the busiest day of the week, however, and that might not work out. "I thought I'd pick up some yarn for my new project."

"Which project? The wedding one?" Knitting had become a bond, a subject of common interest between them, and Ellen almost always knit something right along with her.

"Yes, I was thinking I could knit Courtney something."

"What about a veil?" Ellen said.

That project was a lot more daunting than Anne Marie wanted to tackle. "She probably already has her veil. But Lydia gave me a pattern book and I found a bride's purse I liked. I'd use a cotton yarn with some metallic threads shot through it."

"A bride's purse?" Ellen repeated, her eyes glowing. "That sounds pretty."

"It would have a drawstring and hang from her arm. Courtney could use it on her wedding day."

As she'd expected, Lydia was busy with customers when Ellen and Anne Marie entered the shop. A large table was set up in the back, with pattern books stacked close by. The table was used for classes, too. Everyone who visited the shop seemed to gravitate to this natural meeting place.

Anne Marie chose another pattern book, one devoted to weddings, then pulled out a chair and sat down. She flipped through several pages until she located another bride's purse. She decided she preferred this one, but wanted Lydia's opinion—and Ellen's.

Ellen was at the front of the store petting Whiskers. Baxter and Whiskers tolerated each other and Anne Marie suspected cat and dog were better friends than they let on. Ellen held Baxter on her lap while she stroked the sleeping cat.

Lydia rang up a yarn sale, then joined Anne Marie. "I was just thinking I could use a break. Elise," she called out to the older woman who helped out on weekends, "could you take over for a few minutes?"

"Of course."

Lydia sat in the chair across from her, smiling tiredly. "How are you?"

Anne Marie shrugged. Usually people who asked that were simply being polite. All they wanted to hear was "Fine." That wasn't the case with Lydia.

"I'm coping," Anne Marie said. "Things are…confusing."

"I thought something was up. Tim parked in front of my store on Thursday. He went across the street, read Winter's specials on the board and then headed over to the bookstore."

"Did you see him when he left?" Anne Marie asked.

"I did," Lydia said. "And it was a different story entirely."

"He looked like a man ready to commit murder, right?"

"No," Lydia said softly. "But it didn't take much to

see that he was upset. He stood outside his car for a few minutes, then banged his fist on the hood. After that he talked on his cell."

Anne Marie wondered whom he'd phoned. Then in a flash it came to her. He'd called his AA sponsor. Tim had mentioned the other man numerous times without ever revealing his identity. She was glad he had someone he could talk to whenever he felt the need. She envied him that, although she had friends of her own. Good friends, like Lydia, Barbie and Lillie.

"Mel and I went out last night."

"So I heard," Lydia said, glancing at Ellen, who still sat in the window, petting Whiskers with Baxter curled on her lap.

"We had a wonderful time."

"You always seem to when you're with Mel."

"He's so good to me and Ellen."

"But you aren't in love with him, are you?"

"No," Anne Marie had to admit. She understood what she found attractive about Mel. Her heart wasn't at risk with him. He couldn't hurt her the way Robert had when he'd had his affair—or when he'd died. The shock of both had left Anne Marie emotionally bruised, not quite as resilient as she'd once been. Not only that, she'd met Mel shortly after learning about Tim and Vanessa.

Lydia continued to study her.

"Earlier this week Mel asked me where he stood. I'm afraid I haven't been completely honest with him."

"Don't be so hard on yourself," Lydia said. "The one you haven't been honest with is you."

"I think I might learn to love Mel, given time," she

said. He cared about her and Ellen. While he'd never spoken the words aloud, he showed his feelings in a dozen different ways. Not for an instant did she doubt him. Yes, he was almost twenty years her senior, but that had never bothered her. He'd do anything for her; all she had to do was ask.

"I agree," Lydia said thoughtfully. "Love is a choice. It certainly becomes a choice once the intensity of first love passes and you settle into everyday life. I choose to love Brad every single morning and I'm grateful that he chooses to love me back."

Anne Marie was impressed by her friend's marriage. Lydia and Brad's relationship was strong enough, solid enough, to include Casey, who'd been a difficult and troubled girl. Lydia had told her that Ellen's adoption had influenced their own decision to bring Casey into their family.

"Whatever your decision about Mel," Lydia said, "it'll be the right one."

Anne Marie stayed for tea and then picked out yarn and the new pattern for the bride's purse.

"I want to knit the same bride's purse as you. That's okay, isn't it?" Ellen asked before they left the store.

"Of course."

"Can I knit it without the beads?"

"If you want, but adding the beads isn't hard. Lydia and I can show you how."

"Okay."

"Who will you give the purse to?" Anne Marie asked. She didn't think Courtney would need *two* purses. Maybe

Ellen wanted it for herself, for the fantasies she and April played at.

Instead of answering, Ellen asked another question, this one directed toward Lydia. "Can I knit it in pink?"

"Sure thing," Lydia answered, and led her to the shelf that housed the fingering-weight cashmere yarns. Ellen chose a light rose color.

"Mom likes pink. Right, Mom?"

"I do indeed," Anne Marie said absently, still focused on her conversation with Lydia.

Stepping over to the cash register, Lydia rang up the purchase. "That was a good choice," she assured Ellen. "If you have any problems, your mom can help."

"More than likely I'll be the one going to her," Anne Marie said with a laugh.

Ellen was quiet on the ride home. "Can I go to April's house with Baxter?" she asked.

"That's okay as long as it's all right with her mother." When they reached the house, Anne Marie phoned Natalie, April's mom, and learned that April had been at odds all morning, waiting for Ellen's return. Ellen had taught her to knit, and April was stuck and needed guidance. After a quick lunch, Ellen was out the door.

Anne Marie stood on the porch, watching her daughter race down the street, knitting bag in one hand, Baxter's leash in the other.

It seemed impossible that they'd moved only a week ago. Anne Marie had plenty to do and intended to stay busy. If she spent the afternoon sorting and unpacking, maybe she'd stop thinking about Tim and Mel.

Mel phoned midafternoon, inviting her and Ellen on an outing to the zoo Sunday afternoon. Anne Marie had taken Ellen to Woodland Park Zoo three or four times already, and since Monday was a school day, she decided a quiet afternoon might be best.

Mel accepted her decision graciously and didn't press the point, which struck her as a little unusual.

Not until she ended the conversation did she wonder what her reaction would have been had Tim suggested the outing. Mel might've hoped she'd recommend something else. She hadn't. Neither had he.

The fact was, she didn't feel any excitement, any compulsion about being with Mel. Not the way she felt about being with Tim….

Only he didn't phone.

For the rest of the afternoon, she waited to hear from him. When the phone did ring, around five, Ellen answered; it was obviously one of her friends.

"What's for dinner?" her daughter asked an hour later.

"What would you like?" Before Ellen could respond she added, "*Not* pad thai, and nothing with peanut sauce."

Ellen laughed. "I had that yesterday. I wasn't going to ask for it now. Can we have spaghetti?"

"Sure." Thankfully, that was quick and easy. Anne Marie wasn't in the mood to cook, or, for that matter, eat.

They were seated at the table for dinner when Ellen said, "Dad's eating at Grandma and Grandpa Carlsen's tonight."

"You spoke to Tim?"

Ellen nodded as she reached for the Parmesan cheese and sprinkled it liberally over her noodles. "That was him on the phone a while ago."

Anne Marie immediately lost what little appetite she had. Tim hadn't asked to speak to *her*. She toyed with the noodles, swirling them around her fork, but had no interest in her own cooking.

"Can we start knitting the bride's purse tonight?" Ellen asked.

"Sure," she said, hoping her voice betrayed none of her disappointment.

"Good." Ellen ate with relish, seeming to enjoy every bite. "I told Dad I saw you."

"Saw me?"

"Kissing," she said, and giggled. "You and Dad. You thought I was asleep but I woke up. We were in the car, remember?"

"Ah…"

"That day at the lake."

Anne Marie knew precisely when it had happened. "What did your father say?"

"Nothing at first, then he sort of laughed and said you were a good kisser."

"Did he, now?"

"Is Dad a good kisser, too?"

Anne Marie smiled. "He is."

"I saw Mel kiss you once."

That wasn't nearly as big a surprise.

"You kiss him different than you do Dad."

"Oh?"

"You like it more with Dad. I can tell."

For that matter, so could Anne Marie. "Mel's a good kisser," she said loyally.

"But not as good as Dad."

This wasn't a conversation Anne Marie felt they should be having. "How about dessert?" she asked, desperately trying to change the subject. Ellen shook her head, but the expression on her face said she knew exactly what Anne Marie was doing.

After dinner Ellen cleared the table and together they placed the dirty dishes in the dishwasher, washed the two pots and put them away.

"Church in the morning," Anne Marie reminded her.

"I know," Ellen said. "Can we start knitting now?"

"Okay."

Ellen ran into her bedroom with Baxter at her heels. She returned with the package from A Good Yarn, and they sat on the sofa, side by side. Anne Marie read the pattern all the way through and so did Ellen. It seemed relatively uncomplicated and wouldn't take more than a couple of weeks. Anne Marie cherished her knitting time. She used those quiet moments to think, weighing decisions and mulling over whatever troubled her, letting solutions come of their own accord. The rhythmic action of knitting calmed her mind, making her relaxed and receptive.

"I like the pink yarn," she told her daughter. "You never did say who you're knitting the purse for," Anne Marie said, completing the first row of her own project.

Ellen frowned as she worked the yarn onto the needles. Casting on was the most difficult part of knitting for her, because she insisted on using the long-tail method. At one time Lydia had said she felt it was the best way of starting a project. From that moment on, Ellen had refused to consider any other method.

They'd just finished their first rows when Ellen said, "For you."

Anne Marie didn't immediately grasp what she meant.

"Oh, you're knitting the bride's purse for me?" She smiled. "That's very thoughtful."

"For your wedding."

"My wedding," Anne Marie laughed. "Did I become engaged and forget all about it?" she joked.

"Not yet."

"And just who am I marrying? Mel?"

Ellen stopped knitting, set her needles aside and hurried into her bedroom. When she returned, she was carrying the spiral notebook in which she'd listed her twenty wishes. She sat down next to Anne Marie and reverently opened the book.

In neat and even cursive writing, Ellen had carefully written each of her twenty wishes. Several had been crossed out, including the trip to Paris they'd taken almost a year earlier.

"I have a twenty-first wish."

"And what would that be?" Anne Marie asked, bending forward to read what her daughter had written.

Ellen rested the book on Anne Marie's lap. Sure enough, at the bottom of the third page was her twenty-first wish. *I wish my mom and dad would get married.*

"Your…dad," Anne Marie said. A tingling sensation went down her spine.

"You already said you like the way he kisses," Ellen pointed out.

"That's true." Anne Marie couldn't very well deny it now.

"And he likes your kisses, too." Ellen paused. "Sometimes wishes *do* come true. Look how many of mine already have," she said, smoothing the page.

The trip to Paris.

Finding her father.

Learning to knit.

Anne Marie couldn't read any further because the words began to blur as tears gathered in her eyes. "That's a very nice wish," she murmured. "But you have to remember that sometimes wishes *don't* come true. And sometimes, even if they do, it takes a long time."

# *Ten*

May 5

April knows how to knit really well now. She doesn't even need my help anymore. I told her about the bride's purse I'm making and now she wants to knit one, too, only she doesn't know anyone who's getting married. Her mom is taking her down to A Good Yarn on Saturday and she said I could come. Mom and I have been knitting every night after dinner. I'm glad I showed her my twenty-first wish. I wasn't going to, but I did, anyway.

Anne Marie heard from Mel every day for the next week. He phoned at least once and sometimes twice. Invariably he'd invite her somewhere—dinner, a movie, even just coffee—but Anne Marie always found an excuse. Still, Mel persisted. Finally, unable to put him off any longer, she agreed to meet him for a drink on Friday night, after work. Conveniently, Ellen had a playdate with another girl from school.

Tim phoned, too, but he spoke only to Ellen and, other than a polite exchange of greetings, he didn't have anything to say to Anne Marie. His lack of communication made her realize how much she'd come to rely on him and how much she'd looked forward to their conversations.

Lillie Higgins stopped by the bookstore early Friday afternoon. Lillie was not only a good friend, but one of Anne Marie's best customers. A voracious reader, she'd built up an extensive library and often purchased several hardcovers at a time.

"Oh, the book you ordered came in," Anne Marie said. She'd meant to phone and leave a message earlier, but had gotten sidetracked, which seemed to be the norm lately. She really did need to focus on business, she told herself, instead of the sad state of her personal life.

"I thought it must have," Lillie said as she walked up to the service counter. "It usually takes you about three days to get a special order in."

While Anne Marie retrieved the Mexican cookbook for her, Lillie wandered over to the new display Teresa had arranged. "I haven't heard from you since the move." She picked up the latest bestseller by a popular suspense author and flipped through the pages. "I got your thank-you note. Hector and I enjoyed ourselves."

"I really appreciate everyone's help," Anne Marie said.

"That Tim is quite the character, isn't he?" Lillie commented with a laugh. "While we were loading up the truck, he and Ellen were singing ABBA songs at the top of their lungs. He actually has quite a nice voice. Ellen, too."

At the mention of Tim's name, Anne Marie lowered her eyes. She didn't want to think about him, yet he was constantly on her mind. Not an hour passed without her being reminded of him in some way.

"My dear," Lillie said, placing one beautifully mani-cured hand on Anne Marie's arm. "What is it? Did I say something to upset you?"

"No…"

"Is it Tim?"

Anne Marie nodded. "We had a…falling out."

"Over Ellen?"

"Not exactly." Based on what he'd said to her daughter, he seemed to regret their argument. So did she. Perhaps he felt it best to keep his distance, step aside and give her a chance to work things out with Mel. She wasn't sure how to interpret this painful silence, this…discord be-tween them. All she knew was that she had to find some way of resolving it.

"I remember how awkward it was when Hector and I first started seeing each other," Lillie said. "His family objected, and Barbie had her doubts, too. Neither of us wanted to cause problems, so we ended our relationship. I have to tell you, I've never been more miserable in my life."

"That's where I am right now," Anne Marie told her.

"Then *do* something about it," Lillie said. "If you have feelings for Tim, you need to tell him."

Lillie made everything sound so straightforward. Un-fortunately, Anne Marie's situation was anything but. She liked Mel and enjoyed his company, but he didn't stir her senses, didn't make her feel the passion or excitement she felt with Tim. Mel was attentive and smart and she knew he loved her. But she didn't return his feelings. And there was nothing she could do about that. She couldn't force emotions that simply weren't there.

"You'll tell him, won't you?" Lillie urged.

"I…I don't know yet." One thing was certain: she

couldn't move forward with Tim—if he even wanted to—until she'd broken off with Mel. And that wasn't going to be easy.

Mel had suggested they meet at the Italian restaurant where they'd gone on their first date. So their relationship would begin and end at the same place. That wasn't a comforting thought. But there was no option other than honesty. Anne Marie would drink her glass of wine, then as gently as possible confess she was in love with Tim. After that, she'd be on her way.

She hoped.

By the time she arrived at Ti Amo Sempre, Mel had secured a table by the window. He stood as she approached and kissed her cheek. He'd already ordered her favorite wine, a Malbec from the Mendoza region of Argentina. His thoughtfulness made this final meeting even more awkward.

As she picked up her wine, Mel also raised his glass. "To Fridays," he said.

Anne Marie touched the rim of her glass to his. "To Fridays."

"You had a busy week," he said, leaning back in his chair.

Nervous, Anne Marie reached for a handful of the nuts their waiter had delivered with the wine. Her week had actually been slow, but she'd invented excuse after excuse not to see Mel, most of them related to the business, which led him to believe she'd been overwhelmed by a huge influx of new inventory and custom orders.

"You, too," she murmured, evading the truth for another few minutes—or seconds.

"Very busy," he said solemnly

She responded with a weak smile, then drew in a

deep breath and plunged forward, forgoing any further exchange of pleasantries. "I think you already know why I wanted to meet you this evening," she said quickly. Her stomach was in knots, and all she could concentrate on was saying what needed to be said.

"I asked *you* out, remember?" he said. "Now, relax and enjoy your wine. It's your favorite."

"I know…but I can't relax."

"Try." He gestured for her to take another sip. "The wine will help."

Anne Marie did, and Mel was right; the wine did make her feel calmer. "You came into my life at a turning point," she began.

"And you came into mine when I needed you."

Anne Marie nodded, trying not to wince, wondering how he'd react to her announcement. "I've really enjoyed our times together," she said.

"I have, too, which makes this all the more difficult for me."

Difficult for *him?* Anne Marie glanced up, unsure of his meaning.

"I've met someone else, Anne Marie," he said. "I've been trying to tell you all week, but whenever I called, you had some work problem that demanded your attention and we couldn't chat."

She blinked, certain she'd misunderstood him. "You've…met someone else?"

"Yes, a woman from my office, who's closer to my own age. We have a lot in common."

"When?"

"A couple of weeks ago. Remember the Saturday you moved? Renee was at the office, too. After my appointment, she suggested we grab a bite to eat. We had a great time. I had no idea what a wonderful sense of humor she has."

Anne Marie was having trouble assimilating all this. "Mel, are you being honest with me?" She wanted to make sure he wasn't fabricating this story in order to ease her conscience.

"The truth is, I probably wouldn't have given Renee a second glance if it wasn't for the fact that I already knew I was losing you."

"Oh, Mel."

He gave her a wry smile. "I found out she's had her eye on me for quite a while."

Anne Marie laughed out loud. "You have no idea how much better this makes me feel."

Mel laughed, too, his expression almost boyish. "Tim's a good man."

"I think so, too."

"I regret the way I behaved earlier. I wish you both the best."

Rather than explain that she hadn't exactly worked out the situation with Tim, she let Mel assume all was well between them.

"I hope you and Renee find happiness together," she said. Mel had graciously wished her the best and it seemed only fitting that she do the same. Besides, she meant it. He deserved to be with a woman who cared about him with the same intensity she felt toward Tim.

"Let's keep in touch," he said.

"Let's," she agreed.

"I'll update you on what's happening with me and Renee."

"I'd like that."

They finished their wine, and after Mel had paid the

bill they walked outside into the still-bright evening. On the sidewalk in front of the restaurant, they hugged, then went their separate ways. For the first time in weeks, Anne Marie felt she could smile.

Then she thought of the coming conversation with Tim, and all her anxieties returned.

# *Eleven*

May 7

I doubt that I could be more surprised than I was when Mel announced he'd met someone else. When I got home my head was spinning. But I didn't really have a chance to think about it because Ellen came home soon after I did, talking up a storm about her visit with her new friend Bailey. She's teaching Bailey to knit, too, and wants to start a knitting camp for her friends during summer vacation. The backyard will be perfect, since I plan to get a picnic table and a large umbrella. She's going to invite Lydia to come and teach. Ellen seems to have everything figured out. If she teaches five friends to knit and each of them teaches five friends, by the end of the summer the whole school will know how to knit. Oh, if only life was this simple…

Saturday morning the doorbell rang while Anne Marie sorted laundry. She'd started taking every other Saturday off in order to spend more time with Ellen. When her daughter didn't immediately rush to answer, Anne Marie left the stack of soiled laundry in front of the washer and hurried toward the hall. Baxter was barking wildly. She calmed him and told him to sit—to her great satisfaction he obeyed instantly—then opened the door.

When she saw Tim standing there, she nearly gasped with shock. He was the last person she'd expected—and the most welcome. While she yearned to yank open the screen door and throw herself into his arms, she resisted.

"Hi," she managed, her voice, even to her own ears, sounding breathless and strange.

"Is Ellen here?" he asked stiffly.

"Would you like to come in?"

"Not really. I came by to make sure her bike's working properly after I fixed it."

"It's fine." His excuse was so flimsy, she had to suspect there was another reason—one that had to do with *her*. Now that he was here, Anne Marie had no intention of letting him go. "Come inside, Tim," she said again, opening the screen door to usher him in. "I'm glad to see you."

He met her eyes as if to gauge the sincerity of her words.

"I've missed you," she added.

"Good," he said mildly, although his expression gave nothing away.

"Good?" she repeated. "You *wanted* me to miss you?"

He didn't respond, except with a smile. A very slight smile.

"Did you miss me?" she asked.

"That's not the point."

"As a matter of fact, it is. I want to know if you thought about me in the past week."

He shrugged.

"That's no answer."

"If I admitted you were on my mind every minute of every day, would you lord it over me?"

Her smile was so wide it hurt her mouth. "I might."

"That's what I figured. Women are like that. They demand their pound of flesh—and this time my Shakespearean quote *is* correct."

"Yes, it is, but the context is wrong." Anne Marie frowned. "You were doing very well until you said that. You should know I'm not going to let you make derogatory comments about half of humanity."

"You're the one who was going to lord it over me if I admitted I missed you—which I did."

"I already admitted I missed you, but I'll say it again." There, she'd extended an olive branch.

He grinned and looked so appealing that it was all she could do not to kiss him right then and there.

"Mom!" Ellen skipped out of the kitchen, clutching the phone in one hand. She stopped when she saw Tim. "Oh, hi, Dad."

"Hello, sweetheart."

"Mom, can April come over and play?"

"That's fine."

"Can she bring Iris, too?"

"Yes."

"Can she stay for lunch?"

Anne Marie nodded.

"Thanks, Mom." Ellen brought the phone back to her ear and returned to the kitchen, chattering as she walked.

"Okay, where were we?" Anne Marie asked, her hand on her hip.

Tim smiled again. "I believe you just said you missed me so much that your whole world's sad and gray."

Anne Marie felt her mouth twitch. "Ah...that's not quite the way I remember it."

"I was close, though, wasn't I?"

Anne Marie had a question of her own. "Why didn't you call?"

"I called."

"To talk to Ellen, but not me."

He sobered, and his smile faded. "How's Mel?"

"Very well. We had drinks last night."

A muscle tightened in Tim's jaw. "I see."

"I don't think you do."

"I'm here to check on Ellen's bike. I wouldn't want to take up any more of your time."

"Your being here has nothing to do with Ellen's bicycle." She wasn't going to play that silly game with him.

"If you're still involved with Mel, then I don't think we have much to say to each other."

"Are you always this obtuse?"

"I'm not the least bit obtuse."

That was when Ellen came back into the living room. "April's on her way over."

Anne Marie turned her attention to her daughter. "I'll start lunch in a few minutes. Right now your father and I are having a discussion."

Ellen remained where she was. "Are you fighting?"

"No," Anne Marie said.

"Yes," Tim said.

"We're having a difference of opinion," Anne Marie clarified, glaring at Tim.

"Did you tell him about my twenty-first wish?" the girl asked.

"No." Furthermore, she had no intention of doing so.

Ellen's face fell.

"What's your twenty-first wish?" Tim asked.

"I'll make lunch." Without waiting for anyone to agree or disagree, Anne Marie left the room. She searched the refrigerator, and not finding anything that suited her, took out a loaf of bread and a jar of peanut butter. Ellen would be happy with that, and she hoped April would, too.

The sandwiches were ready when Tim entered the kitchen. He pulled out a bar stool and perched on it. "Did you make me one of those?"

"No. Should I have?"

"It would've been the polite thing to do."

She extracted two slices from the loaf of bread. "At the moment I don't feel like being polite."

"So I noticed." He didn't say anything as she prepared his peanut butter sandwich, cut it in quarters, and set the plate in front of him. "Do you want a glass of milk, too?"

"I might shock you if I told you what I want."

She raised her eyebrows. "And what would that be?"

He leaned forward and braced his hands on the edge of the counter. "I have wishes of my own. I've never written them down the way Ellen has, but I've given those wishes a great deal of thought, especially in the last few weeks."

Anne Marie leaned against the counter, too, and waited for him to continue. "What kind of wishes?"

"Well, one wish was to find my daughter."

"That was granted."

"Thanks to you."

"Go on." She refused to let him sidetrack her.

"Another was to fall in love."

"Vanessa, right?"

"Fall in love *again*," he amended.

Still standing on the other side of the counter, she pressed her palms against it. Their faces were only inches apart. "And?"

"I fell so hard, it was like nothing I'd ever felt before."

"Then…"

"Then I discovered that the woman I loved was involved with someone else."

"If we're talking about the same woman—"

"I think we must be."

"Then that…woman's been doing her utmost to explain that she's no longer 'involved' with this other man."

"No longer involved?" Tim repeated. "Since when?"

"Since last night when they met for a drink. However, the person she's been wanting to tell has been obtuse— yes, obtuse—and is severely trying her patience."

"Is that a fact?"

"It is."

"What I'd like to know is if this woman you mentioned is in love with me."

Anne Marie reached for a quarter of his sandwich and took a bite. "I think she must be."

"You *think?* You mean to say you aren't sure?"

"Well…it's a big decision to love another person." Recalling her conversation with Lydia, about how love was ultimately a choice, she used the word *decision* deliberately. Yes, the emotions, the sensations, might be involuntary, but real love was also something chosen. Something that had to be cherished and protected.

"I agree. Very big."

"There's commitment, to each other and to any children...."

Tim nodded. "One might suggest marriage as a way of keeping that commitment."

"One might."

"That's another of my wishes," he said.

Anne Marie set her piece of the sandwich aside. "Marriage requires a lot of trust."

"Yes, it does. It's—"

He stopped when Ellen and April walked in. Ellen immediately looked at Anne Marie, then at Tim and back again. "Are you two still fighting?" she asked.

"We aren't fighting," Tim assured her.

"We're discussing our wishes," Anne Marie said.

"Wishes?" April asked curiously.

"Mom and I made a list of twenty wishes," Ellen explained to her friend. "I have twenty-one now. I added one."

"I added one to my list, as well," Anne Marie said.

"You did?" Ellen stared at her. "Are you going to tell us what it is?"

Anne Marie nodded. "My wish is that you and Tim and I can one day be a family."

"I like that wish," Tim said in a low voice, a voice full of meaning.

"I do, too." Ellen pointed to the counter. "Is that our lunch?"

Anne Marie handed her daughter and April their plates.

"Can we eat in my bedroom?" Ellen asked.

"Yes, just this once. And don't feed the dogs."

"Okay."

The girls disappeared down the hallway.

"Now where were we?" Anne Marie murmured.

"I believe we were talking about wishes coming true. Even twenty-first wishes."

"I do believe you're right," she whispered.

Tim reached for her with the kitchen counter between them. It didn't take her long to skirt around it and find her way completely into his arms. Then they were laughing and talking between kisses, unable to stop touching and holding each other.

"I wasn't kidding," Tim said. "I want us to get married soon."

"I wasn't kidding, either—" But she didn't finish her sentence because Tim was kissing her again.

They were startled by Ellen's voice. "Mom," she said, standing in the doorway to the kitchen.

Tim and Anne Marie broke apart as Anne Marie straightened her blouse and tried to look as normal as possible.

Ellen wore a huge grin as she put the empty plates in the sink. "You're going to need the bride's purse I'm making, aren't you?"

Tim slipped his arm around Anne Marie's waist. "She is. How fast can you knit?"

"Real fast," Ellen told him, and then with her arms wide open she hugged them both.


September 10

This afternoon Tim Carlsen and I will be married in a private ceremony at the lake house with his family and mine in attendance. I'm so happy I can barely contain myself. Once I allowed my feelings for Tim to emerge, I was astonished at how deeply I cared for him. I had all along, but my pride had refused to let me acknowledge that. Tim is everything I want in a husband.

Ellen told us she's bringing her list of wishes to the ceremony so she can mark off her twenty-first wish as soon as we're officially husband and wife. I have a lovely pink summer dress that goes beautifully with the pink bride's purse she knit me.

This is the second happiest day of my life, the first being the day of Ellen's adoption. Who would ever have guessed when I made my very first wish—to find love again—that God would send me a daughter and then, as a bonus, her father. My husband. Tim.

September 10

Mom and Dad are getting married today. I always knew they would but sometimes adults need help. I can cross off my twenty-first wish now.

\* \* \* \* \*

# Coming Unravelled

## SUSAN MALLERY

My thanks to Debbie and Christina
for including me in this wonderful collection.

### Nikki Mallery—a Puppet Knitting Pattern
### Designed by artist Jean Townsend
### www.jeantownsend.com

My name is Nikki Mallery. My mom is Susan Mallery. You know, the writer. She writes books about love and mushy stuff. Out of all the dogs in the world, she loves me best. She likes to dress me up in pretty little outfits and put adorable bows in my poofy hair. Then she posts pictures on her website, www.SusanMallery.com. In fact, she gave me a whole page of my own on her website. You can see all my video adventures there. I'm very adventuresome! Oh, and I'm the official mascot of Fool's Gold, California. As you can see, I live a very full life.

## MATERIALS:

For puppet:
Small amount of polyfill
1 skein worsted-weight yarn in tan
Small amount of turquoise fingering yarn
Small amount of copper-colored worsted-weight and black worsted-weight yarn
Size 6 double-pointed needles for body*
Size 2 straight or circular needles for eyes

For dress:
1 skein each of fingering yarn in mint-green, purple and orange for dress
Size 3 straight or circular and dp needles

For hair and tiara:
1 skein of bouclé about worsted weight
Pipe cleaner
Felt for a star
Small jewel

*This pattern will fit the average adult hand. For a smaller or larger puppet, use smaller or larger needles. It is also *a right-handed puppet. To make it left-handed, fold the thumb from the left side to the center before attaching the parts.*

## ABBREVIATIONS

st = stitch
dp = double-pointed
inc = increase
k = knit
p = purl

ktog = knit together
ssk = slip, slip, knit (slip two stitches to right-hand needle, put right needle through the back loops, knit together)
pu = pick up

## PUPPET BODY

Using worsted-weight and size 6 dp needles, cast on 44 stitches and divide onto three needles, mark beginning of row.

Work 6 rows in stockinette st, purl one row for the turn of the hem, then continue in stockinette st for 1½ inches from hem line. On next row, dec 2 st evenly spaced. Continue in stockinette st for 2 inches from the hem turn. (42 sts)

Thumb Gore:

First inc round for thumb gore: inc 1 st in next st (first thumb st), k1, inc 1 in next st (last thumb st). Knit to end of round. (44 sts)

K2 rounds even.

Second inc round: inc 1 st in first st, k3, inc 1 in next st, k to end of round. (46 sts)

K2 rounds even.

Continue to increase 1 st in first and last thumb st every third round (4 times) having 2 sts more between incs after each round. (54 sts)

K2 rounds even. Slip to a strand of yarn or a small holder the 15 thumb sts. At the end of the last round cast on 3 sts. There will be 42 sts.

Work even until desired length, allowing 1 inch for finishing, decreasing 2 stitches evenly spaced in the last round.

First dec round: ktog every 3rd and 4th st, 10 times.

K3 rounds even.

Second dec round: ktog every 2nd and 3rd st, 10 times.

K3 rounds even.

Third dec round: k2tog in succession 10 times.

Break off, leaving an end. Draw end tightly through all sts. Fasten off.

Thumb: slip to 2 needles the 15 sts of thumb, with a third needle pick up and knit the 3 cast on sts. There are now 18 sts on the needles. Knit around until thumb measures 2 inches above cast on sts.

First dec round: *k1, k2tog, repeat from * 5 times.

K2 rounds even.

K2tog in succession 6 times.

Finish as for top of mittens.

Finishing: use the tail of the yarn joined at the thumb to pull together any open spaces at the thumb join, reinforcing it. Weave in ends.

Arms and legs: cast on 18 sts on size 6 dp needles, work until desired length, finish off as for thumb. Arms should measure 2 ¾ inches and legs should measure 6 inches. Fill with small amount of polyfill, just enough to fill out the form. Baste top together.

Slip stitch hem in place.

Tail: with a double strand of worsted and 2 size 6 dp needles, cast on 3 sts. * K3, do not turn work. Slide sts to right end of needles. Pull yarn to tighten. Repeat from * until cord is 3 inches long, leaving a long tail of yarn end.

With black yarn, make toenails on the paws.

## DRESS

With green yarn and circular or straight needles, cast on 144 sts, work in moss stitch for 8 rows. In next row, K2tog across. Purl one row. 72 sts.

Change to purple, work in stockinette st for 5 rows. Work 2 rows in orange.

Armholes: K16, slip these sts to holder, bind off 2, K36, slip to holder, bind off 2, K1, SSK, K to end. Purl next row. Repeat these two rows till 8 sts remain, place on holder. (This is left front.)

Right front: Attach yarn at front edge, K to last 3 sts, K2tog, K1. Purl next row. Repeat these 2 rows until 8 sts remain. Place on holder.

Back: Put back 36 sts on needle, with right side facing, join yarn at right edge. K1, inc 1, K to within 2 sts of edge, inc 1, K1. Purl next row. Continue until there are 52 sts. Break yarn.

Knit 8 sts of right front from holder, cast on 2 sts, K52 sts of back, cast on 2 sts, K8 sts of left front. (72 sts) Work 2 rows. In next row, decrease 8 sts evenly spaced along back between armholes. Work 2 rows, bind off.

Sleeves: With size 3 dp needles, pu a total of 30 sts around the arm opening (13 sts on each side of arm, plus 2 sts at top and bottom of opening). Work 9 rows of stockinette st in purple. Change to green, work in stockinette st. for 3 rows, bind off in P st.

Bow: With orange, work an I cord on 2 size 3 dp needles for 19 inches, bind off.

Fold in half. Fold dress in half and match fold marks. Stretch I cord slightly while whipstitching it along the top of dress with purple yarn, stopping ¼ inch before front edge on each side.

Sewing up: Use mattress stitch to sew up front on dress. Weave in all ends.

## HAIR

Make a generous hank of yarn about 20 inches long. Tie piece of yarn in a bow around one end. With another piece of yarn, tie a firm knot 3 inches from the top, wrapping the yarn several times around the hank. Untie the top bow and clip the ends, this forms the top knot.

Separate the section below the knot into two equal pieces (like ponytails). Beginning close to the top knot, use a piece of yarn to firmly wrap a ¾ inch section of the ponytail, securing the ends by using a yarn needle and threading the tail back through the wrapped section. Do this the same way you would wrap a lock of hair around the rubber-banded part of a ponytail to hide the rubber band. Repeat on the other side.

Place the hair across the puppet's head, and secure by stitching with a doubled yarn into the knitted fabric. Placement is important! The bangs should be close enough to the eyes to fall across them. When the hair is in place, trim it so the ears reach to just above the shoulders (generous ears!). Leave the topknot hair longer in back to flop a bit over the back.

Make a small pom-pom, about 3 inches wide, and attach it to the I cord tail.

## TIARA

Affix a pipe cleaner to a star (I used an old felted piece of knitting) by folding the edge of the pipe cleaner over about ¼ of an inch to make a loop, then sew it onto the back of the fabric or paper. Make a bend in the pipe cleaner about two inches from the star and nestle it into the top knot. Wrap the remainder around the base of the top knot and secure ends. Cut off excess pipe cleaner. Glue a jewel into the center of the star (a glue gun is easy and quick). Fluff out the top knot around the pipe cleaner so it does not show. The star should be just peeking out.

## ASSEMBLY

Pull the eye shapes into shape, pointing both the ends, and pin to head for placement. Then sew on with long tails. Use a double length of black worsted to make pupils in satin stitch or French knots.

Place the bobble on the nose spot and use the tails to sew the outer edge of the bobble to the knitted fabric.

Lay the puppet flat and fold the thumb from the right edge to the center. The thumb gore should begin ½ inch inside the body. Place the arms at a diagonal and slightly overlapping. Sew on firmly with a whipstitch. Sew lower legs to inside of hem.

Slip the dress over Nikki arms and tie bow tight enough to hold the dress up along the back (but not too tight).

# *One*

Robyn Mulligan was relieved to find everything in her grandmother's knitting store exactly as she remembered. The bins filled with beautiful yarns in different colors and textures, the big table in back where customers could work on projects while chatting with each other, the good-looking, somewhat scruffy cowboy sitting at the table, the big windows that let in the—

Robyn stepped through the doorway and let her small duffel drop to the floor as her gaze moved back to the table. A cowboy? Here?

Only Ewe was a popular Georgetown, Texas, knitting store, and while there were a few male customers, women outnumbered them at least a hundred to one. Robyn couldn't remember ever seeing a guy sitting down with a project, talking away as if he belonged.

She remembered something about her grandmother mentioning a man had joined their regular group, but Robyn had been picturing someone older and not quite so hunky.

Not her problem, she told herself. Customers, whatever shape, size or gender, were always welcome. That had been her grandmother's philosophy. It made sense. Without customers, the rent didn't get paid.

Robyn glanced around at the bustling space, noting that Adeline, one of her grandmother's two best friends, stood at the cash register, while Marion, the other best friend, helped a young woman who was very pregnant. Eleanor, her grandmother, was probably in back, looking through the new yarns to find something special for a customer.

There was a warmth to the store, she thought happily. A sense of belonging. What on earth had she been thinking, staying away so long? Quick, annual vacations had only made her miss home more.

Adeline completed the purchase and looked up. She spotted Robyn, clapped her hands together and shrieked.

"Eleanor, hurry. She's back. Our girl is back."

Everyone turned to look at Robyn, but she only saw the three seventy-something women rushing toward her. She tossed her duffel, held out her arms and breathed in a sigh of relief as the women who had always loved her hugged her until it seemed like her ribs were going to snap. Nothing had ever felt better.

She inhaled their various perfumes. Adeline, tall and intimidating with a stern appearance, wore the scent of roses. Marion, still coloring her hair a golden-blond, was shorter, rounder and favored White Diamonds. Then there was Eleanor, soft and pretty, wearing Chanel No. 5. The mingling scents had been a part of her childhood for as long as she could remember. Anything she'd made in the store had been infused with the delightful blend, comforting her during stormy nights or when she was sick.

"Let me look," Eleanor said, shooing the other two

back, then putting her hands on Robyn's shoulders. "I've missed you so much."

Robyn felt her own eyes burn with tears. "It's been too long."

"Six years," Adeline said, as if any of them would forget. "Weekend visits don't count, young lady. We were wondering if that city was ever going to let you go."

"New York is like that," Marion said, her hands fluttering. "A difficult place. Oh, but our girl is so glamorous now. And thin." Marion patted her own ample hip. "Thinner than you were when you visited last year. You look like a model."

"High fashion." Adeline sniffed. "You look like you need a sandwich."

"Leave her be," Eleanor told her friends. "She's just barely in the door. Let her get her feet under her." Eleanor smiled at Robyn. "I'm so glad you're home."

Robyn hugged her and then just held on. "Me, too. I should have come back a long time ago."

"To be with a bunch of old women? Why would you want that?"

Six years ago Robyn would have agreed with her. Leaving Georgetown, going to New York, following her dream, had meant everything. But dreams were tricky things and hers had pretty much chewed her up and spit her out. Right now something close to normal was looking really good to her.

"I need to clear up a few things here," her grandmother explained to her, stepping back and smiling. "Do you want to go on ahead to the house or wait for me?"

"I'll wait," Robyn said, bending down and picking up her duffel.

Marion's gaze followed her action, and then she grinned. "Presents?"

It was a familiar tradition. Whoever went away had to bring back something for those left behind. She set the duffel on the counter by the cash register, then opened it.

For Adeline, she had bought an oil painting of New York in the rain. Robyn had loved the artist's work since she'd first seen it two years before. The tall, gray-haired woman stared at the small framed painting for several seconds.

"It's very nice," she said gruffly. "I know just where I'm going to put it. Thank you."

"You're welcome."

Next came the lace she'd found in a vintage shop down in the East Village. "They said the bolt dates back to the 1950s and it's just like the one Grace Kelly picked for her veil," she said, handing the folded fabric to Marion. "Every bride should be a princess on her wedding day."

Marion sniffed, then lunged for her. "Oh, Robyn. It's wonderful. Thank you."

"I'm glad you like it."

"Like it? I love it!"

Robyn turned to her grandmother last. "For your collection," she said, pulling out a tissue-wrapped Steiff bear. "He's a handsome devil, circa 1920, in perfect condition."

Eleanor sighed as she carefully took the present and unwrapped it to see the gift that had cost Robyn her sofa, TV and her last hundred dollars. The price of Adeline's gift had been her bed and nightstand, and the contents of her fridge, while Marion's lace had been the easiest to acquire. She'd only had to give away a Michael Kors cocktail dress she'd bought off the back of a truck and make sure the previous owner of the lace got Robyn's lunchtime shift at the Wall Street bistro where Robyn had worked.

"He's wonderful," Eleanor breathed. "But you're far too generous."

"You're my family. Who else would I be generous with?" The gifts were easy, Robyn thought to herself, it was telling the truth that was going to be hard.

And not something she was dealing with today, she reminded herself.

She zipped the duffel, then flattened it. As she went to tuck it under the counter, she happened to glance toward the table in the back, where the knitters sat. Most of them were busy with their own work, barely paying attention to anyone else in the store. But the man she'd noticed—the tall guy in the Western-style shirt—was focused entirely on her. His dark eyes seemed to burn their way into her skin, and not in a nice way. He looked angry and determined. He looked like he hated her.

His steady gaze made her heart stutter a little. From concern, she told herself. There was no way she found that horrible man appealing.

She stiffened, her chest tight and uncomfortable. "Who's the guy?" she asked, knowing she hadn't seen him before on her infrequent visits home.

Eleanor looked over her shoulder and smiled. "That's T.J. He came to us, what, two years ago?"

"Nearly three," Adeline corrected. "He was in a car accident. Serious injuries. He could barely move his hands."

"His doctor thought knitting would help," Marion added. "He came because he had to. For the first six months he didn't speak a word. Just sat there, trying to knit a row."

"We saved him," Eleanor said, sounding proud. "I think I've told you about him a few times. He's all better now."

"He's not a puppy," Adeline told her. "We helped him. He saved himself. There's a difference."

Robyn glanced over her shoulder, prepared to say that for some reason the man seemed to hate her. But as she looked again, she saw he wasn't paying attention to her at all. When he did look up, his eyes carried the mild curiosity of any stranger.

She faced front again, wondering if the long drive had tired her more than she'd thought. She must have imagined his animosity. After all, how could someone who never even met her loathe her on sight?

Robyn parked in front of her grandmother's pretty house in a quiet, suburban part of Georgetown. The houses all looked pristine—paint and landscaping all kept fresh and neat. This was a part of town where people took pride in their homes.

She got out of the clunker she'd borrowed for the trip home. It was a car shared by a group of people. Robyn wasn't sure who even owned it. She just knew that in two days a guy would arrive to drive it to California. Her job was to make sure it was full of gas and to hand over the keys.

Her grandmother limped toward her. "What can I carry in?"

"I'll get it," Robyn replied, frowning slightly. "Should you ice your knee?"

"At this point, it's beyond help." Eleanor grinned. "But

in a few weeks, I'll have the left knee of a thirty-year-old. I've asked the doctor if he can do that to my behind as well, but he ignores me."

Robyn laughed. "Grandma, are you flirting with your medical professional?"

"Mostly giving him a hard time. Now hand me something to carry."

Robyn passed over the lightest of the bags, then grabbed two more for herself. Deconstructing her life had taken less time than she would have thought, but despite selling or bartering nearly everything she owned, she'd still filled the car with her stuff.

Once they were inside, Robyn followed Eleanor to the room that had been Robyn's since the death of her mother. The windows were clean, the curtains freshly washed. The faint smell of new paint made her frown.

"Tell me you didn't paint this room for me," she said. "You're supposed to be taking it easy until you have your knee replacement surgery."

"I didn't paint the room." Her grandmother winked. "T.J. did it. He's the nicest man. When I mentioned you were coming back and that I wanted to spruce up your room, he volunteered."

T.J. of the glaring eyes? Robyn had trouble believing that.

After leaving the luggage, they went into the kitchen where all important meals, discussions and decisions occurred. Eleanor got out the kettle to make tea. Robyn took it from her.

"Go sit. I'll deal with this."

"You're tired from your long drive," her grandmother protested.

"I can still boil water."

Everything was where she remembered. The delicate porcelain cups and saucers decorated with flowers. The carved wooden box that contained a dozen or so different types of loose tea in worn tins. The tea balls in the drawer to the right and the teapots themselves, in the cupboard next to the stove.

"It's wonderful to have you here," her grandmother told her from her place at the Formica kitchen table. "I've missed you."

"I've missed you, too," Robyn said. "I'm glad you asked me to come back."

"I hated to take you away from your career. However long you can give me is plenty."

There was no career, Robyn thought, feeling both ashamed and guilty. Once there'd been a dream, but it had died a couple of years ago, starved to death slowly and painfully. She'd actually been relieved when her grandmother had called and asked if Robyn could spare the time to take care of her after her knee replacement surgery.

"I'm staying indefinitely," Robyn announced. There was no way she was heading back to New York, but that wasn't a conversation to have her first fifteen minutes back. She would bring it up gradually over the next few days.

While she didn't have the details of her plan worked out, she had a basic premise. She would help Eleanor for as long as she was needed, then she would find a job locally. She was an excellent waitress, with plenty of experience and recommendations. With all the wonderful restaurants in the area, she was confident she could find something nearby. She planned to live cheaply, save money and figure out what she wanted to do with the rest of her life.

When the tea was ready, she carried the pot to the table and poured them each a cup. Her grandmother stirred in cream, then took a sip.

"Lovely," she breathed. "It tastes better with you here."

Robyn laughed.

"How was the drive?"

"Long."

"You got here quicker than I expected."

"I drove straight through."

Her grandmother set down her cup and stared at her. "Robyn, no. Why would you do that?"

"I wanted to get home."

Which was mostly true. There was also the issue of not wanting to spend the money on a hotel room.

"I drank plenty of coffee."

"You must be exhausted."

"My behind is a little draggy."

Eleanor squeezed her hand. "Sometimes I worry about you. All right. I'm going back to the store. You stay here and rest. Climb into bed and don't think about getting out until I get home."

Bed did sound nice, Robyn thought. Her body ached from the drive and her eyes felt gritty.

There was a knock at the front door.

"I'll get it," she said, pushing herself to her feet.

She crossed the living room and pulled open the door, only to find T.J. standing on the wide front porch.

He didn't look any happier to see her than he had before.

Now that he was standing, Robyn realized he was taller

than she'd thought, nearly a full head above her own five foot six. Lean, but with plenty of muscle, he looked like the kind of man who could handle himself in any situation. He had black hair that needed cutting and a determined expression. His dark eyes were cold and assessing as they stared at her over the threshold. If he would smile, she had a feeling he would be devastating…in a good way.

"Marion says Eleanor is needed back at the store," he said. "I came by to see if I could help you unload the car."

The kind words were totally at odds with his expression. It was like looking at a growling dog with a wagging tail. Robyn didn't know which end to believe.

"T.J.," Eleanor said, coming up behind Robyn. "You didn't have to come all this way."

"It's five blocks."

"Still. You're so thoughtful." Eleanor patted Robyn's arm. "After T.J. helps you, dear, get some rest."

"I will," Robyn promised, then had to resist the need to beg her grandmother not to leave her alone with a man who seemed to find her so wanting.

But she'd been fighting her own battles for a long time now, so she ignored T.J.'s steady gaze and ushered her grandmother to her car.

When Eleanor had driven away, Robyn folded her arms over her chest and stared at T.J.

"Why don't you tell me why you're really here," she said.

"All right." He glared at her. "I know your kind and I know what you want. Don't for a minute think you're going to get away with it. If you're going to get to them, you're going to have to go through me."

# *Two*

T.J. had to give the woman credit. She didn't back down. Instead she went to her car and pulled out a couple of boxes, then started for the front door of the house.

He followed her.

"I thought you were here to help," she said.

"Help your grandmother, not you."

She set the boxes in the living room next to her suitcases. "So you're a liar as well as someone who makes pretty incredible assumptions about someone they've only just met. Good to know."

She was pretty, he thought absently, in a too-thin kind of way. Her cheekbones nearly jutted through her pale skin. Her blond hair could be attractive, if it was a little longer. As it was, the sleek, jaw-length bob only emphasized her sharp chin.

She pointed to the door. "You need to go now."

"Not until I find out what you're after."

Her blue eyes turned frosty. "What are you talking about? Eleanor is my grandmother. Has it occurred to you that I'm back to take care of her during her surgery? Where do you get off assuming anything bad about me? You don't even know me."

"And you don't know me." He stared at her. "I'm a friend of hers and her friends. You'd know that if you'd bothered to get involved in their lives, but you haven't even visited except for a couple of days here and there. You've been off in New York, taking care of yourself. Never giving a thought to these women who love you. Instead you're sucking them dry. I couldn't do anything about it before, but I sure can now, and I will."

Her mouth opened, then closed. She shook her head. "Do you think I'm after money?"

"What else? They financed your move there and who knows how much they're spending on a monthly basis. It's expensive to live in the city. You're sure as hell not supporting yourself in the theater." He narrowed his gaze. "They might believe your lies, but I don't. I've looked on the internet. You haven't been in a play in over three years. Although to hear them brag, you're going to be up for a Tony any day now."

She flushed, then ducked her head. "You don't know what you're talking about."

He knew enough, he thought grimly. He knew that she wanted Eleanor and her friends to think she was on her way to making it as an actress. T.J. was willing to overlook a lot of faults, but he wasn't one to forgive a liar. Especially when those lies hurt people he cared about.

He might have come to Only Ewe reluctantly and because taking the knitting class got his doctor off his ass. But over time, he'd found that it was a safe place to be. There were no memories in the store. Just grandmotherly types who fussed over him and made being alive a little less painful.

He spent the first six months resisting their efforts to embrace him. Over time, they'd sucked him into their world. Once he'd given himself over to the process, he'd begun to heal.

Now they were his family and there was no way a skinny, selfish wannabe actress was going to hurt them. He would have to tread carefully—he knew Eleanor adored her granddaughter. But there were ways of protecting the old ladies without them catching on.

"I know enough," he told her. "I'll be watching and waiting."

"You're going to have to do that from the other side of the door," she told him, pointing. "Get out."

He went. When she slammed the door, he only smiled. If she thought a couple of pieces of wood were enough to protect her from him, she was wrong.

Robyn woke shortly after five-thirty in the morning. It took her a second to realize she'd slept for nearly fifteen hours straight. She was starving, but for the first time in forever, she felt rested and at peace.

She was home. She'd moved in with her grandmother after her mother had died. Robyn had been twelve and scared, but never alone. Eleanor had always been a part of her life. They'd been a close family, the three Mulligan women.

She showered in the bathroom across the hall, then dressed. It felt good not to have to put on her waitressing uniform. If she never wore a short black skirt and white shirt again in her life, she would be happy.

Her favorite jeans were loose, she thought, knowing she'd lost another couple of pounds in the past week. All that running around and not so much on the eating. But that would change, she told herself. One of the great things about Texas was the food. There was plenty of it and she would be able to afford it.

Robyn dug around in a bottom dresser drawer to find an old T-shirt to pull on. As she grabbed the one on top, she felt something hard tucked underneath. A book, she thought, pulling that out as well. Only, it wasn't a book.

The worn cover had once been bright blue. Time had left the fabric faded to a more gray color. The pages were a little tattered at the edges. She slipped on the T-shirt, then sat on the bed and flipped through what had once been her diary.

Her grandmother had given her the book years ago. Robyn couldn't have been more than ten or twelve. The first entries were about dance classes and singing lessons, ideas for a sweater she wanted to make her mother for Christmas. Later her thoughts had shifted to boys and fashion, until her mother had gotten sick. Then Robyn hadn't written in her diary for a long time.

Now she turned to the last page and read.

"I head to New York tomorrow. I'm not afraid. I'm going there to make all my dreams come true. Not just for me, but for my mom, too. She never had the chance. It's up to me to make this happen for both of us."

Robyn closed the book. She hadn't been able to make her mother's dreams come true—or her own. Even a few months ago, that knowledge would have been painful. Now she understood that everything had changed. That facing her future with courage was a way to finally be free.

She put the diary back in the drawer, made her way to the kitchen and started coffee.

After opening the refrigerator, she nearly swooned at the sight of eggs and bacon, fruit, and hamburger thawing on a plate. If she wasn't mistaken, her grandmother was planning on her famous spaghetti that night. Robyn's mouth watered at the memory of the delicious sauce smothering a huge plate of noodles.

While the coffee brewed, she moved into the dining room. Family pictures lined the walls. Her mother as a young girl, dressed in a tutu, standing on her toes. Her mother as a teenager, in costume for a school play.

There were similar pictures of Robyn as she'd grown up. At the ballet barre at her mother's dance studio. In high school productions. Their dreams were the same—to be on the stage. To make it on Broadway.

Instead of leaving for New York, Robyn's mother had fallen in love. When she'd discovered she was pregnant, the man who had stolen her heart had taken off, leaving her alone. She'd been determined that Robyn wouldn't follow in her footsteps. From the time Robyn could understand what her mother was saying, she'd heard over and over again that a man only got in the way of a woman's dream. She knew she had to do better. That she had to be successful for both herself and her mother.

Her grandmother had tried to temper the message, saying life was balance, but it was too little, too late. Robyn had gone to New York after college, determined to be the best. Failure hadn't been an option, but it had happened just the same.

She heard footsteps in the hallway and looked up.

"Good morning," she said when she saw Eleanor. "I can't believe I slept straight through."

"You needed it."

"I'm feeling much better." She crossed to the older woman and hugged her. "How are you?"

"Happy to have you home. I thought we'd have spaghetti tonight."

"I saw that. My stomach is still growling at the thought."

They went into the kitchen. While Eleanor poured coffee, Robyn got out eggs and did her best not to whimper in anticipation. She inhaled the smell of the bacon, sipped coffee and dropped toast into the toaster.

"Just one slice for me," Eleanor said. "I'm cutting back a little. I wanted to lose ten pounds before my surgery. Only one more to go. You're incredibly thin, Robyn. What's your secret?"

Not having enough money to buy food, she thought grimly. "I'm on my feet all the time and I'm so busy, I forget to eat." She gave a fake laugh. "The working girl's diet. I'm hoping to put on a few pounds now that I'm back."

"Easy enough. I'll make cinnamon rolls this weekend."

"I'd like that."

They sat across from each other at the table. As Robyn devoured the food, she studied her grandmother, taking in the familiar features, the new lines around her eyes. Eleanor wasn't getting younger, but she was still healthy and active. Robyn hoped to have her for at least another twenty years.

"You looked busy at the store," Robyn said when she'd inhaled the three eggs she'd scrambled, along with four pieces of bacon.

"We are. The Old Town section of Georgetown is always so active and vital. We have our loyal customer base and plenty of new customers. Knitting is very in these days." Eleanor frowned. "Do you young people still say 'in'?"

Robyn grinned. "We understand what it means."

"I want to stay current," her grandmother said primly. "I even text."

"Good for you."

"I see you and T.J. got everything in from your car."

T.J. hadn't been any help at all, Robyn thought, pushing away the last slice of toast. Thinking about the irritating man spoiled the rest of her appetite.

She'd been afraid obsessing about him would have kept her up, but fortunately she'd been too exhausted to let him interrupt her sleep. He'd been so annoying and oddly attractive, which really bothered her.

Still, she couldn't figure out where he got the idea she was a bad person. As for leeching off her grandmother, yes, Eleanor and her friends had financed Robyn's move to New York, but nothing else. She'd been determined to survive on her own and she had.

"You said he'd been coming to the store for a couple of years," she murmured.

"Yes. His doctor sent him. It was very sad. His wife and baby son were killed in a car accident. Apparently he wasn't expected to make it, either. But he did. He was in physical therapy for months. He was told to take up knitting to help with his fine motor skills." She smiled. "I confess Adeline, Marion and I have pretended to be far more helpless than we are to try to bring him back to life."

"That was very sweet of you," Robyn said automatically, not sure what to do with the revelation. The man who had accused her of being a horrible person and a leech was someone she could easily dislike. The injured guy who lost his wife and young son was someone else entirely.

"He's still not healed," Eleanor said with a sigh as she rose to her feet. "On the outside, he's fine, but I do worry about his heart. It's still broken. He's so closed off. Oh, he's friendly enough, but nothing really touches him."

Robyn could think of a lot of descriptions for T.J. and the words *friendly enough* didn't make her list. But he'd apparently become a friend to her aunt and her friends, for which Robyn was grateful. But that didn't mean she had to like the man.

Eleanor carried her plates over to the sink. "I enjoyed having breakfast with you. It's been a long time."

Robyn stood, as well. "It has. Too long. Grandma, I need to talk to you about what happened in New York." It was time to come clean about her past.

Her grandmother smiled at her. "I would love to hear all of it, but I need to get to the store. We have an early class today. Can it wait?"

Robyn nodded. "Sure."

"Good. Come to the store whenever you're ready."

Robyn stayed behind long enough to clean the kitchen, then she walked the five blocks to Only Ewe and let herself in the back. Even though it was a few minutes before eight, she heard the rumble of low conversation coming from the front part of the store. She walked around the corner, through the stockroom and stepped into the main space, only to freeze in her tracks when she saw seven or eight high school guys staring intently at the knitting needles and yarn in their hands. What on earth?

The guys were huge, with broad shoulders and massive fingers. She didn't think she would be more surprised to see hedgehogs knitting. She blinked, then looked again.

Yup, they were still there, with T.J. at the head of the table, giving instructions.

Her grandmother limped over to her. "They come every week," she said in a quiet voice. "Their coach's wife knits and she and I got to talking about how it would help them with their concentration. I mentioned it to T.J. He resisted at first, but we kept on him." She smiled. "The little projects keep him distracted. He's suffered so much."

"He has," Robyn said automatically, her gaze moving to T.J.

He glanced up just then, his dark eyes meeting hers. The annoyance was back, as was the determination. The man obviously hadn't changed his opinion of her.

"I don't think he…" she began, then stopped when she saw her grandmother looking at him with an expression of affection and pride.

She pressed her lips together. There was no reason to point out that T.J. obviously didn't like her. Right now she doubted her grandmother would believe her. It didn't matter anyway. She didn't need T.J.'s or anyone's approval. This was her home. She was back and no crabby man was going to drive her away.

# *Three*

Robyn stood on the step stool and balanced the bucket of soapy water. After raising herself onto her tiptoes, she stretched her arm over the shelf and scrubbed it with the sponge.

From what she could tell, the stockroom hadn't been cleaned since she left six years ago. Not that she would expect elderly women to take on that kind of chore. But there was plenty of dust and grit ready to be washed away. After a good rinsing, she would dry the shelves, then put back the yarn. She figured it would take her two days to get through the entire stockroom.

She didn't mind the physical labor. After the stress that had been her life, she enjoyed getting something specific accomplished. She also liked the chance to think.

Once Eleanor was back on her feet, Robyn would have to see about getting another job. She doubted the store could afford four of them on the payroll. Waitressing was the most obvious kind of job. With her references, she could start at the more exclusive restaurants in Austin. Bigger bills usually meant bigger tips. As long as the place was busy. Fifteen to twenty percent of no customers wouldn't work for her.

She was also thinking she could try to talk to a career counselor. While her degree in fine arts hadn't exactly been long on practicality, there had to be some transferable skills. If not, she wanted to explore other kinds of schooling. Maybe a few business courses would help. She was also toying with the idea of teaching. She'd always loved kids and her favorite times in New York had been helping one of her girlfriends teach a juniors acting class.

She was so engrossed in her cleaning, that she didn't hear anyone walk into the stockroom. She leaned to get the farthest corner of the top shelf, only to jump and shriek when she bumped into something hard and warm.

She turned away from the sensation and found herself stepping out into space. The only thing that saved her from falling was a strong arm wrapping around her legs until she regained her balance.

"Are you trying to kill me?" she snapped, glaring down at T.J. "Why are you sneaking around?"

His normal loathing expression looked almost amused. "I wasn't sneaking. Marion's going out for sandwiches and she wanted me to ask you if you wanted one."

"I brought lunch from home," she said.

"You mean instead of having your grandmother pay for your lunch out, you're letting her pay for you to take her food from her house."

She did her best not to blush. Despite how she felt about him, he was telling the truth—at least about that. She wasn't paying for the food. She hoped that her hard work made it a fair exchange, but she couldn't say for sure.

Part of her wanted to point out that her grandmother

loved her and would do anything for her. Eleanor would never begrudge her a few meals. But saying that meant admitting even the tiniest part of what T.J. thought of her was true and she refused to go down that road.

"I can see I was mistaken," she said, returning to her cleaning. "When I first saw you, I thought you were a cowboy. I was wrong. You talk way too much to be anything but a business type."

He surprised her by chuckling. "That's your grandmother's fault. And those other two. I never used to talk at all."

"You could practice being quiet."

"I could," he agreed. "But I won't."

"Because you're determined to protect them from me."

He nodded.

"Won't you feel like a jerk when you find out you've been wrong," she told him.

"I would, but we both know I'm right."

She drew in a breath and stared down into his dark eyes. "No. We don't."

He studied her for a long time, then turned to leave. He took a few steps. If she hadn't known about the bad accident, she might not have noticed the slight hesitation in his stride, as if he had to think before he moved. When he reached the doorway, he faced her again.

"You're going to have to tell them the truth about your so-called career," he said. "Or I will."

Robyn sat at the big craft table in the rear of the store with the other beginners. She'd chosen a lightweight cotton blend from the sale bin and size seven bamboo needles for her first project. Six years ago she could have whipped out a complex pattern without having to blink. Today the idea of a simple rectangular wrap was daunting.

"It will come back to you," Adeline told her encouragingly. "Your fingers remember."

Maybe, Robyn thought doubtfully. Right now her fingers felt stiff and uncooperative.

She cast on the first row, working slowly, awkwardly. Her hands seemed to work in opposition, rather than as a team. But as she started the second row, she was pleased to see that her stitches were even. All was not lost.

"Oh, no." The young woman sitting next to Robyn stared at her own project, her eyes wide with dismay. "I dropped a stitch. It's gone."

She sounded heartbroken.

Without thinking, Robyn put down her project and reached for the woman's needles. "It's just hiding," she said with a smile. "We'll find it."

The panel looked to be the front of a sweater for a child. The stitches were small and a little lumpy, but the pattern was nice.

Robyn peered at the work, counting stitches, then seeing where the slipped stitch had disappeared. She coaxed the yarn up and over the needle, worked the stitch, then handed it back to the customer.

"There you go."

The woman stared at her. "That was impressive. Are you sure you want to be in the beginner group?"

"I haven't knit in years. I guess there are some things you don't forget."

"Apparently not. I'm Belinda."

"Hi. Robyn. Eleanor's my grandmother, so I might have a genetic advantage."

The petite brunette laughed. "I come from a long line of women who weren't the least bit creative. But I'm determined to learn something. Cake decorating turned out to be a complete disaster, so I've moved on to knitting. I really like it, plus it's something I can do while my daughter is at dance class."

"Absolutely," Robyn agreed with her. "It would be more difficult to travel with cake decorating supplies."

Belinda laughed.

Robyn glanced up in time to see her grandmother smiling approvingly. She told herself to enjoy the moment because as soon as she confessed all, everything would change. For now, it was enough to be here, to feel the yarn in her hands, to see the colors and textures. Even though she hadn't been able to afford knitting supplies while she'd been gone, she hadn't been able to resist going into some of the knitting stores just to look at the yarn, to hold it in her hands and dream about what she could create.

She continued to knit and chat with the other customers. Marion walked around the table, offering advice and giving praise.

"It's too bad you weren't able to keep up with your knitting in New York," the older woman said. "I thought all actors did something on set to pass the time."

"That would be in the movies," Eleanor told her. "Between takes. Robyn was on the stage."

"Oh, of course."

Belinda turned to Robyn. "You're an actress? On Broadway?"

Robyn felt herself flush. "Not exactly."

"She was very successful," Eleanor said proudly. "Practically nominated for a Tony."

"I wish," Robyn muttered. "It wasn't like that."

"How exciting," Belinda said with a sigh. "I've never even been out of the state. I got married right after high school and was pregnant before I was twenty. Now I have three kids. But one day…"

Marriage and three kids sounded kind of nice, Robyn thought. Having a home, knowing where she belonged. At least Belinda hadn't wasted her life and her opportunities. Robyn had worked her butt off and for what? The chance to become a really good waitress?

Thankfully, the subject changed to the empty store next door and speculation about who would lease it.

With the lunch hour came a rush of customers. Robyn put away her project and got up to help her grandmother. As she rang up yarn and talked patterns, she was aware of Eleanor's limping stride as she walked around the store. Had the other woman put off the surgery longer than she should have to give Robyn more time in New York?

Robyn knew T.J. would tell her yes, and blame her for everything from the economy to global warming. While she wasn't willing to take responsibility for all of that, she couldn't help wondering if her grandmother had suffered on her behalf. It wasn't a happy thought.

Tonight, she promised herself. She would tell them the truth tonight, after the store closed.

Robyn kept her word. Shortly after six, when the customers were finally gone and the front doors locked, she walked to the craft table where her grandmother and her two friends were waiting. They'd all agreed to stay so she could talk to them about what it was like living in New York. She was determined to be brutally honest—as much for the sake of her conscience as for their edification.

Now, as she looked at their three loving faces, she

wished she had a different story to tell. Disappointing people was hard enough. Disappointing the three women who loved her best in the world would be like cutting out part of her heart.

Marion smiled at her. "We were just talking about what a pretty girl you were. So talented. I remember your first dance recital."

"Didn't she sing, too?" Adeline asked. "That song from *Annie*."

"You were very special," Eleanor said. "I was so proud when you got the lead in the high school play and you were only a freshman. The other students were furious, but you were the best."

"Oh, and that college production of *Grease*. You were the perfect Sandy." Eleanor sighed. "Such happy times."

Robyn swallowed hard, then pulled out a chair across from the three of them and sat down.

"Those are all great memories," she began, telling herself it was for the best to come clean. "I really thought I was going to show up in New York and immediately become a star." Like hundreds of thousands of other young, foolish dreamers did every year, she thought ruefully. Reality was very different.

"You might not be a star yet," Eleanor told her. "But you've made excellent progress."

"No, I haven't." Robyn looked at each of them. "I wasn't completely honest with you. About anything. My career wasn't going well. It wasn't going at all."

The women exchanged glances.

"What do you mean?" Adeline asked.

"At first I did go on a lot of auditions. I got a few parts. But then everything sort of dried up. In high school and college, I was one of the best. But in New York, there were a thousand other girls just like me. Acting classes are expensive. I burned through the money you gave me in a few months and had to start waitressing just to pay the rent."

"Why didn't you tell me?" her grandmother asked.

"Because I didn't want you to worry. Because I was ashamed of not being everything everyone thought I would be." Robyn stared at her hands on the table. "I haven't had a callback in two years." She forced herself to raise her gaze. "I lived in a sixth-floor walk-up. One small room, with the tiniest bathroom ever. I'm not skinny because it's fashionable, but because I can't afford much food. When I got pneumonia two years ago, it wiped me out financially. I didn't have insurance and the bills kept coming. I've paid them all now, but it's been tough."

"Oh, Robyn," Marion breathed. "You should have said something."

"I couldn't. I had to make it on my own. At least that's what I told myself. I wasn't giving up. But it's been six years. I'm done trying. I want a real life. I want to not be hungry anymore. I haven't had a steak since I left Texas. I haven't been on a date in three years and I haven't…"

She stopped. There was no reason for her grandmother and her friends to know how long it had been since she'd been with a man. That definitely fell into the category of too much information.

"Is this why you always put us off when we wanted to visit?" her grandmother asked gently.

She nodded. "It was easier for me to come here for a couple of days. I could still pretend that way." She paused. "I think dreams are great. But mine turned into a nightmare. I'm ready to be done. I was so grateful when you asked me to come back. Knowing you needed me gave me permission to finally admit the truth to myself. That I was desperate to come back home. This is where I belong."

Robyn tried to smile and wasn't sure she succeeded. "When you're up on your feet again, I'm going to find a job and get my own place. I want to save some money, go back to college and figure out what to do with the rest of my life." She swallowed. "I hope you're not too disappointed in me."

Her grandmother rose and started around the table. Robyn hurried to meet her, then was pulled into a warm, loving embrace. Adeline and Marion joined in, making her feel safe and welcome.

"I could never be disappointed in you," Eleanor said fiercely. "I love you and I'm thrilled you're back to stay."

"We all are," Marion told her.

"Silly girl," Adeline murmured.

T.J. stood slowly. He'd walked in through the back just about the time Robyn started talking to her grandmother and had stayed to listen. After a couple of minutes, he'd thought maybe she was telling the truth. That she wasn't the leech he'd first thought.

She'd had a tough time, he admitted to himself, and he felt kind of bad she'd gone hungry trying to pay her bills. Maybe he should give her a break and let her prove herself to him instead of assuming the worst.

# *Four*

Robyn had forgotten that age twelve began the time of eye rolling. As she explained how to cast on, the girls in the group listened attentively, while the boys looked embarrassed and bored.

The students were part of the Georgetown Partners in Education program that teamed the school district with local businesses. The idea was that getting kids engaged in the community before they were teenagers made for better citizens later down the road. At her grandmother's request, Robyn had set up the table with large, easy-to-use needles and a basket of colorful yarn. The girls were obviously excited by the prospect of learning to knit and the boys had that "anywhere but here" look in their eyes.

"Any questions?" Robyn asked.

No one said anything.

"Great." She heard the front door open and glanced up, then grinned. "Sometimes learning a new skill is easier when you have a mentor or coach to help. I've asked a few people who have already mastered the art of knitting to join us."

Five guys from the high school football team and members of T.J.'s class walked over.

"Whassup?" the tallest of the players asked.

The boys at the table nearly fell off their chairs.

"You knit?" one boy asked, then pushed up his glasses. "For real?"

Inviting the players had been Adeline's idea. Robyn had called the high school and spoken with the football coach. He'd been happy to lend her the players for the afternoon.

The older guys pulled up chairs and squeezed in between the younger kids. Soon everyone was holding needles and slowly casting on.

Marion joined them, going from student to student, offering advice. Robyn did the same, pleased to hear laughter and excited conversation instead of groans.

She glanced up and noticed T.J. at the far end of the store. She'd been too busy with her class to notice his arrival, which made her uneasy. The way the man was always glowering at her, she was more comfortable when she kept tabs on him.

Without giving herself time to second-guess her decision, she walked toward him. As she approached, she once again noticed he was tall—she barely came to his shoulder. Lean, but with an edge about him that spoke of power and determination. Nice looking in a way that made her hungry for something other than food.

"You can stop scowling at me," she informed him. "Or assuming the worst. My grandmother and her friends know everything about my past. And before you ask, I didn't tell them because of you. I told them because I wanted to."

His gaze never left her face. "Anything else?"

She squared her shoulders and raised her chin. "Yes, there is. I appreciate all you've done around here, taking care of Eleanor and her friends."

He raised his left eyebrow. "You asking me to leave?"

"Would you?"

"No."

"Then I'm not asking."

"What's your point?"

She smiled. He sounded both defensive and accusing at the same time. Quite the trick. "I meant what I said. Thank you for taking care of them."

His eyes narrowed. "And?"

She laughed. "And that's all. They're the only family I have. I missed them and should have come home sooner. I appreciate knowing you were here for them."

He seemed to be waiting for something else. She'd never seen T.J. off guard before and found she really liked it.

Finally he cleared his throat. "You're welcome."

Now that was behind them, she had another item to discuss. "Obviously they're important to both of us," she said, nodding to where Marion, Adeline and Eleanor chatted with the students. "For their sake, we should try to get along."

"I can do that."

"Good." Her gaze dropped to his Western-style white shirt. "You're not really a cowboy, are you?"

He flashed her a grin. "No."

The transformation stunned her. He went from angry stranger to handsome, appealing man in a matter of a heartbeat. Speaking of which, hers was doing an odd fluttering dance in her chest.

"Even though you look like a cowboy," she said, pleased she didn't stutter.

"You like cowboys?"

"Not especially."

"Good to know."

T.J. opened the boxes and pulled out armfuls of soft, colorful yarn.

"I love getting deliveries," Eleanor told him as she took the yarn and placed it on the shelves in the back room. "They hint at possibilities. Speaking of which…"

He glanced at her. "Yes?"

"You need to stop hanging out with a bunch of old women."

T.J. chuckled. One of the things he liked best about Eleanor and her friends was their ability to always speak their minds. In his world, too few people said what they really thought.

"Maybe I like old women," he said, and winked.

"Stop that." She shook her head. "I'm serious. You've been hiding from your real life for long enough. Not that we haven't enjoyed the company."

Her insight shouldn't have surprised him, but it did. Insightful and wily. A dangerous combination. Too bad most of society dismissed women "of a certain age." There were plenty of smarts, talent and determination to be had. The country was losing a valuable asset.

He wanted to protest that he hadn't been hiding, but what was the point? They both knew the truth.

"When did you figure it out?" he asked.

Her expression softened. "Since the first day you walked in here. You were so broken and sad. Our hearts went out to you, but we knew better than to fuss. You had to heal in your own time."

She assumed he'd finished healing but he was less sure. There were some things a man simply couldn't get over. Some things that once broken could never be mended.

"Not that we didn't do our best to trick you into living again," she added.

"You didn't trick me. Did you think I wouldn't know you were behind me working with those football players?"

"Coach said he wouldn't tell you!"

"He didn't have to." He stepped around the box of yarn and hugged her. "Did I ever thank you?"

"Nearly every day."

"Now I know you're lying," he teased gently. "I haven't said it nearly enough."

"You don't have to say it," she told him. "You're living your thank-yous, which is the best way, in my opinion."

He released her. "You're too smart for your own good."

"It's a curse I have to live with." She grinned as she spoke, her blue eyes sparkling behind her glasses. "You're always welcome here, T.J., but I meant what I said. You need to stop hiding out here."

What she didn't know was he had nowhere else to go. He'd done a fine job of cutting everything else out of his life. Even his company didn't need him on a day-to-day basis.

The sound of conversation from the shop drifted back to them. Eleanor sighed happily. "Robyn's doing well."

"You're pleased she's back."

She looked at him. "Don't sound so surprised. Of course I am."

"She hurt you by being gone."

"No. I missed her. There's a difference. You young people have to follow your dreams. That's the way of things. But she's back now and staying."

Her mouth curved into a slightly wicked smile. T.J. knew enough to brace himself for whatever was to come.

"I've seen you watching her," Eleanor said pointedly. "Are you waiting for permission?"

A perfect hit, he thought, refusing to let her know that Robyn had been occupying his mind far more than he liked. At first he'd told himself it was because he didn't trust her, but after she'd come clean to Eleanor, he'd run out of excuses.

"I'm not interested," he said flatly.

Her smile never wavered. "You go to hell for lying, same as stealing."

"Fine. I'm not interested in her that way."

"Still lying."

"I don't know what I want."

"That I'll believe. Although you really do owe her, for thinking so badly of her when she first came home."

He opened his mouth, then closed it. There was no point in asking how she knew. Eleanor was, as always, a mystery to him.

"I'll take her out to dinner to make up for what I thought," he grumbled. "But I won't like it."

Eleanor laughed.

T.J. had the uncomfortable feeling that she was laughing *at* him, rather than *with* him.

Robyn locked the front door of the store and turned out the main lights. Marion had left early to have dinner with her fiancé and his college-bound grandson. Adeline had taken Eleanor home. Robyn's grandmother's knee had been especially painful that day.

After finishing closing out the cash register, Robyn locked up the receipts, checked to make sure the alarm was set, then left through the back door. She'd barely made it halfway to the sidewalk when she saw a man standing by a truck.

Before she could jump or scream, she recognized T.J. He'd been noticeably absent for the past couple of days. As much as she'd wanted to ask her grandmother why, she'd held back. She didn't want anyone thinking she was interested in T.J.

Now, as she watched him watch her, she was conscious of the slight elevation in her heartbeat and how her breathing seemed to quicken.

Her reaction wasn't about him, she told herself firmly. It was due to the long drought that was her social life. Her body would have done exactly the same around any other single man under the age of sixty. At least she hoped it would.

"Have you taken to hanging out in back alleys?" she asked as she approached.

"I was waiting for you."

*Why?* was the obvious question but for some reason she couldn't seem to speak.

He'd been leaning against a truck. Now he straightened and looked into her eyes. His were especially dark and she couldn't tell what he was thinking. So what he said next was completely unexpected.

"Would you like to go out to dinner with me?"

If she'd been given three days to come up with possible questions he would ask her, that still wouldn't have appeared on the list. The need to turn around and find out if he was talking to someone else was powerful, but she resisted.

"You don't like me," she blurted. "Why would you want to have dinner with me?"

"I like you fine."

Her mouth dropped open. "You spend half your time glaring at me."

"Maybe I've changed my opinion of you."

"Oh."

One corner of his mouth turned up. "Was that a yes?"

She nodded.

"Tomorrow?"

He was asking her out for a Friday night. She couldn't remember the last time she'd had a date on a Friday night.

She nodded again.

"Seven?"

A third nod.

The other corner of his mouth finished the smile. "Think you'll be talking by then?"

"It's entirely possible."

"I can't wait to find out for sure."

Then he turned and sauntered off.

She watched him go, thinking that it took a Texas-born man to saunter really well, and that she'd missed that and so much more while she'd been gone.

# *Five*

"You want to wear something romantic," Marion said, standing in front of the meager contents of Robyn's closet. "Flowy."

"Forget flowy," Adeline said with a sniff. "Wear a push-up bra and then show it all off. Trust me, when you get to be our age, no one wants to look anymore."

"Stop it, you two." Eleanor spoke from the chair in the corner, where she had her leg propped on a footstool and ice on her knee. "Robyn is perfectly capable of getting herself dressed."

Robyn appreciated the advice, but wasn't so sure she was up to the task. "I haven't been on a date in a long time," she admitted. Besides, the man in question was T.J. and she had no idea why he'd asked her out. There was something about him that compelled her, so saying no hadn't exactly been an option.

If they were in New York, she would whip out a little black dress. Simple, classic, elegant. But she had a feeling T.J. would show up in jeans and she didn't want to look as though she was trying too hard. She settled on a navy pencil skirt that came to a few inches above her knee, a silvery blue twin set in a whisper-soft knit, open-toed high-heeled sandals and her favorite pair of silver earrings.

When she was finished, she twirled in front of her audience. "Well?"

"Lovely," her grandmother told her.

"He'll be dazzled," Marion promised with a sigh.

"You clean up good," Adeline said. "Don't have sex on the first date."

Robyn felt herself blush. "Thanks for the advice."

She had no idea why T.J. had asked her to dinner, but she was pretty confident he wasn't looking for sex.

"Hurry," Eleanor said. "He'll be here any second. The three of us are going to wait back here until you're gone."

"Thanks."

Robyn kissed each of them in turn, then went into the living room to wait.

Fortunately her grandmother was right—T.J. arrived exactly at seven. Robyn opened the door to find that *she'd* been wrong about what he would wear. Gone were the jeans and Western-style shirts. Instead he wore black pants and a hand-knit sweater in graduated shades of green. The expert fit, the complex stitches and the choice of material told her he hadn't bought the sweater at a department store. She would guess a present from either her grandmother or one of her friends.

Information that was meaningless, but a nice distraction to keep her from getting lost in his dark eyes.

"You ready?" he asked by way of greeting.

"Yes." She grabbed her small purse and followed him out.

He drove a silver pickup, the kind that had a step to

get in. What with her slightly fitted skirt, she had to use the step and had a bad feeling she'd flashed the neighborhood as she climbed up.

T.J. waited until she'd reached for the seat belt before closing the door and going around to his side.

"You look nice," he said as he climbed in.

He wasn't looking at her as he spoke, so once again she had to stop herself from glancing around to see if he was actually talking to her.

"You do, too," she murmured.

"Steak all right?"

"Um, sure."

"Good."

And that ended the conversation until they arrived at the restaurant.

T.J. surprised her by using the valet and then telling the hostess they had a reservation. She hadn't expected him to think that far ahead. Not that she had been talking any more than he had on the way over. She sighed, wondering if the evening was going to seem endless. At least she would get a steak out of it, she reminded herself.

They were shown to their table right away and handed menus. Robyn scanned the offerings and was thrilled to see a twenty-two-ounce Porterhouse. As always, she was starving. She pored over the list of side dishes, made her choices, debated soup versus salad and wondered if ordering a glass of wine would be out of line. She glanced up to find T.J. studying her.

"Enjoying the menu?" he asked.

Wow—they were talking now? "It's a nice selection. Do you eat here often?"

"A couple times a month. They know how to cook a steak. Do you want to share a bottle of wine?"

"Sure. You'll have to pick. I don't know much about wine."

"I thought you were a waitress in New York."

"I worked the lunch shift. It was more soda and cocktails than bottles of wine. Although I can do five minutes on the virtues of eighteen-year-old Scotch rather than twelve-year-old Scotch." She smiled. "I took a class."

"On Scotch?"

"The restaurant's liquor distributor offered it and no one else was interested. I didn't have much of a social life, so I thought it might be fun."

"Was it?"

"I got buzzed during the tasting." She grinned. "Plus, once I could talk knowledgeably about Scotch, I sold a lot more and that upped the tips." She tilted her head. "Want to say something snide about me only being in it for the money?"

"Isn't that why most people work?"

"Yes, but you do like to assume the worst about me."

"Maybe I'm over that," he said, leaning toward her. "I asked you out to dinner."

"A confusing turn of events."

"What if I want us to start over?"

He was close enough that she could inhale the clean scent of him and see the long dark lashes that framed his eyes.

"Will you let me know when you make a decision?" she asked.

"About what?"

"You said that maybe you were past thinking the worst about me and maybe you want us to start over. Obviously you haven't made up your mind yet. I'm just asking you to let me know when you do."

He surprised her by laughing. The sound was warm and appealing. It made her want to laugh, too, and maybe to lean in a little farther so that he would kiss her and…

Robyn stiffened in her chair. Kissing? There wasn't going to be any kissing. She didn't kiss on the first date and if she did, it wouldn't be with a man who had, until recently, disliked her.

"Fair enough," he said, smiling at her. "I want to start over. Will you give me a second chance?"

"You don't deserve it," she told him. "But I will because it makes me the better person." She paused, not sure exactly how they would start over. "Tell me about yourself."

He leaned back. "Not much to tell. I grew up in a small town in Oklahoma." The smile returned. "One you've never heard of. We were farmers, mostly."

A farmer? She wouldn't have guessed that. "You didn't go into the family business?"

"I couldn't get away fast enough. Left when I was eighteen and a day. I was headed just about anywhere that wasn't there. Ended up here. Never left."

"What about your family?"

He shrugged. "My parents live in Florida. I see them every couple of years. I have a sister who has two kids. They're in Florida, too."

Their server appeared and T.J. ordered the wine without consulting the menu. She asked for the Porterhouse with salad and a baked potato with everything. T.J. chose the twelve-ounce fillet. The server left and a busboy appeared with bread and water. He'd barely had a chance to put down the basket when she dove in and took two slices.

After setting both on her side plate, she scooped up

some garlic butter, spread it on her first piece of bread and took a bite. The flavors exploded on her tongue, nearly making her moan. Talk about heaven.

She finished the entire slice only to realize that T.J. was staring at her as if she were some kind of science experiment. She reached for her napkin and carefully wiped her mouth before asking, "What?"

"For a skinny thing, you sure enjoy food."

"I've been hungry for a long time." She motioned to her body. "This isn't my natural weight. I'm going to put on about twenty pounds and I plan to enjoy every bite. I am so over being something I'm not. In my world, a little jiggle in a girl's thigh is a good thing."

Something flashed through T.J.'s eyes, something like appreciation and interest. "In my world, too."

His reaction surprised her so much, she put down her second slice of bread. "Why, sir, are you flirting with me?"

"Maybe I am. Is that a problem?"

"I thought you didn't like me."

One of his eyebrows went up. "I invited you to dinner."

"I figured that was just a guilt thing. You felt bad about assuming the worst, then being wrong."

"I think you're complicating the situation," he told her.

"I doubt it."

Their server brought the bottle of wine he'd ordered just then, which was typical, she thought, starting on her second slice of bread. Life was all about timing.

They went through the ritual of opening, pouring, tasting and nodding. Robyn finished her bread, then reached for her glass and sniffed. It smelled like wine to her.

"Ever send a bottle back?" she asked before taking a sip.

"If it's bad."

"Are you a wine snob?"

He chuckled. "Do I look like a wine snob?"

"You could pass for one right now."

He studied her for a second. "I might have been wrong about you."

"Might?"

"I'm being cautious."

"You're trying not to admit you were wrong. If the steak is as good as I think it's going to be, don't worry. I'll forgive you."

"I can't wait." He picked up his glass. "Tell me about life in New York."

She wrinkled her nose. "I was a struggling actress. You've seen enough TV to be able to make some assumptions. Most of them are true. It's hard, there's a lot of competition and while I was talented and brilliant here, when I got to New York I was one of a thousand talented, brilliant young women."

She set down her glass and dug through the bread basket again. "The casting couch is alive and well, I'm sorry to say. Not always, but enough. There was no way I was willing to have sex with some jerk just to get a part. I would rather work for a living. Well…" She bit into the bread. "I guess that's work, too, but not any kind I was interested in."

She spoke honestly and with an edge that told him more than her words that it had been tough.

She wasn't what he'd expected. There was no brittleness, no put-on sophistication. Her level of frankness was also surprising. And intriguing.

He'd done his best not to like her, to assume the worst. He'd been wrong—something that rarely happened.

"Eleanor says you get your talent from your mother," he said.

"I do. She was wonderful. And so beautiful." Robyn smiled sadly. "I'm the blurry version of her. She was the kind of woman who could take your breath away just walking across the room."

"You miss her."

"Always. But I had my grandmother. I've been lucky. I've been loved my whole life. When my mom died, I didn't worry about where I was going to go. I knew I'd be taken care of. And it wasn't just her. Adeline and Marion were a part of every memory." She grinned. "All three of them got me ready for my prom date. They nearly blinded us with all the pictures they took."

"Sounds like a special childhood."

"It was."

"Any regrets about New York?"

She considered the question. "No. I needed to go. I needed to try. Otherwise, I would have always wondered. Like every other unemployed actor, I kept thinking 'what if.' What if my big break comes? What will I do? What will it be like? When I stopped caring about that, I knew it was time to come home. Eleanor's surgery gave me the perfect excuse."

She stared at him. "Don't say anything mean."

"I won't again."

"An unkeepable promise," she told him. "Be careful with those."

Interesting advice, he thought. "What happens now? Any plans?"

"Sure. Get on with my life." She sipped the wine. "My

grandmother's surgery is in a couple of days. Once she's recovered, I'm going to get a job, start saving my money and consider going back to college. My degree in singing and dancing isn't exactly practical." She shrugged. "But it's been my world for so long, it's going to take a while to figure out what comes next."

"You've thought this through."

She smiled. "I appreciate the lack of surprise in your voice."

He laughed, then mentioned a customer who had been in that day.

They talked about the store, weather, even politics. Robyn admitted how every fall she'd watched the reality show on the girls trying out for the Dallas Cowboy Cheerleaders and how it had made her homesick. He caught her staring at the scars on his hands and told her a little about the car accident that had caused them, although he didn't mention his wife and son.

He discovered they both liked old movies and being outside.

"Central Park is huge and wonderful," she said. "But you're still in the middle of a city. I missed the wide-open spaces." She smiled. "I guess I'll always be a Texas girl at heart."

They talked about hiking and camping, she liked museums while he would rather go to a car show. They discovered they both wanted to spend time on the water. She made him laugh, something he knew he didn't do often enough.

When the food arrived, she polished off every bite of the twenty-two-ounce steak, along with potatoes and most of her salad. Watching her enjoy her dinner made his meal taste better. It had been a long time since food was anything but a way to keep his body going.

"Impressive," he said as the waiter cleared the table.

"Everyone has a talent," she told him, leaning back in her chair with a sigh. "That was good. I'm really full."

"You should be ready to explode."

She raised her eyebrows. "Don't be critical. I was thinking of getting dessert."

"Go for it."

She laughed. "Doesn't a fudge brownie sound delicious?"

Watching her eat it sounded pretty good. Robyn was intense about food. It made him wonder what else she liked to focus on in the course of her day...or her night.

Don't go there, he told himself. She was Eleanor's granddaughter and he had no business messing with that.

"You haven't told me what you do," Robyn said suddenly. "Do you work?"

"Sometimes," he said easily, thinking about the company he mostly ignored these days. There were executives in place to run things. While he liked to be a part of nurturing artists, he'd lost his interest in the business aspect around the same time he'd lost everything else important to him.

Robyn stared expectantly.

"I write songs," he said at last, which was true. "Mostly country music."

"Any I'd know?"

"Probably not. I haven't written in a while."

He hadn't done anything in a while, except go through the motions. The only place he felt vaguely normal was at Only Ewe, and that was because it was safe. It wasn't exactly living, but it was better than the half world he usually inhabited.

# *Six*

After his date polished off an entire fudge brownie, along with a side of ice cream and extra whipped cream, T.J. drove her home.

"That was the best meal I've had in years," Robyn told him. "Seriously, I owe you. If there's anything I can do, let me know."

His mind went to a place it hadn't been since the death of his wife and the intensity of his longing surprised him. He had a vision of tangled sheets, a naked, slightly curvier Robyn moaning beneath him as he took them both on the slow road home.

He swore silently. What was he thinking? Sex? With her? Impossible. He wasn't ready to go there.

He pulled up in front of Eleanor's house, intending to let Robyn walk herself to the door. But he'd been raised by a mama who believed in good manners and he couldn't help getting out of the truck and walking around to her side.

She slid out gracefully, then strolled with him to the door. "This was great," she said. "I didn't think I'd like spending time with you, but it was fun."

"That was honest," he responded, amused and a little insulted.

"You don't talk much at the store. I had this vision of two hours with only the sound of clinking flatware to entertain myself. I'd half planned to order a dozen water glasses and play a little tune with them."

They paused by the door. She was smiling as she spoke, her eyes bright with laughter. She was beautiful, he realized and as the thought formed, he knew he was going to kiss her.

Robyn felt a level of contentment she hadn't experienced in years. She was full, happy and ready to crawl into her bed and sleep soundly for a full eight hours. She'd returned to where she belonged, she had people who loved her and dinner had been a whole lot more fun than she'd expected. In her world, that was a big, fat win.

She turned to T.J., ready to thank him, only to find he'd moved close to her. Really close. Then he was leaning in and she only had a nanosecond to brace herself for a very unexpected kiss.

Three hours ago she would have sworn the man would as soon spend time with a scorpion as her. Forty-five minutes ago, she would have said that maybe he didn't completely hate her. But kissing?

His mouth was warm and sure, firm yet gentle. He kissed like a man who knew what he was doing and liked it just fine. Without thinking, she wrapped her arms around his neck. It was both instinct and the need to hold on to something secure in a world that started to spin just a little.

Heat began in her chest and spread out to every corner of her body. Heat and hunger. Not for food, this time, but for a man's touch. Warmth changed to need and nearly took her breath away.

When he stepped back, she dropped her hands to her sides. They stared at each other, his face in shadow, but still handsome.

The man was broken, she reminded herself. He spent an inordinate amount of time with a bunch of older women because anything close to his old life was too much for him to deal with. She was home to get her act together, not take on a new project. They had no business kissing.

Yet she wanted to again and again. She told herself that it was just like being hungry for a good steak. That any old steak would do. But she knew she was lying. The ache inside her seemed pretty specifically about T.J., which wasn't good news at all.

"Thank you for dinner," she forced herself to say.

"You're welcome."

They stared at each other for a few more seconds. There was a moment when the air around them crackled with possibilities. But instead of acting on that chemistry, he turned away. She stood there a few minutes, listening to the sound of his truck driving away.

"I'm the wrong man for the job," T.J. told Marion as he stared around the fussy shop. "Don't you want Eleanor here, or Adeline? What about Robyn? She has good taste."

At least he assumed she did, because she sure tasted good.

He grinned at the private joke, remembering how she'd felt in his arms. All angles and bones, but still exciting. He'd liked kissing her, had wanted to kiss her more. He'd imagined her with more curves and had been aroused for the first time in years.

"You're walking me down the aisle," Marion said firmly, adjusting the front of her pale pink gown. "I want you here. What do you think?"

The dress was floor-length, beaded, with lace and long sleeves. It looked like a wedding gown to him. He didn't know the difference between one and another. The full skirt emphasized her round shape and the age spots on her chest were prominent.

Yet she was as much in love as any bride a third her age and just as beautiful.

"It's perfect," he assured her honestly. "He'll love it."

Marion stared at him hopefully, the wrinkles around her eyes and mouth softer in the flattering lighting. "It's not too much? I know it's formal, but I can't help myself. I don't want to wear a tasteful suit or dress."

"Then you shouldn't. This is your wedding day."

She beamed at him, then patted his cheek. "Thank you. For everything."

He knew she meant more than the dress shopping. After all, he'd been the one to introduce her to her groom.

Six months after he'd discovered emotional rescue at Only Ewe, he'd impulsively invited Marion to join him for lunch. Also at the meal was a retired rancher he knew. It had been love at first sight—both heartening and strange when the couple in question was in their seventies.

"Let me change out of this and we can go back to the store," Marion told him.

"Take your time."

When she'd left, one of the sales clerks offered him coffee. He refused and would have turned to the selection of magazines, but she continued to stand in front of him.

"Yes?" he asked.

She was in her twenties and pretty enough.

"You're T. J. Passman," she said, her voice laced with disbelief. "I've seen your pictures before. You own Long Day Records."

He glanced around quickly to make sure that Marion hadn't overheard. No one at Only Ewe was aware of his business or his success. Success that no longer mattered.

"My boyfriend auditioned for you last year," the girl continued breathlessly. "You turned him down, but you gave him a lot of really great advice. He took it all and one of your music executives signed him last month."

He wanted to be anywhere but here. "I'm glad it worked out," he muttered.

"He is, too. It's so exciting." She glanced toward the dressing rooms. "Is that your grandmother?"

"A friend of the family," he said. "If you don't mind, I'd prefer not to talk business around her."

The girl looked confused, but nodded. "Okay. Sure."

He gave her a smile and waited for her to leave.

Years ago, he'd enjoyed the trappings of success that came with owning his company. But wearing thousand-dollar suits and driving a car that cost more than most people made in a year hadn't saved his wife and son on that slick, wet road. Losing them had nearly destroyed him. He'd been prepared to die that night, too. The joke on him was that he'd lived.

Robyn did her best to keep smiling. Her grandmother had preregistered for her knee surgery and was already checked in at the hospital. They sat together in her private room, waiting for them to come and take her to surgery.

Robyn knew that knee replacement was routine and nothing to worry about, but she couldn't help thinking that stuff happened. People died and Eleanor was the only family she had in the world.

It was her own fault, she thought grimly. She'd been the one to stay away so long. Why hadn't she come home years ago?

"Stop it," her grandmother said firmly. "Whatever you're thinking, I want you to stop it. I'm going to be fine. When I'm recovered, I'm going on *Dancing with the Stars*."

Despite her worry, Robyn laughed. "Well, I should hope so. They've been calling and calling. It's kind of annoying."

Her grandmother laughed and patted her hand. "I'm not afraid and don't you be, either. I'm excited to get back to my regular activities without being in pain all the time. And it's a huge relief knowing you'll be there at the store."

"I'll take care of everything," Robyn promised.

"I know you will, dear."

"I'll even get Adeline to stop talking about her cruise."

Eleanor grinned. "Good luck with that."

Far too soon, the older woman was wheeled away. She waved until she disappeared around a corner. Then Robyn headed for the waiting area. The doctor had promised to come see her as soon as the surgery was over. Until then, her job was to wait and make phone calls. Marion and Adeline were at the store and needed updates every thirty minutes—even if there was nothing to say.

She'd barely settled into one of the chairs by the window, when a tall, good-looking man walked in. T.J. glanced around the room, then headed directly for her.

She hadn't seen him since their date. Under other circumstances, she would have felt awkward. But the impending surgery made it hard to think about anything else.

"They already take her in?" he asked.

"A few minutes ago."

She expected him to express disappointment at missing Eleanor, then leave. Instead he settled next to her.

"Worried?" he asked.

"A little."

"Me, too."

Robyn blinked at him. "Are you staying?"

"Yup."

"Why?"

"To keep you company and because I want to." He frowned. "Maybe not in that order."

Despite everything, she laughed. "That makes it clear."

He flashed her a smile. "She's tough. She'll pull through this. You'll see."

"I hope so."

He put his arm around her. She leaned against him, feeling his strength, knowing the waiting would be easier because it was shared.

"Thank you," she whispered.

"Anytime."

# *Seven*

"Your grandmother now has the knee of a thirty-year-old," the doctor said as he approached.

Robyn sprang to her feet, barely able to breathe. "So it went well?"

"I couldn't have asked for a smoother surgery," the doctor told her. "Your grandmother came through extremely well. She's already in recovery and you can see her in about an hour. She'll still be out of it, so you'll have to keep the visit short."

Robyn nodded, concentrating on sending out prayers of gratitude. T.J. was talking to the doctor, probably asking sensible questions that he would tell her about later, she thought, relieved to know that Eleanor was fine.

"You need pie," T.J. decided when the doctor left. "It's one of those things. Pie after surgery."

"I didn't have surgery."

He shook his head. "Why are women difficult?" He grabbed her hand and tugged her out of the waiting room. "I'll get them to put extra whipped cream on it. You'll like that."

"Pie does sound good," she admitted, following him.

"Now that the four-hundred-pound weight of worry is off my chest."

They made their way to the cafeteria and collected their pie, along with coffee. T.J. led the way to a table by the window. They sat across from each other.

Robyn took a couple of bites, letting the sugar rush restore her.

"Thanks for staying," she said. "It can't be fun, being back in the hospital."

He shrugged. "It's better to wait than be the one in the operating room."

"I'm sorry."

Polite empty words, she thought, wishing there was something more she could offer.

He stared at his scarred hands. "I thought I'd die, too," he murmured. "I wanted to. With them gone, I didn't have anything to live for." He glanced at her. "Fate wasn't that kind. I was left behind to recover without them."

She could intellectually understand. She'd lost her mother, she understood the pain of feeling as if a part of yourself was gone. But to lose a child must be something so much worse. An emptiness that never went away.

"I only went into the knitting store to get my physical therapist off my butt." A faint smile tugged at the corners of his mouth. "Those old women fussed over me. I wouldn't talk, but they said enough for ten people. The first time I answered a question, they nearly fell over."

She touched his hand. "They're good people."

"Yes, they are. They helped me heal—pretty much against my will." His gaze sharpened. "I'm not the man I was before. I don't care about things the same way. I've lost as much as there is to lose."

She wasn't sure if he was sharing or warning her. Either way, there was a message—one she should listen to.

They'd had a single date that had been very nice. She would like to think that they were friends. As his friend, she could appreciate all he'd been through. But to want any more from a man like him was to try to catch hold of the moon. It would never happen.

"I feel guilty about my second chance with my grandmother," she admitted.

"Don't. Be happy that you still have time with her. She's an amazing woman." His expression softened. "They all are. Wait until you see Marion's wedding dress."

"She went for a traditional dress?"

"Lace and beads and a veil from that material you brought her. All dyed pink."

Robyn laughed. "I can't wait to see it. She'll be a beautiful bride."

"I'm walking her down the aisle."

"I look forward to that, too."

Robyn hovered as her grandmother gingerly sat on the edge of the bed.

Eleanor leaned back against the pillows and sighed. "Stop staring. I'm fine."

"You just had surgery."

"Four days ago. I'm feeling good and frankly, compared to the pain I had before, this is nothing."

Robyn wanted to believe her, but she couldn't help worrying. Even though the surgery had gone great and Eleanor's recovery was exactly where it should be, her grandmother wasn't a young woman.

The nurse, an efficient-looking woman in her forties, walked briskly into the bedroom.

"How are we feeling?" the nurse asked as she quickly adjusted pillows and eased Eleanor against them. "That last pain shot they gave you at the hospital will wear off in the next couple of hours. You tell me when it does. We need to stay on top of the pain. Pain stresses the body and for the first couple of weeks, you need to concentrate all your energy on healing."

"Yes, ma'am," Eleanor said with a teasing smile.

Her nurse grinned in return. "That's what I like to hear. Cooperate completely and we'll get along fine."

Robyn stepped back to allow the nurse to check her grandmother's vital signs.

Apparently part of Eleanor's impressive health care had included a private room at the hospital, a drive home in an ambulance and a twenty-four-hour nurse for the first ten days she was home.

She heard the front door open and went to check who had arrived. Adeline and Marion would both come by, although not during store hours.

Robyn came to a stop when she saw T.J. in her grandmother's tidy living room. She shouldn't be surprised that he would visit. He'd been at the hospital every day. Still, she hadn't been expecting him and somehow the sight of him made her breath catch a little.

"How is she?" he asked.

"Great. Happy to be home and the nurse is amazing." She glanced back at the bedroom. "Are you sure the insurance company authorized the private duty care?"

"It's all taken care of. The time is prepaid, so make sure Eleanor uses every minute of it."

"I will and thanks for calling for me."

"You had plenty to do," he said. "I was happy to help."

He'd done more than help, she thought, staring into his

dark eyes. He'd been a rock. When she'd been worried, he'd made her laugh, when she'd been tired, he'd sent her home to rest. Maybe he'd been difficult and judgmental when she'd first arrived home, but that no longer bothered her. T.J. looked out for the people he cared about.

Involuntarily, her gaze dropped to his mouth. He hadn't kissed her since their dinner out, even though she'd found herself wishing he would. Which made her a fool. She wasn't looking to get involved—she had her life to put back together. But even if she was on marriage alert, he wasn't a good candidate. Too much of a past, she thought.

"It's ten," he said gently.

A not-so-subtle reminder that she was supposed to be at the store, helping Marion.

"Do you want me to go to Only Ewe?" he asked.

"No. I need to be there." Her grandmother was trusting her with the business. Robyn wasn't about to let her down. "Are you going to stay for a while?"

"Until Eleanor gets tired," he said. "Then I'll come back this afternoon."

Telling herself he was available because he didn't have a real job or a life might be true, but it didn't make her less hopeful that he would be there when she got home.

"Thanks," she said. "I'll go tell her I'm leaving."

As Robyn returned to the bedroom, she reminded herself that T.J. was the kind of temptation a sensible woman ignored. A man like him was a born heartbreaker. Her woman's instincts made her want to heal what was broken, even as her head pointed out that loving someone like him would only rip her up inside.

Not that she loved him. But she had a feeling she easily could. If she wasn't very, very careful.

# *Eight*

"I was thinking for my sister," the tall, burly high school kid said. "She's only six, you know, and she kind of likes dogs. Is it too hard?"

Robyn studied the knitting pattern Cody held, one he'd downloaded for free online. It was for a knitted toy poodle puppet that was completely adorable, but a little complicated. Maybe they should offer classes for kids, she thought absently. There were plenty of fun projects, like puppets and other toys.

"You could do it," she said at last, "but you'll need help."

Cody, all of seventeen and six feet of testosterone said, "Yeah? You think I could do it?"

Had he missed the "with help" part? "It won't be easy."

"I'm not afraid of hard work. It's for her birthday."

Robyn smiled at him. "Then I guess you're going to do this, aren't you?"

She explained which kind of yarn would be best and left him to figure out if he wanted to find a real dog-colored yarn or go more fantastical with a pink or purple puppet.

It was late morning, on Saturday. Eleanor had been home from the hospital for five days and was doing great. The nurses took care of everything, allowing Robyn to concentrate on the business.

Cody wasn't the only one trying new things, she thought as she chatted with customers and rang up several purchases. She'd started on a new sweater that tested her rusty abilities. The more she knitted, the more she remembered and the more she missed the craft that had always been a part of her life.

"What about this?" Cody asked. "The purple is for the dog and the pink is for the dress."

The yarn was durable and had a sparkle to it. "Your sister is going to love it. The best gifts are those that come from the heart."

Cody blushed, then ducked his head. "Okay. I'll get started, then."

"I'll be over in a few minutes to see how you're doing."

She turned to answer a customer's question, only to feel a slight tingling on the back of her neck. Without looking up, she knew that T.J. had just walked into the store. He came in the back as much as he came in the front and she never knew when he was going to show up.

But she was always *aware* of him, as if she had built-in T.J. radar. If he was in the store, she knew exactly where he was. If he was gone, she missed him. Not good, she thought, refusing to let herself be vulnerable.

After helping a customer find the right yarn for a first pair of socks and gushing over a finished tote bag, she went back to the craft table to check on Cody.

He'd already made good progress on the puppet, completing six rows.

"Nice," she said, bending over his shoulder and studying the careful, even stitches. "You're really getting this."

Cody looked up at her. "Go to prom with me."

Robyn straightened, sure she hadn't heard him correctly.

Cody stumbled to his feet, towering over her, looking humiliated but sincere. "I know I'm young, but I did get into college and I won't, you know, expect anything just because it's prom."

She didn't know if she should be flattered or run shrieking into the afternoon. She felt the tingling again and knew that T.J. was close by, probably listening. Because life was fair.

"Cody," she began.

"There's only ten years between us," he blurted. "It's not a cougar thing."

From somewhere behind her came a noise that sounded suspiciously like a snort of laughter. She vowed to take care of T.J. later.

"Cody," she repeated. "I appreciate the invitation, but I think you'd have a better time with a girl from your school."

"I don't like any of the girls at my school."

"I'll bet a few of them like you." The kid was cute enough and kind. Did high school girls care about kindness in a boy? Or did appreciation of that attribute come with age and experience?

"You're going to say no, aren't you?"

She nodded slowly. "Ten years is a lot of difference right now. So thank you for asking me, but I can't go."

He sighed heavily and collapsed back into his chair. "I figured you'd say something like that. You still gonna help me with the puppet?"

"Of course."

She patted him on the shoulder, then walked back to the cash register. As she passed T.J., she glared at him.

"Don't say anything," she told him.

"I wouldn't. It was sweet."

"He's a good kid."

"I agree." One corner of his mouth twitched. "I didn't realize we had a cougar lurking."

She socked him in the arm and kept walking.

An hour later, Adeline rushed into the store, holding keys and papers in her hand.

"I have the instructions for Mr. Whiskers," she said, as she handed the sheets to Robyn. "He's very particular about his food."

Robyn scanned the instructions. They were two pages long, including detailed instructions about where exactly to leave his plate and how to empty the litter box. She'd always heard that cats were independent and easy. Apparently she'd been wrong.

"Be sure to maintain eye contact," Adeline added. "That's important. You don't want to upset him."

"What will happen if I do?" Robyn asked.

Adeline pressed her lips together. "Perhaps you're not the right person for this."

T.J. joined them. "I'll help," he said. "Mr. Whiskers likes me." He shrugged. "As much as he'd like anyone who wasn't you. Robyn and I can take shifts."

Robyn wanted to say she could handle Mr. Whiskers on her own, but as he was Adeline's treasured pet, it might be better to have a little help.

"That would be a relief," the older woman breathed.

Robyn nodded. "Sure. We'll make sure Mr. Whiskers is happy while you're gone."

Adeline looked doubtful. "I wouldn't use the word *happy* to describe him, but you can try."

Before Robyn could ask more details about this unhappy cat who required eye contact, T.J. was turning Adeline to face the front window.

"I have a surprise for you," he said, pointing to the long, white limo that pulled up in front of the store. "Your ride to the airport."

Adeline clutched her hands to her chest. "For me?"

T.J. kissed her cheek. "For you."

"I've never been in a limo before."

"You'll arrive in style."

The usually stern, slightly difficult woman melted, hugging T.J., then Robyn, waving and rushing out to meet her ride.

For all his attempts to withdraw from the world after the loss of his family, T.J. hadn't been able to stop being who he was—a kind man who truly cared about others. A man who needed emotional connections.

She could relate to that. It was one of the reasons she'd never felt at home in New York. Her family had always been here. She'd had someone to miss. Someone to come back to. What did T.J. have?

"That was nice," she told him. "You've given her a great start to her vacation."

"She deserves it."

She returned her attention to the list of instructions, which included fresh water twice a day, but only from the filtered container on the counter. Never from the tap.

"Want to check this out when Marion arrives?" she asked.

T.J. grinned. "You're going to love Mr. Whiskers."

Robyn was less sure.

They were busy all afternoon and Robyn didn't have a chance to break away until closing. She called her grandmother to let her know she would be a few minutes late, then walked with T.J. the three blocks to Adeline's small house.

The yard was neat, with mature trees and climbing roses. The paint was fresh, the porch swept clean.

"Women of my grandmother's generation are so tidy," she murmured as they stepped through the low gate. "I always feel inadequate. I'm more of a piler than someone who puts things away."

T.J. laughed. "I'm a guy. What do I know about tidy?"

He used the key to open the front door and they walked into the small house.

The living room was filled with large pieces of furniture. Little porcelain figurines covered every open surface. But that wasn't what caught Robyn's attention. Instead she found herself mesmerized by the sight of the biggest cat she'd ever seen outside of a zoo.

Mr. Whiskers was gray, with dark paws and ears. Maybe a little Siamese in his background, she thought absently, as she was captured by a contemptuous green stare.

He was huge—at least twenty-five pounds of pure muscle. Judging by his expression, he was not amused by the interruption to his afternoon nap, or her presence. She had the feeling that he was figuring out if he could take her or not, and if he could, was she worth the effort.

"I don't think I'm a cat person," she whispered.

T.J. laughed. "Don't worry about it. Mr. Whiskers and I go way back."

To her amazement, he crossed to the cat and confidently rubbed it on the head.

Robyn expected there to be a loud hiss, a swipe of claws and blood everywhere. Instead Mr. Whiskers began to purr. The loud rumble practically made the windows vibrate.

"I'll keep him occupied," T.J. told her. "You go prepare the food."

The sacrifice was more like it, she thought as she hurried into the kitchen and began the detailed process of Mr. Whiskers's dinner.

Robyn arrived home an hour later. Mr. Whiskers had been fed and his litter box cleaned. When T.J. offered to take over pet-sitting duties, she gladly agreed. Honestly, if she were alone with the cat, she would fear for her life.

She walked into her grandmother's house and called out a greeting.

"Have you met Adeline's cat?" she asked as she went into the kitchen, where her grandmother sat at the table. "I think he's part mountain lion."

But instead of laughing, her grandmother looked troubled. She sat with the cordless phone on the table, with a pad of paper next to it.

"What?" Robyn asked. "Do you feel all right? Is something wrong?"

"I'm fine," her grandmother said slowly. "It's not my knee. It's…" She motioned for Robyn to sit. "What happened when you called the insurance company about the private nurse?"

"I didn't. T.J. did. Did he get it wrong?" Would there be a large bill? Robyn didn't know much about her grandmother's finances, but while the store was relatively successful, it wasn't a huge moneymaker.

"Not wrong," Eleanor said. "My insurance doesn't provide a private nurse at all. Someone else is paying for that."

"Did they tell you who?"

"Yes. It's T.J."

# *Nine*

"Hey, beautiful." T.J. handed Eleanor the pink roses he'd picked up, kissed her on the cheek, then settled on the sofa across from her. He eyed her knee. "How are you feeling?"

"Very well, thank you." She leaned forward and poured them each a cup of tea.

While her asking him to stop by for a visit wasn't anything new, he had a feeling her request was for more than company.

"What's up?" he asked, taking the delicate cup from her.

Her blue eyes, the same color as Robyn's, narrowed slightly. "How long have you owned Long Day Records?" she asked.

He held in a groan. "How'd you find out?"

"I looked you up on the computer."

"Does Robyn know?"

"No. I didn't tell her. There's a reason you're keeping your business a secret and until I know why, I'll respect your privacy." Her usually warm gaze turned frosty. "However, I don't appreciate you playing us all for fools."

"It wasn't that," he said, putting down his cup. He hesitated before speaking, knowing she deserved the truth. "When I lost my wife and my son, I didn't care about the company. I walked away from it, in spirit, if not in reality. None of that mattered to me."

"But it does now?"

"I've started going to the office again," he admitted cautiously, not sure why she'd thought to investigate him. He glanced at her knee again and knew. "You found out about the nurses."

"That you're paying for them? Yes."

"I did that because I care about you. You took care of me. All of you."

"That was different."

"No, it wasn't."

She pressed her lips together. "Adeline's cruise. The one she supposedly won? That was you?"

He shrugged.

"And the amazing deal Marion got on the wedding. You're supplementing the cost, aren't you?"

He picked up the tea. "I wanted to say thank-you."

"Sometimes the words are enough."

"I seem to have lost my way with words." He stared at the woman who had pulled him back from the brink of emotional death. "How angry are you?"

"I'm not angry. I'm hurt that you would try to deceive me."

"It wasn't like that. I never wanted to hurt you. I wanted to help. Are you going to tell them?"

He meant Eleanor's friends, as well as Robyn. He'd never wanted them to know who he'd been—mostly because he wasn't that man anymore. His interest in his business had changed. Being wealthy wasn't important. But finding a talented artist—bringing him or her to the public—that still excited him.

"I won't tell them," Eleanor said. "Robyn knows you paid for the nurse, so I can't change that, but I said you'd simply paid the difference for me. She believed me."

"You don't have to lie for me. I'll tell her."

"No, don't. It's better this way. If they knew, things would change."

He didn't want to lose the friendships he had at Only Ewe. "Thank you. For understanding and for saving me."

"Silly boy, you saved yourself."

He knew she thought she was telling the truth. That no matter what, he would have come through. But he knew differently. He knew how close to the edge he'd gone and how the three of them had miraculously pulled him to safety. He knew without them, he wouldn't be here today. And he would always be grateful.

Robyn flipped on the lights in the store and set down her purse. She turned to make sure Eleanor was moving easily.

"Are you sure it's not too soon?" she asked, watching her grandmother walk into the store.

"I'm sure. I need to get out of the house. I've learned that I'm not a fan of daytime television."

Eleanor sat in the chair by the register and looked around. Robyn followed her gaze, hoping the store looked as it should. She'd kept up on stock, had taught the classes, taken in the bank deposits and generally managed as best she could. Although she'd worked hard, she'd loved every second of it. This store was like a second home to her.

"You've done well," her grandmother told her with a smile. "I'm very proud of you."

"Thank you. I've had fun. The customers are great. Oh, someone rented the store next door. Tina from First Texas Bank said that she heard it's going to be a kitchen store, which is great. We should have the same demographics for our customers."

"That is good news. Better a girl business than a boy one for our neighbor."

"Are you glad to be back?" Robyn asked.

"I am, but my weeks away gave me time to think. What are you going to do, Robyn? You said you were thinking of staying here, but have you made any decisions?"

"Yes. I'm done with New York. This is where I belong." Robyn outlined her thoughts on getting a job in a restaurant and figuring out what she needed to study to get on with her life. As she spoke, she was aware that she kept one eye on the door, as if anticipating someone's arrival.

Not "someone," she thought with a sigh. T.J. Since her grandmother's surgery, they'd been spending time together nearly every day. She liked him, liked being around him. When he wasn't there, she missed him.

"I wondered if you had any interest in the store," her grandmother said.

"Working for you?"

"No. I was wondering if you would like to buy me out."

Robyn stared at her. Buy her out? As in buy the store? "But what would you do?"

"Adeline and I have been talking. She loved her cruise

and wants to do more traveling. We're both alone and with Marion getting married, we'll be more of a twosome than a trio. I would still want to work here, but I think I'd prefer to be an employee than an owner."

Buy the store. Robyn turned in a slow circle, looking at the familiar shelves, the colorful yarn, the racks of patterns. She did have some ideas, she realized. Different classes to try, advertising experiments.

"I'd love to," she admitted, feeling the wanting swelling inside of her. "But I don't know how it's possible. I don't have any money or assets."

"The business is the asset. I would finance the sale myself." Her grandmother smiled. "I think after all this time I can trust you to pay me back."

Robyn laughed with pure happiness. Taking on the business would be a big responsibility, but it felt right. She ran to her grandmother and hugged her tight.

"I'd love to talk about this," she said eagerly. "We could keep the business in the family and you'd still be here. And I swear I'll pay back every penny."

"I know you will. Plus, you'd get to boss me around," Eleanor teased.

Robyn laughed again. "That would be fun."

"Good. Then we'll talk details tonight." She pointed to the clock. "It's time to open."

The morning went quickly. Marion and Adeline arrived and were told the happy news. Robyn found herself helping customers with a renewed energy and excitement, but she couldn't help watching the front door, waiting for T.J. to arrive.

She wanted to tell him. Maybe it was crazy or she was putting too much on their friendship, but somehow the moment wouldn't be complete until he knew.

\* \* \*

T.J. arrived at Only Ewe a little before noon. He hadn't planned on coming by but Eleanor had called and asked him to.

Ever since he'd learned that she knew who he was, he hadn't been as comfortable around the store. When he was a beat-up, out of work songwriter, he was at ease in his skin. But as T. J. Passman, President and CEO of Long Day Records, he was just a guy who'd lost everything that mattered.

As he pulled open the front door to the store, he found himself looking forward to seeing Robyn. Avoiding the store had meant avoiding her and he'd missed spending time with her. She was different than he'd first imagined. Smart, funny, determined, caring.

He saw her holding out yarn to a girl who was maybe eight or nine. Robyn crouched down, to get on eye level with her tiny customer and said something about yarn. The girl fingered the soft yarn, then laughed. Her mother nodded approvingly and the kid took the yarn.

Robyn stood and turned. When she saw him, her eyes widened and she hurried over.

"You came by," she said, grabbing his hand and pulling him back outside. "I was hoping you would. I have something to tell you."

She was flushed with excitement, practically bouncing in place. Obviously what she had to share was important. But all he could think was that he wanted to kiss her. Right now—his mouth on hers, up against the wall of the building. He wanted to feel the warmth of her body seeping into his. He wanted to tangle his fingers in her blond hair and then run his hands down the length of her body. He wanted her hot and hungry and taking as good as she got.

The image was as powerful as it was vivid. His body actually ached from the need building inside of him.

It had been so long since he'd felt any kind of sexual attraction, he didn't know what to do with the feeling. He hadn't just slowly stirred to life—he'd come back roaring and ready.

"T.J.?" Robyn stared at him, her eyebrows drawn together. "Are you all right?"

"Fine," he said automatically, ripping his gaze from her mouth. "What's going on?"

She hesitated for a second, as if wanting to ask more, and then she grinned.

"My grandmother talked to me about the store. She says she's ready to retire from the business. Not completely. She still wants to work here, but as an employee, not the owner. She says I can buy her out, if I want. That this can be mine!"

She clutched her hands together in front of her chest, as if trying to contain too much excitement.

"Is that what you want?" he asked. "You'd said something about going back to college."

"Sure, because I'd have to. Singing and dancing isn't going to pay the bills. Besides, that part of my life is done. I enjoyed it but I'm not like my mom. I don't want to open a studio. I was thinking business because then I would be trained to do something, but to have this?"

She turned to face the front of the store, then grabbed his hands in hers. "I love everything about Only Ewe. The space itself, the customers, the classes. It's not just a place to buy, it's a community. I'd forgotten that. I belong here. I've always belonged. I guess it just took me a while to figure that out."

Her happiness was tangible. She glowed from the inside and nearly danced in place. On a practical level, the arrangement made sense, but it was more than that, he thought. Eleanor asking Robyn if she was interested in buying the business was an act of trust and acceptance.

"I'm going to sign up for a couple of business classes," she said, still holding his hands. "Basic accounting, a marketing class. I can take them at Austin Community College. They hold classes at Georgetown High School. Did you know that? How come I never knew that? I'm not going to make a lot of changes but I do have a few ideas." She bounced on her toes. "You're not saying anything."

"I'm happy for you."

She stared at him. "Are you really? Are you sure?"

"Very. You're going to be great."

"No doubts?"

"Not one."

Then, because he couldn't help himself, he pulled his right hand free and cupped her cheek. He bent down and pressed his mouth to hers.

She might have been surprised, but she responded immediately, wrapping her arms around his neck and melting against him. Her surrender was nearly as erotic as the feel of her body pressing close to his.

When she parted her lips, he swept inside to claim her. Her tongue met his in a dance that made him both hard and weak. Her sweetness fed his hunger, making him burn. Had they been anywhere else, he would have been tempted to take more, but it was the middle of the day, on a street in town, in front of her store. Reluctantly, he drew back.

Her eyes were slightly glazed, her mouth parted. Uneven breathing filling the silence and he wasn't sure if it came from him or her.

She blinked slowly. "Wow. I wasn't expecting that."

"Me, either."

Her mouth curved into a slow, sexy smile. "Impressive."

He grinned. "You, too."

She glanced over her shoulder at the store, then sighed. "Rain check?"

Wanting still coursed through him—controlled but very much alive. Maybe there would be guilt later, but for now, for the first time in years, he was happy to be alive.

"Sure," he said. "A rain check."

"Can I hold you to that?"

"It's a promise."

She raised herself on tiptoes and lightly brushed her mouth against his. The wanting returned, and with it the need to pull her close. But he forced himself to stay still and she stepped back.

"You're unexpected," she murmured.

"So are you."

"Is that good or bad?"

He thought about the sadness in his past. The loss. How he'd assumed he would never feel anything again. Did feeling something now betray what he'd had before? He didn't have an answer, but wasn't it enough that he'd gotten to the place where he wanted to ask the question?

Or maybe life was about moving on. He'd expected to spend the rest of his days mourning what'd he'd lost. Somewhere along the way, he'd started to heal.

He smiled at her. "It's good."

# *Ten*

T.J. walked into Long Day Records and knew he had to make a decision about the business. Either he got involved again, turned the day-to-day running of it over to his executive staff or he sold it completely. Being half-present wasn't helping anyone. There were nearly a hundred employees at the company—people's lives and paychecks were on the line.

The open foyer was familiar. There was plenty of seating, as hopeful artists tended to show up without an appointment. In the music business, there was always the dream of making it big, if only someone would listen.

Today there were about a half-dozen people. Three guys who were obviously part of a band, a girl duo and a scruffy-looking kid in his twenties with a guitar that had seen better days. All six pairs of eyes were trained on the closed door that led to the audition room in back. If those hopefuls were lucky, someone would call them and they would walk through the door. They would be given a shot. One chance to prove they had "it."

Many a dream had been realized in this building, he thought proudly. He'd discovered his fair share of rising stars. He had an ear for talent, although it had been a long time since he'd used it.

He nodded at the receptionist, then went upstairs, to the executive floor. His office was waiting for him. His desk surface too clean, his in-box empty. No one expected him to show up anymore. The company went on without him.

Across the hall was a large conference room. Gold and platinum records hung there. He could point to at least half the names and know that he'd discovered them. There had been a time when he'd enjoyed taking off for a couple of months and driving through different parts of the country, stopping in small towns to listen to the local talent. He'd given that up when he'd gotten married, but maybe it was something he could start again.

Would Robyn want to go with him? His wife hadn't been interested, but he could see Robyn being excited by the idea. With her background, she would have an ear for potential. Maybe in an RV, he thought, his mind immediately sliding to a built-in bed and tangled sheets.

He forced his attention back to the question about his business. As he returned to his office, he knew he didn't want to sell Long Day Records, but he also wasn't interested in the details of daily management. Which meant it was probably time to officially step down as president and let someone else actually do the job.

He thought of the six kids waiting downstairs, of the dreams they had and the hope in their eyes. He picked up the phone on his desk and punched in the extension for the receptionist in the foyer.

"This is T.J. Send the band back to the audition room," he said.

"Right away." He heard the smile in her voice. "They're

looking pretty nervous. Be careful they don't throw up or something."

He chuckled. "I can handle it. Tell them I'll be down in about ten minutes."

"Sure thing, boss."

He would hear everyone today, he thought as he left his office. The kid last. For some reason, he had a feeling about him. But first he was going to tell his COO that his promotion to president was long overdue. Brandon was more than capable of running the label.

As for himself, T.J. would go back into artist development. He would search out talent and polish the best of what he found until it shined. Making dreams come true had always been the best part of his day.

Robyn's week sped by. By Thursday, she'd registered for her first night class at the community college, had met with Eleanor's accountant and had gone with her grandmother to meet with a lawyer about the details involved with buying the business. As her grandmother would be financing the purchase, no bank approval was necessary, but there was still going to be plenty of paperwork.

With Marion's wedding fast approaching, spending several hours a day learning about inventory and the class schedule and the intricacies of figuring out the deposit every day, there didn't seem to be a moment to breathe. Still, Robyn managed to notice that T.J. hadn't been around. Not since he'd practically made her swoon with his unexpected kiss.

A man who would kiss and run was inherently dangerous. She knew that. But she also couldn't stop thinking about him, not to mention missing him. Being a grown, mature woman, she could easily pick up the phone and call him. But what sounded good in theory turned out to be impossible to put into practice. So instead of simply finding out what was going on with him, she fretted.

Late Thursday afternoon, the UPS guy pulled up behind the store and announced he had a big delivery. Marion had already left for another dress fitting and Eleanor was off at physical therapy. While Adeline manned the front of the store, Robyn went into the back to supervise.

Normally the process took a couple of minutes as a half-dozen or so boxes were dropped off. Today, all the yarn arrived at once. There had to be at least twenty-five boxes, stacked in every spare inch of space. She signed for all of it, then wondered how on earth she was going to get it sorted and put away.

Adeline stuck her head in and gasped. "You're kidding. All that?"

"Apparently. I knew the shelves were a little bare, but still."

"You'll be here until midnight."

Robyn laughed. "Yes, but I'll be doing what I love. Don't worry about me. I'll order in a pizza and get it done."

"Don't get grease on the yarn."

Instead of taking offense, Robyn crossed to the older woman, put her hands on Adeline's shoulders and kissed her cheek.

"I love you very much and I'm so happy to be back home."

Adeline pressed her lips together. "Yes, well, we love you, too. And don't get grease on the yarn."

Robyn laughed. "I won't. I promise."

She organized the boxes, wrestling them into neat

rows, stacked by manufacturer and type. Some of the yarn needed to get out onto the shelves right away. Wedding and baby season was fast approaching and the knitters in the community were already looking for lightweight summer yarns and soft, delicate skeins.

After collecting her order sheets, she put them on a clipboard and went to work opening the first box.

Color seemed to burst out into the storeroom. She couldn't help touching the different fibers and imagining the possibilities. Forcing herself to remember how much work she had to do, she compared the packing slip to her order form, then began carrying the yarn into the store.

At six she locked the front door and shooed Adeline out for the night. She dragged boxes into the main store and got serious about stocking shelves. By seven she was dusty and a little hungry but before she could decide on which takeout she wanted, someone knocked on the back door.

She opened it to find T.J. standing there. As always, he looked tall and lean, handsome. His dark eyes twinkled.

"I got a call that you were in over your head."

She hadn't seen him in nearly a week and she had a feeling their kiss was the reason. It didn't take a trained professional to know he was a man still living in the past. A smart, sensible woman would acknowledge the foolishness of even trying with a man like him and look for someone slightly less broken.

"I'm learning that it is possible to drown in yarn," she said. "Who knew?"

They both spoke lightly, as if they were friends. But the truth was something different. Tension crackled between them. She could practically see the sparks. Despite the fact that she knew it was a mistake, she wanted to throw herself at him.

He stepped into the back room and shut the door behind him. "I meant to come by before. I've been busy."

"Me, too."

"Right. You're buying the business. Everything going well?"

"Yes. We've even met with an attorney. That makes it official."

The room seemed to be shrinking as she spoke, or maybe it was just her. Her chest was tight and her skin felt hot. No matter how deeply she inhaled, she couldn't seem to catch her breath.

Then there was T.J. Looking away from him was impossible and he seemed equally caught up in her. They weren't touching, but she was more aware of him than she'd ever been of a man before.

"I need to tell you something," he said. "About what I do."

"You're a songwriter."

"Not exactly. I am in the music business, though. Just not…"

She didn't know who had moved first. Maybe him, maybe her. One second he was talking, the next she was in his arms, her mouth crushed against his.

He kissed with an intensity, a hunger, that made her knees go weak. His hands were everywhere—her hair, her shoulders, her back, her hips. There was a desperation in his touch—as if he needed the physical connection or he would die. A feeling she could relate to.

She parted for him and he swept into her mouth. She kissed him back, their tongues brushing, but it wasn't enough. The need between them demanded more. It demanded everything they had.

She touched his broad shoulders, felt the heat of his skin beneath his soft cotton shirt. He was strong, every muscle straining. For more or for control, she wasn't sure.

He kissed his way down her jaw, to her neck. He licked the sensitive skin right behind her ear, nibbled down to her collarbone, then pressed an openmouthed kiss at the V of her T-shirt.

Her belly clenched and her thighs began trembling. Wanting devoured her, making T.J. impossible to resist. When he reached for the hem of her T-shirt, she helped him ease it over her head. When he removed her bra and cupped her small breasts in his large hands, she moaned. And when he drew her tight nipples into his mouth, she knew that dying right now would be perfectly fine. Nothing could ever be better than this.

They sank to the floor. Packing paper proved to be a lumpy mattress, but neither of them cared. She tugged at his shirt, he slipped off her jeans. When she was naked, he used his mouth and his hands to make her writhe beneath him.

Even as he moved his fingers in and out of her, his thumb rubbing that single spot of perfect pleasure, he kissed her deeply. She kissed him back, wrapping her arms around him as her body strained toward her release.

It had been so long since she'd been touched like this, so long since she'd felt the building erotic pressure, she started to think she'd forgotten how to get over the top. Then he pushed in deeper still and she was ripped apart by a pleasure so intense, she had to cry out.

He held her through the shuddering release and when she was finally still, he knelt between her still trembling thighs and pushed into her.

She wrapped her arms around his hips, drawing him to her, watching him watch her. Each stroke filled her so exquisitely, she found herself reaching for that place again. The second time, he came with her, his gaze locked with hers, as if reassuring them both, he knew who he was with.

# *Eleven*

Robyn lay on the crinkled paper, feeling both a little slutty and very content. Her body was satisfied, her heart still pounding and she was probably going to be sore in the morning. What more could a girl ask for?

She smiled at T.J., who was next to her. "At the risk of repeating myself, wow."

Humor brightened his dark eyes. "I'm sure I don't know what you're talking about."

"So I probably shouldn't point out you're naked."

He glanced down at his body. "How did that happen?"

"It was one of those things."

The humor faded and he kissed her. "It was more than that." His warm hands moved over her body. "You're amazing."

She snuggled close to him. "So are you."

He drew back after a minute and stood, then held out a hand to help her to her feet. While she was aware they were both naked in the storeroom, he didn't seem to notice.

"We have to talk," he told her.

"Not what I'm used to hearing from a male, but okay. I'm listening."

He grabbed her panties and bra and handed them to her, and reached for his own boxers.

"It's about who I am and what I do. What I want to do."

She knew he was a man with a tragic past, but not much else. "More songwriting?"

"No." He pulled on his jeans and tugged on his shirt. "I want us… I want us…"

He stopped speaking and turned away, swearing.

"I can't believe I did this."

The words were quiet—almost as if she weren't supposed to hear.

He turned back to her. "I never thought… I don't want… What happened before—it can't be this. I can't do this."

At first she didn't understand. Can't do what? And then she knew. He didn't want to have another relationship. Feeling guilty and needing to take a relationship slow was one thing, but not wanting to move on and have a life was something else.

Pain ripped through her as she realized she'd given herself to someone who wasn't free to give himself back. She knew that for those brief minutes, she'd been a part of his life. Maybe his future. And he knew it, too.

His hands slowed and his eyes seemed to see something she couldn't. Which made sense. She hadn't been a part of his past.

She turned away, not wanting to see any more. She pulled on her jeans and slipped into her T-shirt. She'd barely finished stepping into her shoes when he spoke.

"I need to go."

She nodded. "I figured."

"I didn't mean… This wasn't…"

She drew in a breath, reminded herself that she would survive this disappointment, just like she'd survived countless others, then turned to face him.

Gone was the happy, handsome man she knew. Gone was the passionate lover who had so pleased her. Instead she saw the man she'd met when she'd first arrived back home. A slightly challenging stranger who looked as if he blamed her for it all.

"You're allowed to have a life," she said, knowing he wouldn't listen, but having to say the words anyway. "It's okay to be happy."

He stared at her as if he'd never seen her before. "You're wrong."

It was the last thing he said and then he was gone.

Robyn put away the rest of the stock, cross-checking her orders against the packing slips. She moved automatically, not allowing herself to think about what had happened. It was after midnight by the time she was done. She was shaking, probably from hunger and exhaustion, she thought as she walked home through the quiet streets.

Her grandmother had left the light on for her in the living room. Robyn let herself in, then went directly to the bathroom where she showered in water as hot as she could stand. When she had brushed her teeth, she made her way to her bedroom, only to find her grandmother sitting in the corner chair, waiting for her.

"Are you all right?" Eleanor asked.

"I'm fine. I was putting away the new yarn."

"I knew you'd be working late." Her grandmother smiled. "I just had a feeling something was wrong."

Maternal intuition or wisdom that came with age. Something to look forward to, Robyn told herself.

"I don't think T.J. is going to be coming around much anymore," she said quietly, crossing to the bed and taking a seat. "I knew he was a risk. A man with a lost soul seems so romantic on the outside, but there's a place inside of him that I can't reach."

"But you fell in love with him anyway?"

Robyn sighed. She hadn't been able to resist. Not his kindness, the way he cared, his laughter. "Dumb, huh?"

"Love is never dumb."

"Just misplaced?"

"Only the two of you can answer that."

Robyn drew her knees to her chest. "That's the problem. There isn't a 'two of us.' He made it clear he wasn't ready to move on. If he needed time, I could give him that. But he's not willing to go there."

Eleanor's steady gaze never left Robyn's face. "What are you going to do?"

"Nothing. I can't make him heal. Only he can do that."

"But you love him."

"I've only known him a couple of months. I'll survive."

"Maybe he's just not ready now."

Robyn wanted that to be true, but she had a feeling it wasn't that simple. T.J. had suffered a huge loss.

"I can't help thinking he's so defined by grief that nothing else has meaning for him. I'm not sure it matters why.

The point is, he may never be ready. And I didn't come home looking for love."

"But you found it all the same," her grandmother said gently.

"Maybe, but I've just spent the past six years chasing a dream that never came true. I'm not going to waste the next six years waiting for T.J. to figure out that it's okay to be with me." She shrugged. "I'll deal. I'm strong. I can get over him. What I'm going to take from this is I'm ready to have a serious relationship. I want to get married and have babies. I want to love and be loved."

Eleanor rose. She walked slowly, favoring her still healing knee. When she reached the bed, she kissed the top of Robyn's head.

"Have I told you how proud I am of you?" her grand-mother asked. "You've become a wonderful woman."

"I don't feel very wonderful."

"Still, you are. I'm so grateful to have you in my life."

Robyn stood and hugged her. "I'm the one who's grate-ful for everything. You gave me the freedom to test my wings and a place to fly home to." She laughed. "Okay— I'm about to break into a Bette Midler song. I really am tired."

"Then you should go to sleep. Don't worry. Everything will work out. You'll see."

Robyn wanted to believe her, but knew she couldn't. Eleanor hadn't seen T.J.'s stark horror when he'd real-ized what he'd done. She might not be the first woman to realize she couldn't compete with a ghost, but she wasn't going to get caught in the trap of thinking any-thing would change. She'd learned her lesson and now she would move on.

\* \* \*

Thinking about moving on and actually doing it turned out to be two different things. Robyn spent the next couple of days in an emotional fog, going through the motions of living without being able to feel anything but rejection. By Monday she was sleeping better and eating enough to be working toward her goal of putting on twenty pounds by the end of summer. She still tensed every time the door to the shop opened. She still wanted every customer to be T.J. and she still saw him every time she closed her eyes, but the first step of healing had been taken.

Adeline came into the store with an armful of cruise brochures. She and Eleanor pored over them, trying to decide where they were going to go first.

"I can't believe you're traveling without me," Marion said, sounding slightly put out.

"You're getting married," Eleanor said gently. "You'll be traveling with your new husband."

"And having sex," Adeline snapped. "Which is more to the point. Want to trade?"

Robyn grinned as she walked by the craft table where the three of them sat.

"But we're friends," Marion protested. "You'll be having fun without me."

"So will you," Adeline reminded her. "Better fun."

"Maybe later the three of us can go away together," Eleanor said. "How about that?"

Marion brightened. "I'd like that." She glared at Adeline. "And so would you."

"It wouldn't stink."

They chatted about the Mexican Riviera and the possibility of a transition cruise that went from the Mediterranean back to Puerto Rico. Every now and then, Robyn felt them watching her and wondered how much her grand-mother had shared. Whether or not they'd noticed her less energetic mood. They couldn't have missed the fact that T.J. hadn't been in the store. He hadn't called, either. If it weren't for the ache in her broken heart, she would wonder if he'd ever existed at all.

A little after three, Marion called to her. "I think you have voice mail. Your purse is beeping."

Robyn hurried into the back room, telling herself not to expect anything. Anyone could have left a message. T.J. didn't even have her cell number. But as she reached into her purse, she felt her heart skip a couple of beats. Then she glanced at the screen of her cell and saw a familiar 212 phone number.

Her agent, she told herself. Not T.J. The sooner she stopped hoping, the sooner it would all be over.

She listened to the voice mail, which was a curt message asking her to call as soon as possible. She dialed the number, then waited to be put through to Don.

"Finally," he said when she'd identified herself. "I've been hovering by the phone, and let me tell you, I've got a lot to do. How are you? I have news."

Typical Don, she thought, smiling at his fast talk. "Okay. What's the news?"

"You're not going to believe it. You should sit. Are you sitting?"

She perched on a nearby stool. "I'm sitting."

"Great. I got a call." He named a famous and power-ful producer. "It's a new musical and there's a great supporting part that's perfect for you. I mean it, Robyn, it's like they wrote it with you in mind. And get this. They want you. They called me a couple of hours ago and want you in their office first thing. So get on a plane and get here."

Another chance at the dream, she thought, stunned by his words.

"Are you listening?" Don continued. "They called me specifically to talk about you. This doesn't happen every day, Robyn. This is the break you've been waiting for. There's serious support behind this project. We're talking prestige, recognition. Did I mention money?"

Robyn held on to her cell phone and waited for the information to sink in. Her big break. After all this time.

Her gaze dropped to a couple of boxes of yarn she'd yet to unpack. There was a new class for beginners starting next week and she'd found the perfect scarf pattern for them. Eleanor still needed help around the house and what about Marion's wedding? That was in less than two weeks.

The truth was, she was happy here. Happier than she'd been in a long time. Even with T.J. breaking her heart, she wanted to stay exactly where she was. And yet…

She couldn't help thinking her mother would want her to try again, as would her grandmother. But what did she want?

"I don't know," she said softly, interrupting Don mid-sale's pitch.

"…touring company. What? Did you just say no?"

"Not exactly. I have to think about this."

"What is there to think about?" he demanded. "What the hell is wrong with you? This is the chance of a lifetime."

"I know. That's why I have to think. Give me a couple of days."

"One day," he said, speaking between what sounded like clenched teeth. "Damn, Robyn, you're killing me."

"One day," she agreed. She owed it to herself and those who loved her to think this through. "Then I'll call."

"You'd better. I can't believe you're not saying yes."

"I still might."

"If you don't get back to me tomorrow morning, we're through. I won't represent you."

"I understand. Bye, Don."

Robyn closed her phone and put it back in her purse, then stood and drew in a breath. Talk about unexpected. When God closed a door, He really did open a window.

Her grandmother walked into the back room. "Is everything all right?" she asked.

Robyn turned to her and smiled. "That was my agent. There's a part in a play he wants me to audition for. He swears the producers are asking for me by name. It's my big break."

She said all the words carefully, wondering what she would feel if she said yes. Or perhaps more important, what would happen if she said no.

"What did you tell him?"

"I said I had to think about it."

Eleanor studied her. "Why?"

Robyn told herself to breathe. Her stomach was in knots and her head hurt. "I want to be sure. I said I was starting over. That I was done with that part of my life. I'm ready for the next chapter."

"But?"

She smiled. "But you and Adeline and Marion gave up so much to send me to New York. You believed in me. Mom believed in me."

Her grandmother took her hands and squeezed them.

"Your mother would want you to be happy. Would going back and being in this show make you happy?"

"I don't know."

"Then you were right to wait. Whatever you decide, I don't want you to have regrets. Please don't stay because you're worried about me."

Robyn hugged her tight. "I love you so much."

"I love you, too."

# *Twelve*

**T.J.** was perfectly capable of getting a rented tuxedo on his own, but apparently the choice wasn't his. So there he was in the tux shop, accompanied by Eleanor, Marion and Adeline. The three women studied all the different styles before settling on a black tux guaranteed to provide "James Bond allure."

T.J. eyed the sign doubtfully. He was walking a seventy-something woman down the aisle. Allure wasn't required. Still, it was easier to let the sales guy take the measurements, then bring out a sample for him to try.

At one time he'd owned a tux. Custom-made. But he'd gotten rid of it when he'd lost everything. He hadn't wanted the memories.

"Show us what it looks like," Marion instructed, before guiding a still-healing Eleanor into the chair by the three-way mirror.

"He'll need a vest," Adeline announced. "I've never trusted a man in a cummerbund."

"We have several vest patterns over here," the sales guy said as T.J. ducked into the dressing room.

He undid his shirt, then stepped out of his jeans. Being

around the three old ladies wasn't as tough as he'd thought it would be. Once he'd known they weren't bringing Robyn, he'd been able to relax. Not that he could avoid her forever, but he honest-to-God didn't know what to say.

How could he explain that he'd been caught up in passion and desire and that he'd acted without thinking? Not that he regretted making love with her. At least, not until afterward, when the guilt had nearly crushed him.

He'd lost his wife and son. He wasn't supposed to move on and heal.

"Has she decided?" Adeline asked in a low voice.

"I think she's torn," Eleanor replied, also whispering. "It's a wonderful opportunity. A chance to sing on Broadway."

"So why is she hesitating?" Marion asked. "She should go."

"There are complications," Eleanor said. "I'm sure she's worried about me, but I think there's something else. Something that makes her hesitate."

"She should go," Adeline announced, her voice rising slightly. "It's a great part. What she's always wanted. There's nothing to keep her from leaving."

T.J. stood in the dressing room, listening to every word. Robyn had been offered a part on Broadway? She'd said she wasn't interested in going back, but obviously she'd changed her mind. Probably for the best, he told himself. She would get on with her life and he would...

Slowly he shrugged into the tux jacket. He would what? Continue to live his empty life? He hadn't wanted to like Robyn, but over the past couple of months, she'd become a friend. More than a friend. She was important to him. Sure he was confused, but that wasn't any reason for her to leave.

He had to get out of here, he thought, reaching for his clothes. Go find her and talk to her.

And say what?

Who was he to tell her anything about her life? He'd been living in a fog for the past couple of years. Existing without purpose. If she had a dream, if she had goals, no one should stand in the way of them. Certainly not him. It wasn't as if he had anything to offer her.

Someone knocked on the dressing room door.

"Did you get lost?" Marion asked.

He opened the door and did his best to look normal. "What do you think?"

She tilted her head and nodded. "Very nice. This is the one." She smoothed the lapels, then the shoulders. "You're very handsome."

Words that would have sounded a whole lot better if she hadn't chosen that moment to start crying.

"What's wrong?" he asked, feeling helpless and guilty. "Did I say something?"

She shook her head. "No. I'm fine."

He put his arm around her and led her to the bench by the dressing rooms. Neither Eleanor nor Adeline were anywhere to be seen. He sat next to Marion and put his arm around her.

She cried into a tissue she'd pulled out of her purse, then sniffed. "Sorry. I'm a little emotional these days. It's the wedding. Most of the time I know I'm doing the right thing. I'm so happy and lucky to have found love again. But then I think about my first husband. He's been gone ten years."

"You were married a long time," T.J. said.

"We were. And we were happy. Oh, sure, there were difficult times, but he was a good man." Marion glanced up at him. "Sometimes I wonder if I'm allowed to be happy again. I know that's silly, but I can't escape the question. How can I move on without him?"

He thought about the love in her eyes and how beautiful she'd looked in her wedding gown. "You're allowed to be happy again. It doesn't take away from what you had."

"That's what everyone says. What they don't talk about is that the sadness never really goes away. I will always miss him. Moving on isn't as easy as people think."

He knew that firsthand. He missed his wife and son every day. Sadness was easy, he realized suddenly. It was healing that took work.

"You have moved on," he told her. "Don't let your past keep you from having a future. You deserve this."

She smiled through her tears. "Thank you. I want to believe you. Sometimes it's hard."

"Do you want to break an old man's heart by changing your mind?"

"No," she said firmly. "I wouldn't hurt him for the world."

"Then you're going to have to accept being a beautiful bride and making every other man in the room jealous."

Marion laughed. "You're too sweet to me. To us all."

He hadn't been sweet to Robyn, he thought grimly. He hadn't even talked to her since that night. He'd walked out and left her alone, probably hating him. Not that he deserved better.

Marion stood. "Thank you for listening. My weepy moment is passing. Come show Eleanor and Adeline how handsome you are. I can't wait to see you dance at my wedding."

He allowed her to lead him into the main part of the store. But as the old ladies fussed over him, he found himself thinking about Robyn and the opportunity she had back in New York.

Adeline had been right. Robyn had no reason to stay here. Unless someone gave her one.

T.J. paced restlessly in the back of the church. For the past week, he'd been determined to figure out what to do, what to say, how to fix things. The reality was, he had no right to stand between Robyn and her dreams. If she needed to go back to New York to be on Broadway, he had to support that. But he also believed he couldn't let her go without telling her how he felt.

It had taken several sleepless nights, two days with his former in-laws and getting drunk enough to endure the granddaddy of all hangovers before he'd figured it out.

When he'd finally come to his senses, it had been four in the morning. A little too early to make calls. He'd spent yesterday dealing with last-minute wedding details for Marion, then chauffeuring Eleanor around. As much as he'd tried to see Robyn, he'd been thwarted by a senior citizen at least a dozen times. If he didn't know better, he would say there was a conspiracy to keep them apart.

Maybe there was. For all he knew, they believed Robyn was better off going back to New York and wanted to make sure he didn't mess with her dreams. He wouldn't stand in her way, he thought now as he waited for the bride to decide it was time to walk down the aisle. He would tell her how he felt, then let her decide. If she was going to New York, he was going with her. There were a lot of talented musicians in the city. He would find them and bring them to the label.

The truth was, he didn't want her to go. He wanted them to stay here, in Texas. He wanted roots and connections and all the messiness of life. But this wasn't all about him. It was up to Robyn, too.

What if she didn't love him back? What if she didn't want him to go to New York with her? What if he was turning into a woman with all this introspection?

Marion stepped out of the bridal room, a petite pink flower of a woman. "I'm ready."

He crossed to her and held out his arm. "Then let's make an honest woman of you."

Marion giggled. The lady from the church motioned to the organist and the wedding march began.

They moved slowly down the aisle. He was aware of the fifty or so people in the church, the sunlight streaming in the stained-glass windows and Marion clinging to him as they moved toward her groom. But all he saw was Robyn.

She stood on the bride's side, her blond hair nearly to her shoulders now. She was beautiful enough to take his breath away, and looking at him as if everything was all right. In fact, she smiled.

There could be a dozen reasons for her good mood, he thought frantically. Everything from the smug satisfaction of knowing she was leaving him without a second thought to pleasant memories about their night of passion. Or maybe she wasn't thinking about him at all. Maybe…

He swore silently. He had to know. He couldn't wait another second.

Without considering where he was or what he was supposed to be doing, he stopped in front of Robyn. Surprise widened her eyes, but she didn't look angry. That was something. Now if only he could figure out what to say.

* * *

Robyn was aware of every person in the church staring at her. She wanted to give T.J. a little shove. The minister and groom were waiting, only a few feet away. But the tall, handsome man watching her so intently didn't seem to be moving at all.

"T.J.," she whispered. "The wedding?"

He glanced at Marion. "I just need a second."

"That's all right. Take your time, dear."

T.J. turned back to Robyn and reached for her hand. "I was a jerk," he began. "I'm sorry. I shouldn't have walked out that night. I should have stayed and explained."

She felt herself flushing as she desperately hoped he was going to keep the information vague. Not only didn't she want to discuss their sexual encounter in front of a crowd, church really seemed the wrong place to go into it.

"When I lost my family, I thought I had lost everything," he said. "I didn't want to live anymore. Then three women came into my life and forced me to keep moving forward." He gave her a faint smile. "Against my will, they helped me heal."

His fingers were warm and strong against hers, his gaze intense.

"Then I met you," he continued. "I didn't want to like you, but you were amazing. Warm, caring, funny, determined." He paused. "I found myself wanting to be with you. I didn't know how to reconcile those feelings with what I'd gone through."

"I sort of figured that out," she admitted. "It's okay."

"It's not. I hurt you and you're the last person I want to hurt." He drew in a breath. "I love you, Robyn. I love you. I mean it. I'll even go to New York with you, if that's what you want."

His words washed over her, filling her, making her feel all floaty inside. She felt herself smiling.

"Really?"

"With all my heart."

"I love you, too."

"I'm glad to hear that, because I want us to be together. Even if that means moving to New York."

"Why would we go anywhere?"

"That part you want. The opportunity of a lifetime?"

Robyn glanced at her grandmother. "You told him about that?"

Eleanor shrugged. "I might have mentioned it."

She turned back to T.J. "Did she also mention that I decided not to go because my life is here?"

He raised his eyebrows. "No. That wasn't discussed."

"Someone needed to push things along," Adeline said with a sniff. "We're not getting any younger, you know."

Robyn ignored that. She leaned toward him. "I'm staying. Does that change anything you just said?"

He brushed his mouth against hers. "Not in the least. I love you and I want to marry you."

There were a few gasps, one loud sniff and a couple of sighs. She felt her heart racing in her chest. "I love you, too, and we can talk about the marriage thing. Maybe after a few more dates?"

"Sure." He turned back to Marion, then held up his hand. "One more thing. I'm not exactly an out-of-work songwriter."

"Is that what you told her?" Marion asked.

"I own Long Day Records."

Robyn blinked. "The one with all the big country stars?"

He nodded. "So if you ever want to make a record, I'm your guy."

"Not today, but thanks for asking." T.J. owned Long Day Records? She never would have guessed. "You must have a really good staff to take care of things. You spend most of your time at Only Ewe."

"I do. In fact I just promoted my COO to president. I want to spend my time finding new talent. I thought maybe you'd like to join me. After all, you have a great staff yourself."

It was too much, she thought, swaying slightly on her feet. "I don't know what to say."

"Tell me you'll still be mine after this wedding."

"That I can promise."

"And that you'll love me forever."

"Even longer."

"Good."

He kissed her again, then tucked Marion's arm through his. "Ready to get married?" he asked.

The beautiful bride beamed at him. "This is already the best wedding ever."

"I'm thinking your groom is getting impatient."

He led the bride the rest of the way up the aisle. Robyn watched them, her heart overflowing with love. Eleanor squeezed her hand. Adeline sniffed loudly into a tissue.

Robyn watched the man she loved give away the seventy-something bride. Then he returned to stand by her side. A place she knew he would stay, for a very long time.

\* \* \* \* \*

# Return to
# Summer Island

## CHRISTINA SKYE

To Celia,
Knitter, crocheter and crafter extraordinaire

Thank you for showing me the world
through Caro's eyes—

And thanks for being so amazing
at the work you do.

# Caro's Purple Twisted Rib Wristlets.

Right and left hands are the same.

Using worsted-weight yarn and size 7 needles, cast on 63 stitches using a fairly loose long tail cast on. (Video tutorial at www.knittinghelp.com. Walk, don't run. You'll be *thrilled* you learned it!)

Row 1 (WS) K2, p5 *(k4, p5)* and repeat pattern between asterisks, through to last 2 stitches. End k2.

Continue in rib pattern as established for 4 more rows.

Row 6 (RS) Decrease row, using a centered double decrease (video tutorial at www.knittinghelp.com).

P2, *(k1, slip 2, k1, pass 2 slipped stitches over, k1, p4)*. Continue repeat inside astericks through the row. End last ruffle decrease with p2 instead of p4.

Row 7 (WS)

K2, p3, *(k4, p3)* Repeat */* to last 2 stitches. End with k2.

Row 8

P2, *(slip 2, k1, pass 2 slipped stitches over, p4)* Repeat */* and end with p2 instead of p4.

Next row and all remaining odd (WS) rows.

K2 *(P1tbl, k4)* End P1tbl, k2.

Next row and all remaining even (RS) rows.

P2 *(k1tbl, p4)* End k1tbl, p2.

Continue in pattern to desired length. Caro chose 7 inches. Your choice!

**Bind off**

Work loosely in rib pattern (knit the knits and purl the purls.)

*Notes:*

TBL = through back loop.

Pattern stitch purls and knits are *both* done TBL for row definition on right and wrong sides.

Trust me, it is worth a little ~~irritation, clumsiness, fuming~~ fiddliness.

(Is *fiddliness* a word? It is for me.)

On decrease rows 7 & 8: be sure to slip the 2 stitches as one, knitwise, then pass them over together, making a neat, centered decrease. Any other decrease will put the ruffle off balance. And we don't want that, not after the lovely, crisp line of raised twisted stitches!

Video links (these were current at the time of this writing, but may change.)

Long tail cast on—http://www.knittinghelp.com/videos/knitting-glossary
An excellent and immensely helpful site.

Centered double decrease—sl2, k1, p2sso (or S2KP2), YouTube has a dozen listings.

Twisted knit stitch, ktbl knitted through the back loop—http://www.knittinghelp.com/videos/knitting-glossary
Same for twisted purls.

## Finishing

Turn wristlet wrong side out and fold vertically, matching the sides. Mark thumb hole on your hand using a hair clip or sewing pin. (Plastic, spring-loaded orchid clips work perfectly here. Check your local garden or home-supply store. Who knew?)

Sew seam with matching yarn and a blunt darning needle, working up from the bottom, through both layers close to the edge, catching yarn outside of one stitch on each side of the hem, back and forth. (Finishing tutorials are available at my blog. Or email me—scarfaholic@gmail.com). Pictures work best for this.

Continue sewing until you reach the bottom of the marked thumb hole. Break yarn, leaving 8 inches to weave in. Sew top of seam above thumb hole. Ditto 8 inches. Break yarn and weave in all ends.

All done.
Wear and enjoy your toasty hands, just as Caro does! Gage loves her red pair, knit in Malabrigo Twist yarn. So soft.

Come visit my website, www.christinaskye.com, for a full charted version of this pattern, along with more free knitting designs and tutorials.

Happy knitting!

Note—I am delighted if you knit this pattern for gifts, charity donations or resale. Feel free to use the pattern on your blog or website also. Credit is requested, and highly appreciated: *Copyright Christina Skye 2010.*

# *Prologue*

*Knitting Journal Entry*
*Caro McNeal*

*Bags packed. Knitting ready.*
*Leaving today. No more ocean.*
*No more Summer Island.*
*Why is it so hard?*
*But if I don't go now...*

Around Caro the attic was quiet, rich with memories and dreams. She leaned down, doodling in her worn leather knitting diary. The big maple tree in the front meadow gradually appeared beneath her pen. Patiently she added balls of yarn for fruit and knitting needles for stems. The knitting always stayed close, part of her now. Yarn had calmed her journey, soothed her harsh losses, stitch by stitch, for a decade and more.

For Caro knitting was more than a hobby, more than simple entertainment. When she held her needles, her mind soared and dreams turned clear. Part meditation, part therapy, knitting was an interior journey where she learned to see herself.

Not that she ever spoke of it that way. It would have been outright embarrassing.

But it was true, just the same.

Down below in the kitchen she heard her grandmother, clanking cups and preparing water for tea. It was one of their favorite rituals. But this time would be the last. She had to go, even though it hurt to leave.

Tonight she would be in Chicago.

She printed the word in her knitting diary using big block letters, feeling her heart pound. Her pen moved, sketching big apartment buildings. Crowded streets and bright, expensive shops.

Out beyond the trees Caro saw the gleam of water where the Pacific hugged the narrow harbor in a bright curve of teal. Gulls raced and plunged, shrill in the face of a coming storm. Even in summer, the Oregon coast was unpredictable in its beauty.

*I'm going to miss this place, all storm, sea and changing light. How will I feel at home anywhere else, without the sight and sound of the sea? Without the laughter of everyone I love…*
*So many changes.*
*Is this crazy of me? Is it reckless?*
*Or is it just selfish?*

A car motor growled somewhere over the hillside, beyond the banked red roses and the big green meadow. Time to go. She'd put it off for too long.

She would help others the way she'd always hoped to—because more than anyone, Caro knew the pain of sudden violence and aching loss.

She'd already found an apartment. Cramped and cheap, it had a tiny water view—if she squinted hard enough. She'd even tracked down a yarn store with a weekly knitting group. Knitting was a solace she couldn't live without. The flow of wool and silk in neat, even stitches reminded her who she was and kept her calm when her life was in turmoil.

The way it was now.

Leaving a place that made you feel safe was never easy. Summer Island had sheltered her in its cobbled streets since she had lost her parents as a girl. Islanders stuck together, and Caro had felt protected and loved, safe within a community of friends. The island had been a perfect home for a sad eight-year-old girl.

But Caro was no longer that girl. Losing her parents had made her see other people's pain, and she was called to help them heal as she had done in the wake of loss.

She cradled her diary, touched the pages filled with three years of dreams, regrets and plans. A knitting diary at first. Now it held far more of her life than simply yarn and stitches. It held dreams and regrets, joys and plans.

Caro McNeal turned to the ocean and leaned through the open attic window, taking in the salty air, catching this moment for her memories. Her brown hair gleamed, restless and sleek just as she was.

A dust mote danced through a bar of sunlight and she remembered how much she loved this house, loved this town. And despite all that love, she had to break away.

She felt guilty about that, though her grandmother hadn't complained or protested about her plans. Not once.

Guiltyguiltyguilty.

She scrawled the words fast. Her fingers clenched and her pen tore through the paper.

Yes, all true. Guilty as charged. But she still had to go. She had to find her own legs and see what she could become.

She needed new streets. New responsibilities. New faces across a busy café.

If I don't go now, I never will.
Never. Never.

Caro stared at the words. On the page nearby she saw her latest notes for a sweater, sandwiched between rough sketches of cabled sleeves and long ribbed cuffs. Yarn possibilities for future projects, taken from old knitting.

But Caro wouldn't repeat anything.

She would move on and keep growing. The past was too often a cold, sad place, with too much loss.

"Caro? Are you about ready, love?" Teacups rattled. Footsteps crossed to the bottom of the stairs. "The tea is done, and Grace and her grandfather just pulled up."

The crunch of gravel. A car door slamming.

Grace, her oldest friend, called out. Laughing the way she always did, calm and smart, knowing exactly what she planned to do with her life.

Caro took a last look at the sunny attic and its distant view of the sea. She touched her old diary and then scrawled a few last words.

That's all. No more to say.

I'll write from Chicago. Everything will be different then. New, busy. Full of possibilities.

After so much waiting and so many dreams, the car was outside, the plane ticket in her pocket. Caro closed the diary and took a deep breath. Time to go.

"Coming, Gran," she called. "Tell Grace I'm all ready."

She closed the attic door, holding her diary tight. Then she ran down the stairs and didn't look back.

# *One*

She was going to be late. Horribly late. And Caro McNeal *hated* being late, especially for work meetings.

Gripping her worn leather document case, she raced across the street, trying to ignore an icy wind that snarled off Lake Michigan. She was going to miss her last meeting of the day if she didn't hurry. This was what her life had become—always running. Always playing catch-up.

Traffic was stopped all around her—more of Chicago's interminable road work. How long had it been since she'd taken time to stroll along the Oak Street Beach and enjoy the sunshine? What about watching the dogs romp at Belmont Harbor? She used to love that.

As a senior victim advocate with a demanding caseload, Caro couldn't even find time to window-shop in Lincoln Park these days. Thanks to recent budget cuts, her client load was worse than ever. She hadn't even gone home to visit her grandmother in ages.

At least she had her knitting. Rosewood needles and

soft wool. Red mohair and pink alpaca. Their threads kept her sane when life was tangled and work was very, very grim. Which it usually was.

As she thought of her current knitting project, Caro's tension lifted. She was making a lush scarf with big, complex cables in palest blue alpaca. She was halfway through, and her fingers itched to finish it so she could wrap the soft folds around her neck.

But unfortunately work came first. It wasn't easy shepherding crime victims and their families through the complexities of the legal system. It wasn't pleasant seeing police photos and sharing the pain of those who had lost a beloved wife, son or sister. And her job was important. Caro was careful and caring and thorough in everything she did. Right now the thick leather bag under her arm held three domestic-violence cases and two homicides, but she had never regretted her choice. She wasn't good at math and didn't have an artist's clarity of vision. She didn't understand the stock market and couldn't translate French poetry. But she *could* smooth the way for those who suffered. She had seen the fear and confusion in the eyes of frightened families and knew that her job helped them untangle the threads of their lives in the aftermath of violence.

And how could she have forgotten? Tonight her grandmother was coming!

Caro took a slow breath of sheer happiness. She actually had three days off coming, and how she needed it. She and her grandmother were going to shop to their hearts' content and then enjoy long, leisurely dinners. *Sheer heaven.*

A sudden gust of wind ripped at her throat. A second icy blast pulled her hand-knit scarf free and swept it high into the air. Caro gasped, watching the delicate pink lace drift over taxis and trucks, landing on the far side of Michigan Avenue.

A fire truck raced past and promptly tore the fragile pink stitches into a long, jagged mess. Ruined.

In a span of five seconds all her careful hours of knitting were suddenly just a memory.

But what did one scarf matter? Tonight, after she picked up her grandmother from the airport, she would start on another scarf. But first, Caro had her last appointment mediating with a school psychologist on behalf of one of her victim's children.

A drop of rain struck her cheek. She scanned the street and saw that the next light had just turned green. If she moved fast, she might actually not be late.

Behind her Caro heard the whine of a car motor. Shouts rang out and a green van raced around the opposite corner, skidding hard. The driver was waving his hands wildly through the open window.

Why wasn't he slowing down?

Everything around Caro slid into slow motion as the van skidded sideways again, spun in a wild circle, then jumped the sidewalk.

A heartbeat later she was struck hard from the side. Pain slammed down her arm. She staggered, gripping her side, crying out as rain drenched her face. Her grandmother—who would meet her at the airport?

Around Caro the street began to blur.

The last thing she remembered was a second wave of agony burning down into her right wrist and her own hoarse cry of pain.

# *Two*

*White tile.*

*White uniforms. Voices that ebbed and flowed.*

*Caro drifted in and out on thick waves of pain. White walls. White shoes. People moving. Shouting. Hooking up machines and looking worried.*

*The world spun again. The floor shifted. Everything was still white. After a long time Caro stopped fighting the pain and let herself drift back down.*

The gray pain went on for hours. Caro heard nothing but the rasping sound of her breath and her heartbeat.

She drifted again, and when she next opened her eyes the pain was still there, but it seemed distant now, part of someone else's world. Caro saw a tall woman studying a clipboard beside a bed. Her hair was braided and her chiseled black features were elegantly beautiful.

*Nice face. Strong face.*

She must have said the words out loud, because the nice face turned and a pair of gentle hands reached out to take her pulse.

"Good to have you back with us at last, Ms. McNeal. I'm Dr. Clarke."

"Where—" Caro's voice cracked. "Where am I?"

"Cook County Hospital. You've been here for six days. We were starting to think you didn't like us." The nice eyes narrowed, looking thoughtful. "How do you feel?"

But Caro heard only one thing. *Six days? What had happened?* She tried to sit up and blanched at the searing torment in her right arm and shoulder.

"Better not to move, Ms. McNeal. Your body has been through a great deal. Healing is going to take some time. What you need to do now is sleep. Everything else can wait." The nice face came closer.

Caro saw a syringe.

"My arm—burning. And my grandmother…" Caro closed her eyes and swallowed. "Supposed to pick her up from…airport."

"Try to relax, please. Your grandmother's fine."

Caro didn't want to frighten her grandmother. Her gran worried too much. She was certain that life took the things you loved most.

Not surprising, given that she had lost her only daughter and son-in-law in a car accident when Caro was eight. After Caro had lost her parents, she had gone to live with Morgan McNeal in Oregon. Caro needed to protect her grandmother from any more suffering.

*No, I have to see her. She'll worry. I need to explain.* Caro couldn't manage the words. Her mouth felt funny, as if it was coated with steel wool.

Someone raised her arm. The sight shocked her.

Her arm was covered with bruises. Angry welts cut into her skin and disappeared beneath a long strip of white gauze. Caro remembered the flash of lights and burning pain.

There had been a dusty green van. A man waving his

arms. Then an explosion of pain as she was thrown side-ways. She closed her eyes at the searing memory.

The doctor kept speaking quietly. Caro closed her eyes and felt her mind begin to drift. Pages rustled. The doctor opened Caro's right eye and focused a light.

"Try to take it easy, Carolina. Everything's going to be fine." The doctor spoke quietly. "We'll call your grand-mother and let her know you're awake."

She shouldn't be here. There were people relying on her. Caro should have been with them right now, offering comfort and support. She frowned at a sudden memory. "My knitting—is it here? I—I had my diary and my knit-ting bag when the van... I need my yarn. My best needles were in that bag. My knitting diary, too." She couldn't manage to say anything more. She tried to sit up, but could barely lift her head. "I can't lose those things," she rasped. "I can't replace my diary."

"Everything will be fine," someone said in a calm, distant voice used to soothe a child who knew that some-thing bad had happened, but didn't understand that her world had just changed forever. It was the kind of voice you used to hide the worst sort of news.

"I need my knitting bag. And my diary. All my notes—my sketches are there."

"Soon," the voice repeated quietly. "For now, you should rest." A penlight flashed in Caro's eyes again. "How many fingers do you see, Carolina?"

"Six," she muttered. She wasn't blind, at least. "And my name is Caro. No one calls me Carolina now. But you can't call my grandmother. She'll worry. I'll call myself. Later..." She frowned down at her arm, motionless on the crisp white sheets. "Why can't I feel my hand?"

"Don't worry about that now."

As a victim's advocate, Caro had seen violence. When they told you the details could wait, when they told you to relax, that meant it was very, very bad. "I need to get up," she said hoarsely. "Now. You don't understand. I have a case. I'm supposed to contact the family—"

"Someone else was assigned to take over your caseload. You're going to have to rest, Caro. Just rest now."

She felt a prick at her hand. "I don't want to rest. I want to know what's *happened* to me. What's wrong with my hand?" She fought in vain against the thick gray wave of sleep that wrapped around her. "Tell me the truth."

She felt a blanket pulled up around her and her eyes closed. "Please," she tried to say.

Footsteps moved away toward the door. "Her grandmother's not answering," a man's voice said quietly. "I left a message, but no one has called back."

"Keep trying. She's going to need her family once she's lucid."

The man moved away. "I'll keep trying her grandmother. She's probably going to be upset."

"Tell me something I don't know. The right thumb was fractured. And her new wrist X-rays are just coming in. Hell." The doctor sounded angry, tired. Frustrated at things that she couldn't understand or change. "One thing is certain. That young woman is damned lucky to be alive. All she wanted was her knitting bag," the low voice went on. "But I don't know if she'll *ever* do any more knitting. Not with that hand the way it is."

*No more knitting?*

The words haunted Caro as trays rattled and doors opened. People came and went. Her head hurt.

*Not knit?*

She drifted back down into sharp, troubled dreams.

* * *

Caro opened her eyes and saw sunlight on the far wall. The room went in and out of focus. "What day is it?" she rasped.

An orderly turned from his cart loaded with lunch trays. "February 14. You woke up just in time for Valentine's Day, ma'am."

Caro gave a dry laugh. "That's romantic. Where am I?"

"Cook County Hospital. Intensive Care Unit." The man's voice sounded low and distant.

Someone spoke to the orderly, and he rolled his cart outside.

"How do you feel, Caro?"

*Bad.* Her shoulders aching and her throat raw. Little slivers of memory dug into her brain. There had been car horns and snarled traffic. A dusty green van skidding over the curb.

Caro struggled to sit up, trying to clear her head. Suddenly she was aware that something else was wrong. "Why can't I feel anything in my hand or my arm?"

"We can talk about that a little bit later."

"No, *now*." Caro remembered this voice. This was the doctor with the nice face. She felt a crippling wave of fear. "Why did you say I wouldn't be able to knit again?"

The doctor blew out an irritated breath. "I shouldn't have said that. I'm not God and it's not for me to predict the future. The truth is that you are the one to determine what will or will not happen. You have torn ligaments, several fractures. One wrist was badly hurt. But you can come back. I've seen it happen. It is going to take a whole lot of work though."

*Be tough,* Caro told herself. "I want to start today."

The doctor nodded in approval. "I have an orthopedic

expert set up to evaluate you. Together we'll plan a comprehensive program of rehabilitation. The sooner you can start, the sooner you can have your life back."

Caro looked down at her right arm, encased in a heavy cast all the way to her shoulder. Only the tips of her fingers were visible. Right now having her life back seemed like a very dim hope.

"Okay." She took a deep breath. "I'll do whatever it takes."

Through a haze of pain Caro started to ask about her treatment and surgery options. She was stopped by a bustling sound outside in the hall. There was a flash of red at the door. Gold and silver chains dangled against glazed glass beads.

"Gran," she whispered. Relief surged over her in a warm wave. She felt the prick of sudden tears. "You came. I—I'm so glad to see you."

Six feet three inches tall, Morgan McNeal was an imposing sight. Her silver hair lay in stunning waves that cascaded around her shoulders. Her keen eyes took in everything around her as she dropped a big leather bag on a chair and shook her head. "I came as soon as I heard you'd woken up." Morgan leaned over the bed and touched Caro's cheek. "We've all been worried sick."

Caro squeezed back more tears as she felt her grandmother's hand gently smooth back her hair. Her grandmother was an accomplished artist whose coastal Oregon landscapes were shown in collections around the world. The White House had recently commissioned two paintings for a state gift, but none of it went to Morgan's head. Every sale was like her first, and she still burned with an artist's fire every time she opened her studio door.

*How could you miss your mother when you had a grandmother like this?* Caro thought.

Morgan kissed Caro's face and then turned to study her heavy cast. "You definitely know how to keep life interesting." Then she smiled slowly. She opened her big leather tote bag and pulled out a smaller woolen bag with soft fabric handles. "I thought you'd want this."

"My knitting bag! How did you get it?"

"A woman—a knitter, I might add—saw it on the street after your accident. She called and found out where you were and insisted that your yarn and diary be returned to you."

Caro took the bag, feeling as if a small part of her world had returned to normal. "She knew how I would feel. Another knitter would understand that I could never replace this diary."

"You knitters are something special, you know that?" Morgan pulled a chair closer to the bed. "I checked and your yarn and diary are fine, so you can relax. And just for the record—I'm here as long as you need me, my love."

# *Three*

"Yes, I understand that her strength and dexterity are going to be limited. I will monitor all those things closely." Morgan sat very straight, her eyes on the X-ray framed in a box beside the doctor's desk. There were long and short gray lines through the bones at Caro's right elbow, wrist and fingers. The gray lines were fractures. The picture left no doubt about the extent of Caro's injuries.

"I know you and your team have done a wonderful job here. I can't thank you enough for all you've done, helping Caro move from a full cast to an elbow-to-finger cast. In time my granddaughter may need more surgery, and we will be prepared for that. But for now—I want to take Caro home. She needs that most." Morgan's voice was firm. "She needs to be in safe, familiar surroundings right now."

Dr. Mildred Clarke tapped her pen on the neat desk, looking undecided.

"I'll take care of all the details. I'll see that she's seen regularly by the orthopedist at Oregon Health and Science in Portland. You've approved their physical therapist already."

The doctor looked at two more X-rays. She flipped through Caro's most recent tests and blood work. Then she closed the thick file and pushed her glasses up on her forehead. "It will take hard work and there are no guarantees that your granddaughter's hand will ever completely heal. Forgive me, but I think it's best to speak clearly to you. You've both worked so hard and Caro has improved nicely in the last month." She rubbed her eyes. "But the damage was severe."

"My granddaughter is stubborn, Doctor, and I'll be right beside her. We'll do whatever it takes. Caro is going to recover all her strength. *That* is a promise. Just watch us."

It rained on the way to the airport in Chicago and it rained while the plane taxied to the gate in Portland. Tired as she was, when Caro finally saw the ocean she forgot all about the clouds and her pain.

They stopped at the same place they always stopped— around a bend in the road above a small headland by the sea. The rain hadn't made it to the island, it seemed, and the sun was shining from behind a few wispy clouds. As a girl, Caro had sat in that same spot, shaded by a rugged oak tree in the middle of a broad meadow. With her knees drawn to her chest, Caro had drowsed in the sun, dreaming of grand passion and great adventure. The oak tree looked the same, but now its scarred trunk showed signs of age and hard weather. Things always changed. You could bank on that.

Beyond the meadow the hillside dropped sharply to a small harbor where scattered boats rocked at anchor.

Despite all the places she had been and all the friends she had made, this meadow and this old tree meant home, the magnet for Caro's soul. A deep feeling of welcome and peace wrapped around her.

At least *some* things hadn't changed.

She heard the crunch of gravel, and a second later her grandmother touched her shoulder. "What do you think of it?"

"The meadow is lovely and the sea looks just the same. Vast and deep. New as my dreams. I guess the sea never changes, even when we do."

Morgan sat down on the grass beside her granddaughter. "This was always your favorite spot, wasn't it?" She pulled a blade of grass and chewed it thoughtfully. "But not everything's the same. Rafe Russo—you remember him?"

Oh yes, Caro remembered Rafe. Summer Island's bad boy, Rafe had set every girl's heart on fire with pure lust. "Of course I do. How is Rafe doing these days?"

"He joined the Marines. He's stationed over in Afghanistan right now. His aunt still lives near the library, and he stays in touch." Caro's grandmother shot her a look. "Are you sure you're okay? You look pale, honey."

"I'm fine." Caro cradled her arm carefully. She didn't want to think about the pain in her wrist. This was her first glimpse of home in three years, and she wanted to savor the moment, letting the wind and waves speak to her. A fishing trawler cut through the harbor toward the main pier, while noisy seabirds circled above the wake. Caro turned her face to the sun and closed her eyes. "What else has changed on the island?"

"Well, you know the old grocery burned down last year. Thank heavens no one was hurt. We needed a new one anyway." Caro's grandmother cleared her throat. "What else? Let's see, some mainlander bought the Harbor Café. They put in Wi-Fi and an expensive wine bar, which lasted all of three months." Caro's grandmother sniffed. "But the animal shelter is still running strong. And Grace Lindstrom, your friend from high school? Well, she's in Paris now, writing cookbooks—historical cookbooks, I think. Her grandfather still manages the animal shelter. Dr. Lindstrom told me Grace was coming home to visit sometime this spring." Morgan slanted a careful glance at Caro. "Maybe you'd like to volunteer at the shelter once you're feeling better. Dr. Lindstrom—Peter—could certainly use your help. I think he keeps the shelter afloat with his own money these days since state funds were cut last year, during the fiscal crisis. Closing the shelter would have meant that all those poor animals..."

She didn't finish. Caro got the picture well enough.

"Yes, I'd love to help out, Gran." Caro gritted her teeth as she cradled her right arm. "Just as soon as I can." She smiled crookedly. "Next week should be good."

"I wish that were true," her grandmother murmured. "But you've made excellent progress, far better than your doctors expected." She studied Caro's face. "You're tired and I think you're in pain. Let's get you home."

Caro wanted to stay longer, but the pain was building. She stood up slowly, feeling the wind in her hair. "Yes, I've seen the meadow and the old tree. Let's go home." She felt her grandmother's hand on her shoulder.

Neither moved, caught in memories. Caro had stood on this spot as a girl desolate and lost in the wake of her parents' sudden deaths. She had come to this hill as a restless teenager, desperate to grow up and see her future. And through everything, her grandmother had supported her. The responsibility of raising a young child had come when she'd least expected it. She had been building a successful career as a painter, but she had put everything on hold for her granddaughter. She'd swept Caro up in island activities and kept her busy with new friends and new hobbies. Together they had tackled a new craft project every week. Her energy and enthusiasm had made the perfect antidote to Caro's terrible loss.

It felt wonderful to be home, Caro realized. Why had she stayed away from the island for so long? She paused beside the car, resting her good hand on the door. "I'm ready to go, Gran. I'd like to rest a little, but then maybe we can drive down to the harbor. Is the little bookstore still there?"

"They closed last winter, I'm sorry to say. Tourism has been down and they just didn't have enough business. But the day is all yours, my love. Wherever you want, whenever you want. I forgot to mention there's a new restaurant near the harbor. I've seen your old friend Jilly Peterson working there. I heard she was accepted at a prestigious cooking school in Scottsdale, so she'll be leaving soon. She always seemed so restless, so anxious to get away from the island. Now it looks like she's on her way."

Then Morgan's update on Caro's old friends ceased. As she drove over the ridge of the hill, red roofs emerged above twisting streets that hugged the water. Caro had always loved the quirky cottages snuggled beside the harbor. Decades before, a pair of English artists had moved here, bringing with them the traditional thatching techniques. Now a dozen whimsical cottages still boasted thatched roofs carved into scrolls and rolling curves. There had once been talk of making up note cards and a Summer Island calendar with photos of these cottages, earmarking the revenue to benefit the local library, but Summer Islanders were a careful lot. No one wanted to be flooded with crowds of loud summer tourists or off-season photographers on the prowl for "local color." In the end the plan was scrapped. Life stayed slow and quiet on the island, just the way it had been for decades.

"The dragon roof is just up ahead." Caro's grandmother slowed the car, smiling. "Remember?"

Caro saw the sleek gray body rising and falling along the top of small dormers, above walls covered by climbing roses. Cut into thatch, the dragon's body curved along the roof ridge in the afternoon sunlight. It was a work of great skill, Caro saw now with the eyes of an adult. But for a child, it had been a creation of pure magic, sprung from dreams, not everyday metal tools. Its beauty made her breath catch, driving away her pain and her worry. "Is it still haunted, Gran?"

"So I hear. The last deal for a buyer from Seattle fell through. It's on the market again."

Caro felt a pang. Buying the dragon cottage had been one of her childhood dreams, but the current owner, a wealthy movie exec from L.A., was asking an exorbitant price—certainly far beyond her reach. Besides, she wasn't nearly ready to move back home.

As the car turned onto a tiny cobblestone street overlooking the harbor, Caro caught the perfume of roses. She saw the gleam of the gold-and-blue stained-glass windows in her grandmother's studio.

Caro closed her eyes, feeling she was truly home.

"I'll make you a pot of tea, love. I thought you'd like your old room under the eaves, the one where you can see the harbor."

"That sounds wonderful, Gran." But Caro was fighting

to hide her pain and exhaustion from long hours of travel. "I think I'd better rest first."

"You go on ahead. I'll bring up your bags." Her grandmother frowned. "Do you need help? Should I stay—"

"I'll be fine." There was an edge of determination in Caro's voice. It was too early to begin full-scale therapy on her hand, but she had to start adjusting, learning how to be independent again. With two pins in her right wrist and an elbow-to-fingertip cast in place, the process wouldn't be easy.

As she passed the little window at the landing, Caro yawned. "I'm so tired. It must be all the fresh air and the water." She yawned again. "It's lovely to be home, Gran. Thank you for everything."

"Thank me for what? Of course I would come and help. It doesn't bear discussing."

"Well, then thank you for keeping everything in the house just the way it was. The roses are still the same and you haven't changed the old twig furniture on the hill. I always thought that this house was perfect. Growing up, it felt like sheer enchantment to live here." Caro yawned again, half asleep on her feet. "It still does."

As she trudged upstairs, Caro didn't see the smile of pride that lit up her grandmother's keen blue eyes.

"Yes, we're finally home, Peter. It's been a rough month, I don't mind telling you. Then our flights were delayed and Caro's luggage was lost. My poor, dear Caro. You wouldn't recognize her now. She's lost fifteen pounds and looks terrible.... No, of *course* I didn't tell her that. *Men*." Morgan blew out a breath. "Her hand? I can tell the pain is bothering her all the time, but she refuses to take her pain medication unless she's right on the edge of screaming." She sighed. "Stubborn girl."

"I wonder where she got all her stubbornness," Peter Lindstrom, Summer Island's veterinarian, said wryly. "I've been doing some research about her hand. I also spoke to an old friend in Minnesota who highly recommends the physical therapist you chose. You're going to be busy. He told me that Caro's compliance with the therapy schedule will be crucial to her recovery."

"She's a determined woman, Peter. So am I." Morgan's voice fell, and she looked up cautiously before she continued. "Caro's going to need a great deal of rest and moral support in the next few months, Peter. I'm afraid that means that I can't...that we can't..."

"I already guessed that, my love. And I've waited for you twenty years, so I suppose I can wait a few more weeks to announce our marriage."

Morgan drummed her fingers on the big wooden table. "I was going to tell her during my visit. Then the accident happened and there was no time."

"I understand." Voices rose sharply. Barking echoed over the line.

"Peter, is something wrong at the shelter?"

"No. Just some new arrivals. Heaven knows where we're going to put them. Since I converted our back storage room into sleeping areas for the animals, there's no more space left anywhere. I'm using an old trailer for supplies now. And with more funding cuts ahead..." He cut off his complaint. "But we'll manage. We always have."

"You're a wonderful man and an amazing veterinarian, Peter Lindstrom. I *love* you. I hope you know that."

"Just keep telling me, Morgan. I can't seem to hear you say it often enough. And I warn you, I'm going to drop by Saturday night. I won't give up seeing you entirely. But don't worry. I'll use the excuse of showing you pictures of our newest rescue animals." Shrill barking filled the air. "Now I'd really better go. We just got four more abandoned puppies and it's starting to look like World War III back there."

Peter Lindstrom put down the phone and rubbed the knotted muscles at his neck. It had been the Friday from hell. He hadn't stopped moving since dawn, when a stray puppy was brought in, bleeding and abandoned by the side of the road. Fridays were always the worst, he thought grimly. Fridays were the day people made desperate decisions or pulled up stakes to leave town; on Fridays, in the heat of the moment, people sometimes decided to dump their cat or dog behind an empty building or outside a busy shopping center. They told themselves it was for the best, convinced that someone else would pick up the responsibility.

He bit back an oath, furious as always at how irresponsible people could be. But the truth was, they did what they could. Peter knew that times were hard, and sometimes people simply ran out of options. If it came to a choice between feeding four hungry children or feeding a dog, who was he to point an accusing finger? Day by day he did what he could. The shelter would keep its doors open for as long as he was alive. He was drawing from his own savings now, something he knew Morgan suspected. But even she didn't realize the extent of the costs to run everything.

But no matter. He was an old man and his tastes were simple. He didn't miss the money, and he loved the pets that he could save. He loved them *almost* as much as he loved Morgan McNeal—as he had loved her for decades now.

And he worried about Caro. From his conversations with

his orthopedist friend in Minnesota, he knew that Morgan's granddaughter faced a grueling ordeal. Peter had already arranged for his friend to visit Summer Island during his yearly vacation. Peter wanted his opinion on Caro's case, and he didn't want Morgan to feel responsible for any cost involved. She had enough on her plate right now.

And if Morgan, stubborn as she was, didn't like his interfering, so be it. When you loved people, you meddled. Peter Lindstrom had grown up in a big and close-knit family. Now his siblings and nieces were spread all over the globe, but they still meddled.

Out of love and caring, they protected their own. They argued and laughed and bullied. So would Peter.

But he was a wise man at seventy-two years old; he knew when to keep his meddling to himself.

His lanky teenage volunteer knocked on the door. "Sorry for the noise, Dr. Lindstrom. The Doberman escaped again. I barely caught him before he raced across the road in front of a truck. He's in his cage now."

The loud, incessant barking was noisy testimony to that fact.

The boy cleared his throat. "And the mail came. I…I put it on your desk." He didn't meet Peter's gaze, which probably meant there was a new pile of bills. Another hit to his savings.

"No problem. I'll have a look later."

The tall vet rubbed his neck, pulling his thoughts back to the rear operating room, where the injured puppy was in recovery. It had been a straightforward operation. With luck and good care, the little dog would be active and ready to tackle the world again in a week.

He prayed that Caro McNeal's outcome would be equally successful.

# *Four*

*One week later*

There was too much to do and not enough time to do it.

First Lieutenant Gage Grayson had three days left before his return flight to Afghanistan, and he had every second planned. He had visited his sister, who was suffering through her first bout of chemotherapy and had no other relatives. Because of the advanced stage of her cancer, Gage had asked for and been granted emergency leave to accompany her for two weeks at the beginning of her treatment.

After his stay with his sister in the hospital, Gage had made a bereavement call to the family of one of his youngest men. His sergeant had given his life to save four civilians under fire, and his heroism would never be forgotten.

With that emotional visit done, Gage had two days left to transfer his pets to the home of an old friend, who was going to care for them during the remainder of Gage's tour in Afghanistan.

Curled up on the seat beside Gage, a big white cat looked up and meowed. A golden retriever poked his head between the seats and licked Gage's face with happy abandon. Since his sister had been diagnosed with cancer, she would no longer be able to take care of two active animals until after her chemotherapy was complete. So Gage had scrambled, relieved when his friend had volunteered to take over.

"Jonas will take good care of you two, I promise."

He scratched the retriever's head. "You both be good." Gage was taking Bogart and Bacall to their new home—assuming that he could find the way back to the interstate. Twice he'd lost his way on the narrow coastal roads and his GPS wasn't picking up anything in this isolated region. Gage checked his watch. He still had one more errand before he could head north to Jonas's place. If he was lucky, it wouldn't take long.

Through the clouds he saw a glimpse of red roofs above a harbor dotted with trawlers and a few pleasure craft. He didn't remember seeing a town on the map. Where was he?

Gage checked his rental truck's GPS again and muttered an oath.

*Out of service area.*

Didn't that just figure?


Caro sat by the window, watching the ocean churn and froth at the foot of Summer Island's main pier. In the weeks since the collision, she had worked hard. She had worn a full arm cast and was recently upgraded to an elbow-to-fingertip cast. Then she had begun the complex therapy recommended by her specialist, making slow but steady progress with her grandmother's help.

She was sick of getting by with one hand. She wanted her strength and her life back. She wanted to be able to manage by herself and not keep bothering her grandmother for help with simple tasks. And she wanted, more than anything else, to knit again.

Caro closed her eyes, feeling a physical yearning for the touch of soft silk and springy merino wool sliding through her fingers. It had been too long since she had picked up her needles, too long since she had watched colors play and twist, caught in changing patterns. Knitting had become a deep solace, a meditation in touch and color. Every day that Caro didn't knit seemed painfully incomplete.

You couldn't explain the feeling to someone who hadn't felt the lure of the yarn. Caro had long since stopped trying.

The unused muscles in her right hand strained as she squeezed the soft exercise ball her specialist had given her. The movement was uncomfortable, but Caro kept right on working.

The McNeals were fighters, and Caro swore that she would be knitting before the week was out, even if all she could manage was a few sloppy stitches.

She pulled a ball of teal yarn from her knitting bag and took a deep breath. Eagerness mixed with fear as she lifted a pair of wooden needles. She had been depending on her grandmother for everything during these past weeks. It was time to push herself a little harder and see if all her exercises and therapy had begun to pay off.

Sunlight played over the big wooden table and the boxes stacked at one end. Her grandmother had been unusually frazzled on her way out that morning, turning at the door to warn Caro that she was expecting two more packages today. Or maybe she had said someone was coming to pick up two packages. Caro couldn't remember.

She would call her grandmother to be sure. But first she had to find out how much she had lost and how far she had to go. She needed to do that alone, without anyone who could see her frustration and fear.

Would she ever be strong again, able to do the things she had once taken for granted? She stared down at the neat rows of stitches, caught exactly where she had left them on the needle during her last project. Her hands trembled, touching the row of knitting. Every movement had seemed so easy. It had been part of her life for years. What if she never regained these soothing skills that she had taken for granted for so long?

*Push, wrap and lift. Then slide off a new stitch.*

Caro's hand clenched as she slid her needle into the first stitch. But she couldn't control the movement and, to her dismay, knocked all the stitches off. Her needle slipped free and plunged to the floor.

*Never mind,* she told herself fiercely. *Try it again. Just keep going. Each time you'll get better.*

Ten minutes later Caro knew the sad truth. Even the simplest kind of knitting was beyond her. All she had to show for her struggles was an aching right hand and a pile of dropped stitches. Her fingers wouldn't work the way they should. She had no strength and no control.

She closed her eyes, rubbing her temples with her good hand as a headache boiled across her forehead. Maybe a cup of tea would help. Her gran had left a pot with Caro's favorite Earl Grey on the middle of the kitchen table, inside a wool tea cozy. Maybe a break was all she needed. Feeling a little more optimistic, Caro bent to lift the handle. As she did, her sleeve caught on the spout, and the beautiful blue-and-white Royal Copenhagen teapot shot across the table, fell on its side and tumbled off, shattering into pieces on the tile floor.

Caro blinked, stricken by the sight. The teapot had been her mother's favorite, part of her parents' wedding set. Her grandmother had wanted to use it that day to celebrate Caro's progress and growing strength.

Now Caro had broken it, shattered it in her clumsiness and determination to do too much too soon. Maybe that was the story of her life, always pushing, always racing to be at the next destination without taking time to appreciate the place where she actually was. How strange that she had never really learned how to slow down.

Her eyes blurred with tears. She still had dim memories of the last time her mother had used the tea set, during one of her grandmother's visits. It had been a magical afternoon, and none of them had imagined the terrible loss in their future.

Kneeling carefully, Caro collected the broken porcelain. The teapot would never hold tea, but with care and patience Caro could glue it back together, making it look like the lovely piece that her mother and father had used every Sunday afternoon. But it would be only an illusion—pretty, but unusable.

*Worthless.*

You couldn't put the pieces back together again, not in any way that was functional or true. What was the point of holding on to an illusion when a thing was shattered beyond repair?

Just like her hand.

She felt blood on her finger. Tears burned her eyes as she remembered Sunday dinners around the big wooden kitchen table with the faint smell of her mother's lavender perfume and the low boom of her father's laughter. So many years ago, yet the pain still lingered.

The sound of a car on the driveway made her turn. She

didn't move, clutching the small porcelain fragments in her hand. Footsteps crunched over gravel, and the front doorbell pealed a long cadence from Chopin, one of her grandmother's favorites. Caro used her left hand to shove back her hair. Was this one of her grandmother's friends? It wasn't unusual for an islander to drop by without notice.

But the shadow in the window looked very tall, and when Caro opened the door the floor seemed to tilt. The man on the steps was well over six feet, his hair touched with hints of warm brown and dense mahogany. Yet what drew Caro in were his eyes, focused and clear, as if he looked at you and saw everything but judged nothing. His gaze seemed to say that he was someone you could trust to hold your life's secrets—even your life. All of this flashed through Caro's mind as he stood at the front door. She stared at him awkwardly, with the doorknob gripped in her left hand as a bar of sunlight fell around them.

"Yes?"

He cleared his throat, frowning at her. "Are you all right, ma'am?"

"Why wouldn't I be?"

"Because that looks like an awful lot of blood on your finger." His voice was just as calm and focused as his eyes, yet there was warmth in his low tones.

"Bleeding? Me?" Startled, Caro looked down and saw a line of blood on her palm. *Must have cut it on the teapot fragments. Funny, it didn't hurt.* But her hand was throbbing now and she felt a little queasy. "I guess you're right." She opened her fingers, staring at the handful of broken porcelain pieces, angry that she had broken something so beautiful.

His eyes narrowed. "You've got blood on your cheek, too. Are you okay?"

"Sure." But the truth was everything hurt suddenly. Her hand and wrist and elbow and the little spot below her shoulder blade that had been tight and knotted for weeks. Caro wondered whether they'd always hurt. She felt a little dizzy, so she put her good hand on the wall, staring at the man in the plain black turtleneck. For some reason she couldn't stop the words that tumbled out next. "You're very handsome."

"Me?" He laughed good-naturedly. "No way. I'm as average as blown sand."

Caro shook her head and tried to stop feeling so dizzy. "Sorry to be rude, but why are you here?"

"To pick up a package. This is Morgan McNeal's house, right?" When Caro nodded he pointed down the driveway. "Look, I've got a medical kit in the truck. If you want, I can clean that cut for you, ma'am. I've got some field medical training."

"You're a doctor?" Somehow the image didn't fit.

"Not a doctor. U.S. Marines."

The air seemed heavy, charged with energy. Caro tried to clear her sluggish thoughts. "Well, thanks, but there's no need to bother. I'm…fine. So what kind of package are you looking for?"

She saw his hands open and then he shoved them into his pockets. "A painting. I was told this was where Morgan McNeal lived, and I've come to pick up a painting she made for my friend. My name is Gage. Lieutenant Gage Grayson."

The name suited him. Strong, and a little unusual. So he wasn't actually a total stranger knocking out of the blue. But she still wasn't ready to let him inside.

"I think my grandmother mentioned it, but I'm afraid

I wasn't listening too carefully. Let me go look inside on the table."

As she turned, the screen door shut, bumping her arm and making her wince. Still so clumsy. Maybe she'd always be clumsy. Maybe this was as good as it would get.

"Are you *sure* you're okay?"

"Oh, I'm great. Just perfect, Mr. Grayson." Caro realized her voice sounded hoarse, even a little desperate. "I mean Lieutenant. Really. Perfect."

"How long has it been?" he asked quietly from outside the door.

"How long has *what* been?"

"Whatever happened to leave your arm in that cast and make you feel so frustrated."

"I don't feel—" Caro stopped and then turned back toward him. "Is it that obvious?"

"To me. Maybe not to others."

"So why do you notice things that other people don't, Lieutenant Grayson?"

"Just a habit. And the habit has turned into a survival technique where I'm headed." He sighed and then glanced over at his truck. "Look, ma'am, I could come back at another time, but my schedule is tight. I fly back in forty-eight hours and I've got a list of things I need to do first."

"Back where?"

Gage gave a little roll of his shoulders. He looked as if he didn't particularly want to talk about this. There was a movement in the blue truck on the driveway and his mouth hiked up in a sudden grin. "I'm almost done, Bogart," he called out loudly. "Hold on, boy."

A furry head rose over the driver's seat. A wet nose pressed against the window.

"Sit, Bogart," Gage called.

Loud barking came from the truck.

"Sit and be good," Gage ordered.

The barking just grew louder.

Caro hid a smile. "He's very well trained, I see."

"He used to be and that's a fact. But I've been away for a while and he's…excited to see me." Gage looked a little harassed as a cell phone chimed in his pocket. When he scanned the number, his smile faded. "I need to take this. Sorry. It's my sister and she's been sick."

"Of course." Caro hesitated, watching the sun play over his shoulders. When he was done with his call, Caro held open the door. No point in being rude, she decided. "Why don't you come in while I find your painting?"

"Glad to, ma'am."

He had a rich voice, the kind that seeped under your skin, and Caro liked the direct way he met her eyes. But if he called her ma'am one more time, she was probably going to scream.

She was picking up the last pieces of broken pottery when he crossed the room. "Need some help with that?"

"I'm good, thanks. I'd offer you some tea—but I just smashed the pot."

"What happened?" Gage gestured to the cast on her right arm. "Accident? Or a motorcycle crash?"

"Car. It's been a while now, but I'm still kind of a mess." Why had she told him that? "Sit down, Lieutenant Grayson."

Instead of sitting, he paced the room, looking restless. He moved to the window, studying the blue stretch of the sea below. It was an arresting view and visitors almost always stopped there. While his back was turned Caro had a chance to study him closely. His military bearing was unmistakable now, and so was a sense of contained energy. But he looked worried about something.

"Is your sister okay?"

"About the same."

"I'm sorry."

"Yeah, so am I. Anna's worked hard for a lot of years. Now this." He paused, running a hand over his neck. "It's cancer." He stared out the window at a single trawler heading out to open sea. "I won't be around to help her."

Caro had a dozen questions to ask. Where was his sister? Where would he be going and for how long? What were his plans when he came back?

*Not your business.*

"Tea is out, but how about some coffee?"

"No need to go to any trouble. I'm good here just watching the sea. This is one heck of a view, ma'am."

"Call me Caro, please. I'm Morgan's granddaughter." She started to hold out her right hand, frowned, then raised her left hand instead. Despite the strength of his fingers, his grip was gentle. Caro felt a ridge of calluses on his broad palm as their hands touched.

The air seemed to hum. Caro watched a tiny dust mote dance through the sunlight and brush their joined hands. His skin seemed warm under her hand, meeting hers in a perfect fit. She glanced into the depths of those keen eyes and felt herself pulled in, caught by questions that suddenly seemed very important.

She stepped back, feeling a little light-headed.

"Did you say army?"

His mouth twitched. "Marines, ma'am. I've got a flight from Portland the day after tomorrow."

"I see." Caro liked the way he stood quietly as if he was soaking up the room, soaking up the normalcy of this moment. "And you can stop calling me ma'am. It's Caro. Have you been in the military long?"

"Long enough." He shoved his hands into his pockets, again deflecting a question he didn't seem to want to answer. "How about I help you with those paintings? Maybe I can spot the one I'm supposed to pick up. It's a landscape of the sea during a storm."

"There's a big pile of packages here. It should be in there." Caro reached out, misjudged her motion and sent two thick padded envelopes skidding across the kitchen table. She muttered under her breath. "Stupid hand."

"Let me help you." Without a sound he moved beside her and Caro felt the brush of one powerful shoulder followed by the sudden warmth of his body. He pulled half a dozen packages into a line, scanning the names and addresses. "This one is mine, I think." He turned the padded envelope so Caro could see his name. "Your grandmother has beautiful handwriting. You don't see that very often anymore." His broad, tanned hand opened on the package, tracing one edge. "So you're Morgan McNeal's granddaughter. They told me down at the café that you might be here."

All Caro could do was nod. There was a weight of energy between them, churning in the quiet room. She had the strangest sense, just for a moment, that she could see dim images around him.

Sand and smoke.

Driving dust and the cries of men caught in pain and confusion. "You've seen some fighting," she murmured, sure of it without knowing why.

He slid his hands into his pockets again. "I thought wearing civilian clothes would make me look like a civilian, but it doesn't seem to work."

"It's not about the clothing. There's something about you, the way you stand, the way you look around. It's very silent and thoughtful. Were you in Iraq?"

He shook his head. "Afghanistan." He looked back at the window, but his eyes seemed focused on a very different place. As the stillness and intensity clung to him, Caro had an urge to reach out and touch his shoulder, to offer some measure of warmth he could take with him. Strangers or not, it was the least she could do.

But she didn't move. She didn't make spontaneous emotional gestures like that. Besides, she reminded herself, he was almost a stranger. As Caro turned, one of the stacked paintings wobbled and fell. The others collapsed like dominoes. The last one hit her hand, making her gasp in pain.

"Careful."

There was blood dotting the cuff of her white shirt. As she bent over for a paper towel, her knitting needles escaped from her pocket, still dangling yarn.

"So you knit?" When Caro didn't answer, Gage reached around her and rescued her needles. "Are you always this stubborn?"

"Afraid so."

"My friend's wife knits, and I don't recall ever seeing her without yarn and needles. She made us all helmet liners last winter. They were a big help." Gage took the paper towel from her hand. Quietly he went to the sink and dampened it with hot water. "Let me have a look."

Caro wanted to refuse, but something about his voice calmed her. It was the most natural thing in the world to hold out her hand and feel his palm brace her fingers. He was careful as he cleaned the jagged cut, and she could sense that he was careful in everything he did.

"You'll get stronger. Just give it time."

"I hope you're right." Her cheeks flushed. "These days...I'm not so sure."

"I am. You're stubborn and you're a fighter. I can tell. You're probably more of a fighter than you know." He finished working, his head bent over her hand, focused on her completely until she felt the force of his intensity and care wrap around her.

There was something special about Gage Grayson. He had a way of making her feel safe and protected without saying a word.

"So...you're leaving town soon?"

He lifted his eyes at her question, and nodded.

"Do you have plans right now? Like maybe—for coffee. Or how about lunch at the Harbor Café?"

Caro cleared her throat. Had she just asked him *out?* A man she barely knew? This was totally wrong. Absolutely *not* like her.

Gage's eyes crinkled a little. "Are you asking me to lunch, Ms. McNeal?"

"It certainly sounds that way. And I don't ask men out very often, so you'd better snap at the chance, Lieutenant Grayson."

He cocked his head. The smile that opened over his face took away the weight of worry and duty that Caro had seen when he first arrived and again when he received the phone call from his sister. That look let her know she'd done the right thing.

He finished cleaning her hand. "It would be my pleasure, Caro. For the next hour I'm at your disposal."

# *Five*

Gage stared out the front window while Caro got ready to leave. He hadn't expected to be charmed by Morgan McNeal's cozy cottage above the harbor. He hadn't expected to enjoy the muted sound of waves or feel the sun so warm on his shoulders.

And he definitely hadn't expected to meet Caro McNeal, fighting with pain, clearly struggling to put her life back in order. The fact was, Gage felt a little disconnected. There were parts of him scattered in too many places. One part was with his sister as she fought her way through her first course of chemotherapy in California. Part of him was already back in Afghanistan, feeling sand whip at his face as he scanned the nearby ridge for signs of hostile troop movements. Another part was grieving with the family of his dead fellow Marine.

And the rest of his mind was alert above this restless sea, marveling at its beauty and the idea that life could be so quiet, so calm.

So *normal*.

Who knew that he would run into a woman like Caro McNeal, tall and stubborn and beautiful, when he least expected it? Gage had earned every break that life had given him. He never expected—or even wanted—a free ride. The gift of meeting Caro had landed like a body blow, hard and low to the stomach.

It had also hit at his heart, in the hidden place where he'd boxed up most of his boyhood dreams. It hadn't taken him long to realize that Caro was in pain, though she was working hard to hide it. He had also guessed that she would be harder on herself than anyone else could be. She struck him as that kind of person.

Her invitation had surprised him because he was sure she didn't make many offers to men she didn't know— probably not even to men she *did* know. But something left him curious, and that same subtle awareness made Gage restless and intrigued.

So he would squeeze an hour into his tight schedule and see where it took them. He didn't have any serious expectations—just some quiet conversation and a little laughter. Caro seemed as if she could do a lot better than a Marine first lieutenant with less than $3,000 in his bank account and his next ten or so years promised to Uncle Sam.

"Why are you frowning?"

"Was I?" Gage held open the front door for her, enjoying the way she walked, smooth and limber and determined. No artifice or seduction, but graceful just the same, despite the careful way she protected her right arm. "I was thinking about how strange it feels to be back in the States in this quiet town. Things are normal. No guns. No blowing sand." No wounded comrades, he thought. No munitions dumps to secure. No death stalking you in a predawn ambush.

Though Gage realized there was death here, too. Caro

must have come close in that car accident, and right now his sister was fighting with death. Maybe normal was more complex than it looked, and there were all kinds of bravery.

He waited for Caro to lock the house, then followed her down the gravel walkway to his rental truck. It would be a squeeze with his pets, but they were both fairly well behaved. Something told him Bogart and Bacall would like Caro. The sight of his pair in the truck brought back a pang of sadness. They would take it hard, but Gage knew his friend Jonas would do fine by them. Jonas had sounded a little tired when Gage spoke to him the day before, but it was just a touch of flu, he'd insisted. Nothing important.

When he realized Caro was talking to him, he shoved his worries deep. Leaning down, he quickly pushed two empty coffee cups into a paper bag under his seat. Rueful, he scratched Bogart's head. "Sorry. It's kind of a mess."

"No need to explain." Caro smiled at the retriever. "Is this Bogart?"

The dog barked excitedly. "Hold out your paw for Ms. McNeal. That's a good boy."

Tail banging against the seat, the big retriever barked again and then lifted his paw through the open window. Caro leaned closer and saw a white cat pressed against the retriever.

Her eyes widened. "Your cat is beautiful. And she gets along with your dog?"

"You bet. Bogart here took care of Bacall ever since she was a kitten. I found them huddled together in a storm sewer, both strays, nothing but skin and bones. These two are best friends."

He put his head down and was rewarded by barking

and wiggling and hectic pressing of happy bodies. His face was licked with the sheer, unbounded joy that only a pet can share.

Caro leaned against the truck and laughed, and the sound seemed to do strange things to the sunlight, making Gage feel dizzy and calm at the same time.

"They're beautiful, Gage."

*So are you,* he thought. Suddenly he wanted to stay at this quiet, normal house above the snug little harbor. He wanted to hear Caro laugh again. He wanted to remember that the world could be calm and sane.

But Gage would have to leave, and soon. His responsibilities couldn't be ignored. So he forced a smile and scooped up Bacall, setting the white cat high on his shoulder.

"How about we go find that cup of coffee you mentioned?"


What was she *doing?*

Caro was regretting her decision before she reached Gage's truck. She didn't know the man, didn't know anything about his past. It was doubtful he would buy a painting just to cover up theft or some other crime, but these were strange times. Who knew what people were capable of?

Meanwhile she looked like a wreck. Her hair spilled everywhere, and she was painfully aware of the scars on her arms and hands from the collision. She hadn't been out with a man in months, even before the accident, and she hadn't been out of her grandmother's house for any kind of social event since she had come home.

And yet...

Caro stopped walking.

All of these things were true, but they weren't the real problem. The real problem went deeper and was far more frightening, she realized.

"Caro?" Gage stood with his purring cat on one shoulder as he held open the passenger door. "Did you forget something?"

"Oh, I definitely forgot something." She stared at the truck, flooded by a wave of frustration.

And beneath that lay fear. Because Caro knew she might never come back from this, and all her good memories could be behind her. The future might be about making do and getting by, about adapting to very diminished abilities.

She didn't think she was brave enough to accept that.

"Caro, talk to me," Gage said quietly. "What's wrong?"

"What's *wrong?* Everything. This is a mistake—a huge waste of your time. My prospects aren't really very good, and I'm wondering if I'll *ever* be able to manage simple tasks again." She took a raw breath, reached for the truck door and muttered as her fingers slipped on the latch. "I can't even open a door. I—I hate being so weak. So helpless."

She felt the slam of her heart as buried emotions suddenly churned inside her. "That's what's wrong. And that's why I'm going back inside right now."

"Caro." It was just one word, just two syllables, but the power in the word made her look up. His hand curved over her shoulder and he looked down at her face, deadly serious. "You'll come back. You'll be even more than you were before this happened, not less. How do I know that? Because of the way you don't complain even when you're gritting your teeth in pain. Because of the careful way you touched your knitting needles while your face filled with good memories. You'll definitely be back, Caro. So let's go have lunch and I can watch you get started."

"I'm frightened." She ran her good hand over her eyes, stunned at what she was saying. "What if I can't?" Somehow it seemed easier to ask these hard questions of a stranger, someone who wouldn't be offended by her honesty. She held up her cast and stared at her nearly useless right hand, then closed the fingers slowly, gritting her teeth at the pain. "What then?" she whispered.

"You'll drop things and curse. You'll ask for help, even though you won't like it. Then you'll get up and try again. We all fail, Caro. It's part of the human job description. When it happens, we just get up and try something new."

"How can you be so certain?"

"I have to have good instincts. Knowing who to trust keeps you alive during a dawn attack or on a crowded street with civilians who might actually be hostile combatants. I know how to watch people. When I look at you, I see a strong woman—one who doesn't know half of what she's capable of yet."

"You do?" She flexed her right hand carefully. Was it her imagination or did the simple movement hurt just a little less than it had that morning? "Are all the men in your unit as smart you are, Lieutenant?"

"I like to think so."

She nodded, believing him, accepting his decisiveness. It had been wrong to bury her fear and anger. It had taken a stranger's calm optimism to make her see that.

"There's still a problem. I can't put any pressure on my hand yet. I may need some help getting into your truck."

"I can help you." A smile flashed across his face. "But you'll have to share seat space with the rest of my family."

"Your family?"

"These two are all I've got except for my sister." Gage put the cat on the front seat and then reached inside to scratch the dog's head. "Bogart and Bacall, meet Caro McNeal. She's going with us." The dog barked and put two paws on Gage's chest. "Move over, Bogie. Give the lady some room here." Gage turned, frowning as he took in how high the passenger seat was beside Caro. "You are definitely going to need some help there. How about I lift you?"

Caro hesitated, then nodded. When Gage's arms slid around her waist, she knew it was just a friendly gesture, the impersonal brush of two bodies, yet touching him still left her blood racing. Once she was settled, Gage slid behind the wheel and leaned over without asking to clip her seat belt in place. The minute the door was closed, Bacall stretched gracefully across the seat and curled up in Caro's lap, purring loudly.

She placed her hand gently on the cat's back, savoring the feel of warm fur beneath her sensitive fingertips.

"I can move her, you know. Otherwise she's going to get fur all over that nice skirt of yours."

"I wouldn't hear of it. This feels wonderful. I had a cat when I was a girl, but only briefly. Unfortunately, my grandmother is allergic."

"You grew up with your grandmother?"

Caro nodded. "I lost my parents when I was young, but Gran was fantastic. She never believed in pointless rules, and she kept her own artist's hours. When her muse was afoot, nothing stopped her. It was an unusual way to grow up, but I wouldn't trade those memories for all the world. And in case you're wondering, I haven't got a hint of artistic blood. Gran gave me painting and drawing lessons when I was a teenager, but nothing took. My only creative skill is knitting. Not that I'm complaining. For me knitting is more than enough—craft, therapy and meditation all in one." She looked out the window, remembering the patronizing comments of her coworkers back in Chicago. "Most people don't understand how it calms you and focuses your mind."

"Oh, I do. Dex—that's my friend—says he knows one thing by now. *Nothing* gets in the way of his wife's knitting night. He says she's always in such a great mood when she comes back that he wouldn't dream of begrudging her that three-hour piece of happiness once a week."

"Wise man," Caro said. "I never had time to attend mine regularly in Chicago. Something always seemed to come up. And now—well, it may be a long time before I can knit again."

*Maybe never,* a cold voice whispered.

"Stay with it. You'll get there, Caro. Remember, attitude is everything."

"Is that a Marine motto?"

"No, my personal motto."

Her fingers moved gently over the cat's fur. "I like it." Caro nodded, feeling a little drowsy with the low purr of Gage's cat, curled in her lap. "So you have no family but your sister?"

"Afraid not. I lost my dad when I was four. I lost my mom two years later. I think it broke her heart when Dad passed on. But maybe that was just the imagination of a grieving boy." He drove carefully, as he did everything else, missing nothing as they passed Summer Island's winding cobblestone streets, past banked roses and small quirky cottages painted bright colors of blue and green. "My sister and I were in and out of foster care for a few years. I can't complain. We got to stay together and lived with some very nice folks. Then I joined the service, and I found a different kind of family. My men are the best, bar none. I've got no regrets." Gage's voice was firm. "But enough about me. Where would you like to eat? I remember passing a pizza place and a café down near the harbor."

"Let's go to the café. They have great sandwiches and some wonderful desserts."

"The café it is." He was already turning right, without asking for directions.

"How did you know where to turn? Have you been on Summer Island before?"

"I spent a week here one summer as a boy. I just remembered as I was driving to your house. Back then this place seemed like something out of a book. Every house a different color. And those crazy thatched roofs."

"Amazing, aren't they?"

He nodded and looked across at Caro. "What was it like for you to grow up here? Was it as good as I imagine?"

Caro nodded. "After I lost my parents, Gran's friends pulled together and helped take charge. It was a big transition for her. She's a very independent woman, and she didn't count on having a young child in her care, not at the height of her painting years. But after a few rocky spots we worked things out. We were best friends then and we still are."

"So you stayed here after school?"

"No, I went to Chicago."

"Why would you give up a wonderful place like this?"

Caro watched clouds blur the horizon. "Leaving the nest. Solo flight. You know the clichés."

"What happened?"

"Nothing. I love my job and I think my work in victim advocacy is very important."

He nodded thoughtfully. "I imagine there's a lot of pressure with the job. So what brought you back here? Was it because of the accident?"

"Yes." Caro stiffened at the memories. She cradled the brace on her arm.

"You want to talk about it?"

"No, I don't think so. I'm just a statistic, the kind that comes when you put a bad driver with faulty brakes on a crowded street. I'd rather focus on tomorrow than yesterday. Maybe that does make me a fighter." Caro smiled as the cat stood up and stretched on her lap, then licked Caro's fingers. "And…about lunch. You don't want to leave these two guys out here in the truck while we eat. I've got a better idea."

It took them less than ten minutes to gather everything they needed. Caro knew the perfect spot to go after that. Gage followed her directions and parked near a big meadow on the hill, where granite ridges overlooked the lighthouse and the restless sea.

"I never would have thought of this. It's been years since I've had a picnic." Gage took the blanket that Caro had borrowed from the owner of the Harbor Café and spread it over the soft grass beneath a dense willow tree. "I'm not sure if I remember how."

"Simple. Leave the details to me."

While he straightened the blanket, Caro slowly opened small take-out boxes. "Close your eyes," she ordered.

"Is this going to hurt?" Eyes closed, he leaned back against the tree.

"You'll have to take a chance. Ready?" When he nodded, Caro held a fully cooked hamburger to his mouth. "Well, what do you think?" She watched him bite into the hamburger, savoring every bit.

"You have no idea." He took another slow, almost reverent bite. "Not that I'm complaining. Uncle Sam does a darn good job for us over there. But it's just not the same as fresh, locally made food like this. So why aren't you eating?" He looked down and frowned. "Are you in pain? I know how hard it can be to recover from a wound." He didn't wait for her answer, locating a plastic fork and giving her a bite of the food on her plate.

Caro's face flushed. "You don't have to do that."

"I know I don't. Now be quiet and eat."

She took the bite of potato salad, seeing the determined look in his eyes. There was no point in arguing, especially since she had done too much that day and her hand was feeling cramped and weak.

Acutely aware of every old bruise and healing scar, Caro made a mental note to knit herself a pair of gloves, the cute fingerless kind that was so popular right now. At least they would cover the worst of her scars. But for the moment she had to be satisfied with tugging her sleeves down as low as they would reach.

When they were finished, Gage lay back on the grass and tucked his hands behind his head, watching the clouds race along the horizon. Across the meadow a red-tailed hawk circled high and returned. Sometimes it was good just to sit in the sunlight and let life unfold, Caro thought.

Right now it was a relief not to worry about tomorrow or next week. Sitting here beside Gage filled her with a sense of peace.

As she leaned back, Caro saw the old dragon cottage through the trees. Its beautiful thatched roof and stained-glass windows seemed to glow golden in the afternoon light. As a girl Caro had dreamed the house was haunted.

If so, it was haunted by beauty, she decided.

Gage's golden retriever dashed by her, nearly overturning a bottle of apple cider, and Gage lunged forward to prevent a mishap. He caught the bottle in one hand, and in the process his arm slid along Caro's waist. The air felt hot and heavy as the retriever barked and then put his paws on Gage's shoulders, knocking him back onto the blanket in excited demand for more play.

"They're going to miss you. Will they be staying with your sister?"

Once Gage managed to struggle out from under Bogart, he ran a hand over the dog's ears, calming him. "No, it would be too much for her. An old friend is going to keep them until I get back."

*Until I get back.*

The words hung between them, pressing at Caro's chest. There was a chance that he *wouldn't* come back and they both knew it. In war, loss and death were grim and ever-present possibilities.

Gage glanced at Caro, his fingers smoothing Bogart's fur. The movement was slow and careful, and Caro found herself imagining the pleasure of that touch. The images made heat skim over her skin, and something shimmered to life, growing between them, restless and hungry. Awareness seemed to snap between them like a hot electric wire.

Neither one moved.

Gage looked down at Caro's mouth, then down at her hands. He cleared his throat and pushed onto one elbow. "Would you mind—that is, I'd like to write to you. It would be nice to have news, nice to know how you're doing. It always helps to remember that somewhere there's a normal world and normal people going about their lives," he said quietly. "But maybe…you won't have time for that."

"I'll be happy to give you my email address. How long do you expect to be gone?"

"It's better not to focus on time. I'll be back when I'm back. If I'm counting minutes, living in a world of *what if,* I can't focus or do my job." He took out a little notebook, tore out a sheet of paper and waited while Caro wrote down her email address. "I can't guarantee I'll be able to answer quickly, if I'm out in the field…"

"That's fine. I'll keep writing, Gage. Just drop me a line and tell me how you are."

A rabbit appeared in the bushes beside the meadow and Bogie tore across the grass in hot pursuit. Unconcerned, Bacall simply yawned and curled up on top of Gage's leg, purring in the sunshine. The sense of peace on the hillside was deep and almost tangible. Caro closed her eyes, feeling the sun on her face, gathering these layers of peace like a soft alpaca shawl around her shoulders.

Suddenly a shrill ring made Gage shoot up and dig at his pocket. His eyes darkened as he glanced at the screen of his cell phone. "Excuse me, Caro. I need to take this." He stood up and walked away, speaking quietly into the phone. Caro couldn't hear the words, but the tension in his shoulders was unmistakable.

When he came back, the calm had left his face and his eyes were bottomless. She felt as if she was looking into the face of a different person. A professional soldier's face.

"Is everything okay?"

"I have to go. My transport time has been pushed up. I'm sorry, Caro. This last hour…it was more than I expected to have. I thank you for that, and for making a stranger feel at home here for a little while."

Caro's throat burned. She reached out without thinking, using her injured right hand to close over his. Ignoring the pain it caused, she pressed his calloused palm. "I enjoyed it, Gage. I wish you had more time. I wish—" She stopped, then glanced at Bogie and Bacall. "How far do you have to take them?"

"My friend lives about an hour north of here. They'll be fine with Jonas. He loves animals. But I need to get going. I'll take you home, get that painting and then move out." Methodically he collected their food and plates and stowed everything in the back of his truck. "Take care of yourself, Caro. Remember, you can fight your way through this. I'm counting on you." He smiled suddenly. "I'll write to my friend's wife and ask her to send you some of her knitting designs. She was pretty badly messed up several years ago in a car accident and it took her about fifteen months to get back to knitting. My friend said she was really surly for most of that time. Dreaming up her own patterns kept her going."

"Fifteen months without knitting?" Caro rolled her eyes. "If that happens, I'm going to need heavier medication."

Gage chuckled as he herded his animals back into the truck. Then he and Caro stood in the sunlight with the wind off the sea and the sun on their shoulders. "Be sure you write to me," Caro said softly. "I want to know…"

He cut her off with one finger against her mouth. "I'll write. Count on it. Meanwhile, you take care of yourself. I know we only met this morning, but being here with you feels…" He didn't finish. Instead Gage leaned down and kissed her very gently. His thumb traced the line of her cheek and he sighed. Caro leaned into him, feeling the strength of his arm against her shoulder.

Just for a moment, the world was at peace. Everything slid into place and felt right.

Then Gage straightened. He brushed a strand of hair out of Caro's eyes and stepped back. Emotion churned in his eyes.

"Come back here," she said quietly. Surprise filled his face but he bent down, and she rose to kiss him back, this time not so lightly.

The meadow was very still, and Caro could almost hear the pounding of her heart. She wanted more time. She wanted lazy Saturday mornings by the harbor and long walks in the rain. She wanted to know everything about him.

But Gage had to go. This was no time for questions or flights of fancy. She felt his hand close over her cheek one last time, as if he needed to remember the curves of her face, holding the image close as support for darker times.

Then he stepped back. "We'd better go," he said gruffly.

Caro was suddenly aware how impossibly sad three simple words could be.

They said nothing else. He was clearly distracted by the change in his travel plans and they rode in silence to Caro's house. Her grandmother was back when they arrived and she confirmed the painting for his friend. Gage was clearly becoming restless, so Caro said goodbye, cutting off her grandmother's questions. The last thing Caro saw was his hand raised in farewell from the window of his truck as he leaned over to smooth Bogart's head, which was pressed against his side.

The big hawk glided over the ridge.

The world seemed to tilt as the truck vanished around a bend in the road.

Caro felt her grandmother's hand on her shoulder. "Are you okay, honey?"

"Of course, Gran." But the truth was, she missed him painfully already. How was it possible to feel so connected with a man she'd known for only an hour?

It wasn't until she turned to go inside that Caro glanced down and saw a folded piece of paper near her foot. She realized it was the sheet with her email address. Gage must have dropped it when he helped her out of the truck. How would he contact her now?

"He seemed like a nice man." Morgan stood beside Caro at the front porch, watching the last rays of sunshine burn above the trees on the ridge.

"Yes, he was."

"Is everything all right? You look pale."

*No,* Caro wanted to say. *I wanted him to stay. I wanted to feel the careful way his fingers moved through my hair when I kissed him. For once in my life I wanted to be dizzy and reckless and I have no idea why.*

But dreams like that were pointless. He was gone. So she shrugged and managed a smile. "I think I'll go work on my exercises, Gran. Then I'll help you organize the rest of those packages to be mailed."

All so normal.

Yet *nothing* seemed normal now. Caro sensed that her world had changed irrevocably in the past hour.

All because of a tall, quiet stranger whose smile would haunt her dreams.

# *Six*

Gage glanced at his watch and felt his shoulders knot with tension. It was going to be tight. Too darned tight. Military transports were never firm, and he had known he would have a narrow window on this trip.

But then his friend Jonas had called. What he'd thought was a bout of flu had mushroomed into full-blown pneumonia, and Jonas was on his way to the hospital. Now Gage had no one to care for his animals and he had a military flight to catch in a few hours.

He gripped the wheel, thinking frantically. For a moment he was tempted to turn back and ask for Caro's help, but he remembered her saying that her grandmother was allergic to animals. So that was not an option. He had no friends and no family in the area. No help and no options left.

But he couldn't dump his two best friends.

Bacall pressed against his arm, purring loudly, and Gage fought to lock down his emotions. "I'll find a place for you two." His voice was raw. "I swear it. I only have two hours, but there *must* be something." Memories of Caro's slow smile and dark, intense eyes kept intruding as he fought to force them away. Maybe he should go back to her house after all. Maybe she knew a friend who could help. Maybe…

Night was falling as the beam of his headlights outlined a row of pine trees along the road. In front of the trees Gage could see a neat white building with a handmade wooden sign. Gage rubbed his eyes, feeling hope surge through him.

The sign read: Summer Island Pet Clinic And Animal Shelter.

The distinguished older man at the front desk looked Gage over thoroughly as he walked inside. "What can I do for you, young man?"

"Do you…?" Gage's mouth was dry. He couldn't believe that he was in this situation, not after all his careful planning. What was he going to do if this failed? "Do you take in stray animals?"

"Definitely, when it's possible. Right now we're full, I'm afraid. Why don't you come back next week?"

*Next week.*

Gage felt his hope crumbling. "I won't be here next week." He might not even be alive next week, but Gage didn't mention that brutal truth. Instead he focused on his duty and the task at hand. "So you see, coming back won't be possible, sir." He held Bacall against his chest and stroked the cat's back. "I'm deploying at dawn. The person who was going to take them can't do it because of illness. I need—well, I hoped that…"

The man put down the file he was holding and crossed the room. "I see. Come in, son. Let's go back to my office and discuss this. I think there's something we can do to help," the older man said quietly. "But first, tell me the name of that handsome cat you're holding?"

Gage took a hard breath. "This is Bacall, sir. And my retriever sitting at the door is called Bogart."

*"To Have and Have Not?"*

Gage nodded. "Best movie ever made. But about my animals—I need to know they will be with a good family. I have to be sure they're safe, sir. I owe them that."

"I'm glad you're so responsible, son. And I'm going to see to their care. I'll take them myself—Mr...."

"Grayson. First Lieutenant Gage Grayson."

"Navy?"

"Marines, sir. I'm heading back to Afghanistan in the morning."

"Well, Lieutenant, that is a fine and well-trained dog waiting for you at the door. He'll be in good hands here. So will your cat. Count on it."

"Thank you, sir. You don't know how much that means to me." Gage ran a hand across his face and then looked up at the clock. "I was afraid—well, how could I just drive away and abandon them? What kind of person could do that?"

"I'm Peter Lindstrom, Summer Island's vet. And believe me, Lieutenant, I've been trying to answer that same question for almost fifty years. Can I get you something, Lieutenant? Some coffee? I think we have a box of doughnuts in the back."

"No, thank you, Dr. Lindstrom. And I really do appreciate this."

"I'm glad I could help. I guess you have a plane to catch."

"Yes, sir. If you don't mind, I'd like a little time with these two before I go."

Peter Lindstrom tried to suppress a pang of sadness as the big dog pressed uneasily at his owner's side, sensing the change of mood. Pets were smart that way. As he walked back into his office, he saw the tall Marine bend down in front of the retriever. He stroked the dog's head gently. "Well, I guess this is it, Bogie. Time for me to hit the road."

The vet closed the door to his office, feeling a lump in his throat.

Gage knew that his time was gone. Yet some kind of miracle seemed to have brought him to this shelter and a safe haven for his pets. Gage trusted his instincts, and this Dr. Lindstrom seemed like a good person who would stand by his word. He was buoyed by relief that his two pets would be safe. And they would be close to Caro, he realized. Maybe he could ask her to check on them occasionally.

Bogart bumped at his chest, whining, and Gage scratched behind the dog's ears, just where he liked it. "Now you listen, Bogart. I won't be gone forever, but while I'm away I expect you to do everything that the nice vet says. No getting up and roughhousing in the middle of the night. No whining or turning up your nose at the food. I gave him your ball and I'll be sure he has all the rest of your toys that I packed."

Then Gage reached down and scooped up his cat. "Bacall, you take good care of Bogie when he feels bad. I'll expect you to keep a good eye on things. Both of you know that I love you, whatever happens. This place will be a good home until I get back. Now, we've all got our work to do, and I have to go do mine." Gage knelt, grabbed the two and held them tight, burying his face in their soft fur.

And then Gage Grayson lost it. He had too many memories of fallen comrades—most recently of the young son whose family Gage had seen this week. The mother had looked back at him from a dark place, as if there were no words for what she was feeling.

How did you deal with so much pain and hold it all together? Because there was one thing that he knew without question. He did have to stay strong for himself and for his men, bunkered in a dusty outpost on a dusty hill in Afghanistan.

So Gage didn't whine or curse. He forced his fingers to let go of his two beloved pets and then stood up slowly. His eyes felt gritty as he took a step back. He didn't have any family except his sister. These two were all he had.

Saying goodbye was going to be about the hardest thing he'd ever done.

He took a deep breath. "So that's it. You know I love you. And I'll be back, you two." Gage managed a crooked smile. "One day I'll come rattling back here in my truck and my pockets will be full of treats, all for you rascals. That's a promise."

After Gage left, Peter Lindstrom reached down and scratched the retriever's head.

"Nothing's going to happen to him." Peter made his voice firm and confident. "He'll come home safe and sound."

But the dog and cat stayed at the window staring out at the road, looking listless and anxious. An hour later the cat gave a low meow and began to groom the dog's ears carefully. The dog curled up with his paws held protectively around the cat. Both gave each other the only comfort they knew. They stayed together that way all night, curled up close, wary and alert.

Waiting for Gage to come back for them.

*Dusk*
*Northern Afghanistan*

Gage had lost track of the hours he'd traveled, shuffling from airport to airport and country to country. Night turned into day, and then into night again.

When he finally stepped onto the crowded runway in Afghanistan, he caught the distinctive smell of cordite, diesel oil and burned mutton from clay cooking ovens. Men ran and walked past him, pushing weapons and luggage and heavy equipment containers. He nodded to a dusty trio who had passed through his camp a month before, on their way to disrupt insurgent bases in the south. The whole scene was oddly familiar yet also surreal, as if he had stepped out of one life and dropped hard into another.

"Lieutenant Grayson, your chopper is ready to leave, sir." A lanky corpsman with a sunburned face pointed behind a row of stacked crates where a personnel helicopter was being readied for takeoff.

"But first you need an updated set of vaccinations, sir. There's some new strain up north, maybe a cholera variant. It'll just take a minute."

Gage took off his camo jacket and unbuttoned his sleeve. He had dropped Morgan McNeal's painting with his friend's wife on the way to the airport in Oregon. The reception had been ecstatic. In return, he had a gift packed carefully in his mess kit. Those homemade double chocolate brownies were going to be a nice treat later that night.

But thinking of food made Gage remember hamburgers and apple cider in a meadow overlooking the sea. From there it was just a short jump to thoughts of Caro's husky laughter and her extraordinary strength under difficult circumstances. He had thought about her during all the long hours of his travel.

As he received his injections, Gage used his other hand to pull out his wallet to retrieve the inevitable paperwork needed to record his updated status.

"Thank you, sir. And now I'll need your medical card and your form CD-492A to stamp."

"Right here, Sergeant." Gage pulled out the papers and then frowned at the empty space in his wallet. He had tucked the sheet with Caro's email address in that spot for safekeeping. He was sure of it. How could he have lost it?

"Something wrong, sir?"

Gage rubbed his neck, watching wind kick sand over his boots. How was he going to write to her *now?*

"Sir, they're waiting for you."

Frowning, Gage shouldered his gear and ran through the dust toward his ride.

# *Seven*

For three days Caro checked her email, waiting to hear from Gage. She didn't like to think of a near stranger as an obsession, but the attachment between them felt far stronger than she expected or even wanted. Her grandmother had managed to find a way for her to contact him, to her relief.

"Gage Grayson? Yes, I believe he wrote me via email last month. Let me look him up." Her grandmother slanted her a questioning look. "Was there a problem with the painting he picked up for his friend?"

"I don't think so. It's just that—we went to lunch. Nothing more. And I told him he could write me, but after he left I found the piece of paper with my email address. He dropped it near his truck, and I haven't heard from him yet."

Caro's grandmother started to say something, then closed her mouth abruptly. She looked down and flipped through a thick binder. "Here he is. Lieutenant Gage Grayson. I have an APO address, a cell phone number and an email address for him. I'll write down all three of them for you." Morgan's voice was carefully neutral. "I spoke to him twice on the phone last week and he seemed like a very nice young man. He was only visiting here temporarily, as I recall."

"He was going back to Afghanistan. Then something happened and his flight was moved up. But there was something about him, Gran. We both felt it. I'm not sure that I can explain."

Morgan McNeal nodded slowly. "Sometimes things aren't logical. Never ignore the feelings that don't seem to make sense. Those can be the most valuable of all. If I had ignored that small, nagging instinct, I never would have met your grandfather."

"Really? You knew he was—special, right from the start? You never told me that."

"I can keep some secrets, can't I?" Caro's grandmother stared out the window. "And that story will have to wait for another day, my love. We have work to do." Morgan closed her binder, brisk and efficient as usual. "Now let me look at your hand. You've got another physical therapy visit tomorrow in Portland, and I don't want him to say you've been coasting. Have you managed any knitting yet?"

"Nothing to speak of." Caro laughed wryly. "I took it all for granted, Gran. First cables, then lace, even color stranding in the old Nordic style. Knitting was always there for me when I needed comfort or focus or just plain entertainment. I was beginning to learn crochet, too, with all those beautiful motif squares. And I loved all of it." She took a deep breath. "Now I can barely hold two needles at once, much less knit an even row of stitches. The day that Gage came here, I broke Mother's old teapot from clumsiness. All I wanted was a cup of tea. But I misjudged and knocked the pot to the floor."

"Just give it time, Caro."

"I have. It's been over a month, but nothing works right."

"You're in pain, too," her grandmother said quietly. "I can tell."

Caro closed her eyes. "I'm lucky to be alive and mobile. I'm blessed to have you helping me. I know and believe this, Gran. The accident could have been far worse." She smiled a little. "But why is it that I keep thinking about what I *used* to have?"

"Call it being honest with yourself. You *have* lost a part of your life, after all. But a very wise and experienced victim's advocate once told me that in her work, brutal honesty was always the first step to recovery. Do you remember telling me that, Caro? It was your second year and you had a very difficult case at the time."

"I remember. So I'll follow my own advice and keep being honest. Forgive me for any whining. In fact, just give me a nice sharp bang on the head and tell me to shut up."

Caro's grandmother laughed and gave her a quick hug instead. "No banging will be required. Now, why don't you go and butter those scones that Melissa sent from the Island Diner while I get out your therapy bag. Something tells me this session is going to hurt more than your others. I think that you're at a transition point. If you push harder, you can break through to a new level. But it's going to cost you."

"I can take the pain, Gran. What I can't take is these reminders of all the things I used to be able to do. It's like running into a brick wall with a picture on it, and that picture is yourself the way you used to be, but you can't get there because you're all blocked off. Everything is changed. Does that make any sense?"

"It makes perfect sense. And we will tackle that wall together, you and I. Even though it came about in this horrible fashion, I'm so happy to have you here, Caro. Never think that you're a burden on me. And while we work, you can tell me more about this charming lieutenant you had lunch with." She stopped suddenly, looking thoughtful. "Wait a minute—he had two animals with him, didn't he? It was hard for me to see into the truck when he left."

"That's right. A cat and a dog. Why?"

Morgan drummed her fingers on the big antique farm table. "Peter Lindstrom saw him. At least, I think it was your lieutenant. The description fits. I think I'll call Peter and find out." Her eyes twinkled. "But not until you finish your exercises. That will give you some incentive to work harder."

Twenty minutes later Caro reached for her towel with trembling fingers. She was wrung out and sweating, but she'd made clear progress. She had to be grateful for that.

"If Gage had a problem, why didn't he say something to me? He could have brought his pets to me. I would have found a way."

"He barely knew you, Caro. Probably he didn't want to bother you. You didn't by any chance happen to mention that I'm allergic to cats, did you?"

Caro blew out a sharp breath. "You're right. We were talking about his cat, and I said how wonderful she was, but I couldn't ever have a pet because you were allergic."

"There's your answer. That young man chose not to saddle you with his problem."

"So what happened? Dr. Lindstrom wouldn't have taken Gage's animals away to another shelter, would he?" Caro shot to her feet, grabbing for her coat. "Let's *go*, Gran. We need to find those two before anything happens to them. I have to—"

Morgan laughed. "Sit down and relax, scatter-head. The matter is well in hand. Even though you think of Peter and me as ancient, we still have a few brain cells left. I found out that Gage's cat and dog are living with Peter."

"You're sure?" Caro felt some of her tension ease. "They're definitely safe?"

"Absolutely. Tomorrow they're going home with Peter. He has been rehabilitating a wounded hawk and couldn't risk an encounter until he freed it. So everything will be fine with Bogart and Bacall."

Caro stood holding her coat, unable to relax. "They're at the shelter now? I want to go see them, Gran. I want to help Dr. Lindstrom take care of them. And when I get back," she said slowly, "I'm going to write to Gage. Maybe I can send him some photos. Do you think he would like that?"

"I think it would be wonderful. We'll go just as soon as you finish your last set of exercises."

Caro stuck out her tongue. "Have I ever told you you're a dictator?"

"Only twice today. But I'm determined to see you knitting again by the end of the month." Morgan raised an eyebrow. "My studio gets cold, remember? You promised me a new pair of fingerless gloves. I'd like pink. And you can make a matching pair for yourself while you're at it," Morgan added slyly. "I'm sure that your dashing lieutenant will think they're very cute."


Caro's grandmother helped her carry a big plastic bag up the steps to the animal shelter. Inside the bag were cat treats and dog toys purchased at Summer Island's only grocery store. The veterinarian opened the door and welcomed her inside, looking a little tired but very happy to see Caro and her grandmother. Dr. Peter Lindstrom was still handsome at seventy-two, and he worked the hours of a man three decades younger. Caro had always suspected that he and her grandmother had a secret attachment. Dr. Lindstrom's wife had died seven years earlier after a protracted battle with lupus, and Caro had thought they might marry after that, but the two seemed happy to live independent lives.

It figured, she though wryly. Caro never expected her grandmother to do anything the normal way.

"Come in, come in," the vet said, waving them into his office. "Have you come to help me clean out cages or to administer enemas?"

It took Caro a moment to realize he was kidding. "That's a joke, I hope."

"Of course it is. I'm pleased simply to have your company, Caro. And your grandmother's too," he added, slanting a look at Morgan. "You'd better not stay long, Morgan. Your allergies—"

"I know my own limits, Peter. Five minutes will be fine. Then I'll just go outside. But Caro wanted to see how Bogie and Bacall were doing."

Peter Lindstrom's eyebrows rose. "Yes, your grandmother told me you spent some time with the lieutenant."

"Only a little." Caro brushed a strand of hair off her cheek, feeling self-conscious. "I had lunch with him before he had to leave. He told me that a friend was going to take his pets while he was in Afghanistan."

"Yes, I believe that was all arranged. Then his friend had to be hospitalized. Gage didn't have many options by then, but he landed at the right place and his animals are safe with me. They miss him, of course." The vet shot a thoughtful look at Caro. "I suspect they're not the only ones."

Caro didn't hear, too focused on opening the door to the back treatment rooms, where she could hear Bogart barking. The big dog almost knocked her over when she went inside. Caro scratched his head carefully, wary of her wrist, while the dog pranced in delight around her. Bacall was curled up in a wicker basket lined with a flannel sheet. The cat looked thinner than she remembered and seemed to be lethargic. "Dr. Lindstrom, how is Gage's cat? Has she been eating? She doesn't look so good."

"She's taking it harder than the dog, but they're both missing their owner, Caro. It's not scientific, but I can tell." The vet stood in the doorway, frowning. "People or animals—all of us suffer from the force of our emotions."

For a moment Caro read something deeper there as the older man glanced back at her grandmother who had walked out to the front porch. Then the vet cleared his throat and leaned down to search through his well-stocked drawers. "Gage left this for them." He held out a plastic bag. "It has two of his old T-shirts and an old sweatshirt. He figured these would help them make the transition. He's very intelligent, that young man. Maybe you'd like to give them to the animals, Caro. It should be okay now."

"Now? I don't understand."

"I waited so they'd have a clean transition. I didn't want them strung along, hoping Gage would walk back through the door. They have to adjust to him being gone. As it was, it took me twelve hours to even get them into my office. They stayed right at the front door, hoping he would come walking back through it."

Caro felt a lump in her throat as she took the bag with Gage's clothing. Bogart bumped against her side as she crossed the room, but the cat stared up at her without any interest. The poor creature was clearly suffering.

Caro knelt next to the basket and spread Gage's old T-shirt on her lap. "Do you want to come here, honey? I've got a treat for you." The cat's head rose. Ears back, she sniffed the air. Her eyes snapped open and she jumped from the basket straight into Caro's lap, sniffing every corner of Gage's old T-shirt intently.

"That's a good sign. She remembers Gage. These will make her feel calm. Give her a few minutes, Caro. Let her get comfortable and then try a couple of those treats you brought. This is the most alert she's been since Gage left."

The cat sniffed and stalked, exploring every inch of the worn T-shirt, her tail straight up in the air. Caro heard a low rumble of a purr. Then Bacall rolled onto her back, rubbing her body against the T-shirt in a frantic display of excitement. "So cute. She definitely remembers. Is there anything else I can do to help her?"

"I'd say you just did the best thing possible. Just give her a few treats when she's ready. And now, since there are more cages to be cleaned out, I think I'll go and deal with that. Maybe you wouldn't mind staying here with Lieutenant Grayson's animals. Once I finish, I'll take your grandmother down to the house for some coffee."

"I guess that makes *me* a cheap date," Morgan called through the open door to the porch.

"You two go on and have your coffee." Smiling, Caro reached out to stroke the cat's white fur. "Once my hand is better, you can put me down for any kind of work you need done here at the shelter, Dr. Lindstrom."

The vet stood in the doorway. "Any idea when that might be?"

"A few more weeks. My physical therapist says I should have some real strength back by then—probably enough for simple jobs like cleaning cages and changing litter."

"I'll keep that in mind." The vet rubbed his neck. "With funding the way it is, I can use all the help I can get. And if you're certain you'll be okay, I could definitely use some coffee. We won't be long."

"Take all the time you need. We'll be fine here. Won't we, Bacall?"

The idea came to Caro while she was listening to Bacall purr. The cat had wolfed down four treats and now was sleeping contentedly, curled up in Caro's lap.

For no reason she could name, Caro itched to grab one of her grandmother's sketching pencils. She had no great talent, but Caro had lied to Gage about being completely without artistic genes. As a girl she had delighted in making quick cartoon sketches of her friends. She had even sold a few to their parents. But the skill had never seemed very important to her.

Caro decided she would begin a little diary with daily sketches of the two animals. Even though any kind of drawing would be a challenge, Caro was determined. It would be her gift to Gage.

After all, a soldier in a faraway place needed a little sunlight in his life.

*Forward Operating Base Wolverine*
*Afghanistan*

"Lieutenant, you've got a call coming in. And I think there's an email for you."

Gage took off his helmet and swept the sand out of his face. Flies buzzed in through the window, along with the smell of mutton fat carried over the ridge. Another spring day in paradise, he thought wryly.

*Semper Fi.*

His days had passed in a blur of work since he'd returned from the States. A journalist had come to research a story on the recent campaign to disrupt insurgent supply lines. Satellite equipment and medical supplies were being restocked. The valley's main road had to be rebuilt after a minor earthquake.

Gage was glad to be busy. He didn't want to think about the loss of good men and women and the potential for losing more. He didn't want to think about his sister's illness or his cherished pets, living with strangers back in Oregon. He didn't even want to think too much about Caro McNeal, because feelings could become a dangerous distraction. He had to focus on his duties so that he could safeguard his men at this strategic outpost.

Gage grabbed a cup of strong coffee and headed to the small room that served as the camp's electronics center. He scanned the reports from the past twenty-four hours and checked for security updates from Kandahar. Gage was a twenty-first-century officer fighting a twenty-first-century war, requiring hydrology, computer and physics skills right along with assault tactics.

He finished his coffee and then poured another cup. Finally finished with his duties, he opened his private email account.

A grin swept over his face when he saw the address and the sender's name.

Summer Island Pet Report #1

Bacall slept on my bed last night. I stayed over at Dr. Lindstrom's house to help him at the clinic.

How do you sleep through all that purring? It woke me up twice.

Bogart ate Dr. Lindstrom's socks and three hamburgers. He would have eaten more if we hadn't stopped him. Socks, I mean.

We all miss you.

Stay well.

Caro

P.S. I knitted three stitches today. Three in a row! Progress! I seem to be able to hold a pencil, so this will be my therapy. Don't laugh at my bad drawings.

A little sketch of a dog and cat filled the bottom of the message, clearly his two rascals. She had drawn them and attached the graphic to her message.

Gage sat back and smiled.

She missed him. She had come right out and said it. And Bogie and Bacall were doing well with Summer Island's vet. That was a huge weight off his mind.

"Lieutenant, are you—" From the doorway his communications officer stopped and cleared his throat. "Sorry, sir. I didn't mean to interrupt you."

"No, I'm done here, Sergeant. Do you have new satellite updates for me?"

"They just came in, sir. There's been some activity in the valley."

Gage took the new file, his mind racing.

So much for free time.

# *Eight*

*Summer Island*
*Two weeks later*

"Good dog. That's it, bring me the branch." Caro was standing outside the animal shelter, tossing a small branch to Bogart, who was covered in mud and deliriously happy. They'd been exercising for twenty minutes in the sunshine and Caro was surprised that her wrist ached only a little. She had also developed a tremendous appetite. Maybe she'd even try to cook today. Her grandmother loved chipotle corn bread, which happened to be Caro's specialty. Why had she not cooked it in such a long time?

The answer was clear. She had been caught up in her busy life in Chicago, doing intense work that was both difficult and draining. For years she had helped others put their lives back together. But now it was time that Caro helped herself.

From her pocket, she heard the ping of the email program on her cell phone. She had tried not to think about the email she'd sent to Gage, or the possibility that he had just been polite when he'd suggested they keep in touch.

Every time her email program alerted her to a new message, she had grabbed for her phone, keeping it beside her even when she slept.

She wasn't usually impulsive like this. There had been a few men in her life, but none of them had stuck. Yet from the first moment she set eyes on Gage, Caro had felt as if a switch had been flipped on inside her. When she was around him, colors were brighter. Sounds were more intense. She couldn't explain it, and she wasn't sure she wanted to try. Explanations might destroy the fragile thing growing between them—whatever it was.

"Bogie, come here. Heel." Caro knelt on the ground with the dog's face pressed against her neck. She tried to stay upright, eventually landing flat on her back when Bogie pushed her over in his noisy exuberance.

"Down, Bogart. Sit."

By the time she fumbled her way free, the dog was calmer. With a noisy sigh he turned once and then settled down with his head across her knee.

Caro pulled out her phone and scanned her incoming mail. A wave of happiness settled over her when she saw the most recent message.

Watch those socks.

Bogart has a real sock problem. He ate two of mine once. Threw them up right after.

I'm real jealous of the hamburgers.

Hey—you said you couldn't draw, but those sketches were great. Keep them coming, okay?

Gage

She laughed as Bogie rolled over, his tail banging as he made it clear that rest time was over and he wanted more play. Caro reached down and rubbed the dog's ears. "He's definitely got your number, hasn't he?"

She drifted happily, remembering Gage's laugh. He liked her message and had enjoyed her drawings! Bogart barked, and brought her a stick, so Caro held it in her good hand, tossed it high and watched him leap into the air for the catch.

Another image filled her mind. She'd sketch Bogie in midjump just like this and add a picture of Bacall, curled up in a neat circle, sleeping on Gage's old T-shirt.

And she would label them in one line: "Attitude is everything."

Caro didn't look up when the front door opened. Keys rattled and she heard her grandmother's footsteps. "Anything urgent I should know about? You were working at that desk when I left. I don't want you to overdo things, honey."

"I'm almost done, Gran. I'm just having trouble capturing the line of Bogart's body when he jumps. It's harder to draw less, isn't it? Every line has to count extra."

"So they tell me. Now that I've found my niche with watercolors, I doubt I'll ever go back to charcoal or pencil." Morgan McNeal leaned over Caro's shoulder and laughed. "Very nice. You've caught that dog just right. I swear I can hear him bark on the page." She took off her coat and sat down next to Caro, helping herself to one of the chocolate chip cookies Caro had baked that morning. "Have you heard anything from Bogart's owner?"

"Just one email. But he's doing fine. I think he was very glad that his pets are in good hands." As she spoke, Caro sketched quickly, stopping to erase a line or smudge a shadow. Once she dropped the eraser and muttered under her breath. But her hands were finally getting stronger.

She still couldn't knit more than a row, but her drawings were coming along surprisingly well. She couldn't wait to share this one with Gage in her next email.

"What?" She looked up, surprised to see her grandmother shaking her head.

"I've only asked you a question three times. Did you decide what you wanted for dinner? Or maybe we should go out tonight. I hear that Peter Lindstrom's granddaughter is back from France, and we could meet them somewhere. Grace has been gone for what—three years now?"

"Three and a half. I'd love to see her." Caro's voice faded as she vanished back into her drawing.

"Tonight, then. That will be very nice." Morgan McNeal smoothed back her hair in a little unconscious gesture of happiness. "Where would you like to eat?"

No answer.

"Honey?" Still no answer.

Caro didn't look up, busy drawing, so she didn't see the thoughtful look on her grandmother's face as she left the room to call Peter.

*One week later*
*Tuesday p.m.*

Caro hunched over her laptop, gnawing at her lip. She had sent Gage four emails now and she usually received an answer quickly.

It was just friendly chitchat, she reminded herself sternly. No reason to let this go to her head. So she was careful to keep her tone casual.

Pet Diary #5
We gave your pair baths today. I got soaked, but I didn't mind.

You won't believe it. Dr. Lindstrom lost his hat in the field behind the shelter and Bogart found it. He came trotting up the path as proud as possible, carrying the hat in his mouth. Then he dropped it right at Dr. Lindstrom's feet. Did I mention that your dog is really smart?

He is also really hungry. He tried to eat my shoe tonight. Second time this week.

As for my knitting, I can still only manage one row. But I can feel myself getting stronger.

Caro

Wednesday p.m.

No kidding. He loves to track. Maybe I need him helping me over here.

Your last drawing of Bogart with your shoe made me laugh so loud I spit out my coffee. And you say you can't draw?

You really got Bacall down to the last whisker. Are they still sleeping curled up together?

Take your time on the knitting—you'll get there.

Gage

Wednesday p.m.

You bet. I stayed with them at Dr. Lindstrom's again. His granddaughter is home from France and we had a lot of news to catch up on. But why didn't you tell me Bogart's a pillow hog? I'm lucky to get one tiny corner. Plus—he snores.

Really, really snores!

Bacall slept curled on my chest, purring again. But they don't go to sleep without your old sweatshirt.

I've decided to knit you something. At the rate I'm

going, it will be months before it's finished. But it helps to think of someone when I'm working—it makes the pain seem worth it.
Be safe.
Caro

Caro didn't mention that she slept with the sleeve of his sweatshirt by her cheek, too.

Gran wants to know if your friend's wife liked her painting. Even after all these years, my grandmother is still a little insecure about her work.
But please don't tell her I said that....
C.

She loved it.
She wrote her husband a letter and said it was the only thing she'd carry out in a fire—well, after their two kids.
Knitting something for me? I can't wait—that's something I'll definitely look forward to.
G.

You know what I think? I think that you should get these sketches published. You're good, Caro. My guys are cute, but you make them look beyond cute. You catch something...something that's universal about them. I don't know how you do that. If your knitting is anything like your sketches, it's going to be incredible.
Well, gotta go. Chow time—
G.

But it wasn't chow time.
It was a high-priority alert about hostile activity targeting Gage's area.

*0400 Zulu time*
*Northern Afghanistan*

Sand blew over the ridge. Stars gleamed, bright and cold, above the horizon.

Gage stood beside his communications officer and both scanned the rough terrain with night-vision glasses.

"Lieutenant, did you see that? I'm picking up something just where I did the last time."

"I'm on it." Gage didn't look up from his glasses. The night was cold, but the activity level was hot—and getting hotter. They'd had two quiet nights in a row, and quiet worried him. Quiet usually meant that someone nearby was marshaling forces, getting ready for bad deeds.

There it was again.

A small movement on the opposite ridge. Light glinted for a second, then vanished. That made the fourth time in ten minutes, in a piece of rough terrain where drone surveillance had picked up new insurgent activity.

"Saddle up, Marine. We're going out for recon. Three squads." Gage knew there was only one way to assess the movements in the strategic ridge that faced them across the valley. And that was with boots to the ground.

Caro shot awake, clutching her pillow.

Something was wrong, something that she couldn't name. She listened for a sound in the night—the tread of stealthy footsteps or the clink of metal tools, forcing open a window.

Nothing. The house was quiet. Her grandmother had gone to sleep a while ago, exhausted from a long day of painting. Caro pulled on a fine wool shawl that had seen better days. Gripping it close, she walked to the window and peered out. A light rain fell, dappling the sidewalk and the gravel path outside her window. Roses swayed in the rain, but there was nothing to make her feel tense and uneasy.

She looked back at the clock and made a quick calculation of the time in Afghanistan.

The feeling of *off* persisted, growing stronger.

Gage, she thought. Something was wrong.

*He's hurt or in danger.* Somehow, she just knew. And she'd never felt so scared.

# *Nine*

"Alpha, do you copy?"

Gage heard two brief clicks on the radio transmitter, signaling that his first squad leader was in place, no enemies sighted.

"Duke?"

Two more clicks.

The responses came, quick and nearly silent. When he was sure that his squads were safe, Gage began the steep climb to the top of the ridge. This would put him roughly two hundred yards from the last location of the movement he had seen earlier that evening. So far there had been no signs of activity during their reconnaissance, but he knew that someone could be dug in deep here in the boulders, nearly invisible until you were right upon them.

So he was erring on the side of caution. Taking it slowly and going by the book.

A piece of gravel shifted, dropping on the trail in front of him. Instantly he lifted his hand, and the order to halt was relayed around him. Slowly Gage sank down, and he knew that all his men were doing the same, becoming part of the night and the scrub of the high desert terrain. Just the way they had been trained to do.

He glanced at his watch, noting the time, aware that in the silence and the dark every sensation could be untrustworthy. Nothing moved. All the men stayed motionless, flat against the ground.

Another piece of gravel fell on the trail. This time it was followed by a flash of light. A scrawny goat moved slowly behind two boulders about ten yards away from Gage. He waited.

A second goat appeared. And behind this one walked a boy, head and body wrapped in felted wool and sheepskin against the high desert night.

Gage forced himself not to move, not to prejudge a situation that could be exactly what it seemed, a shepherd boy returning home after foraging with his goats.

Yet it could be something else entirely. A civilian scout, tracking the perimeter of an insurgent base. Civilians were part of warfare here, just as they had been for centuries. It could be a deadly mistake to forget that fact.

He watched the boy slap one of the bigger goats on the rump with a small branch. The goat snorted and bucked his hind feet, and instantly the boy froze, glancing around furtively as the sound echoed in the night.

Suddenly the same goat turned, staring directly into the small tangle of bushes where Gage knew one of his forward squad leaders was hidden. He felt a surge of adrenaline as he ran through scenarios. The boy could have a machine gun hidden behind the rock; he could have a cousin or older brothers just over the top of the ridge.

But Gage would not shoot an unarmed, innocent civilian just because of a suspicion. He tapped out the forward leader's number and then a danger alert, which was acknowledged just as briefly via encrypted radio set.

Then Gage rose slowly to a crouch and headed away from the boy, on a wide and indirect route along the far slope to the top of the ridge.

Twenty minutes later all hell broke loose.

Caro paced the room, worried but unable to say why. After an hour she went to make a pot of herbal tea and then returned to her drawings of Gage's dog and cat.

At least, she tried to draw. But she couldn't relax, couldn't find her focus. The blurry sense of *wrongness* had become an acute stab of danger. And there wasn't a single reason for it.

She heard the rustle of clothing behind her. "Caro, love, what's wrong? Is it your hand?"

"No, Gran. It's—" She frowned and jammed shaky fingers through her hair. "I feel a sense of danger." She pulled on a sweater and shivered. "I can't explain it and maybe it's nothing. But why don't you and I check all the doors and windows? And after that, maybe you could call Dr. Lindstrom. I just want to know that Gage's pets and the clinic are okay. Something just feels…wrong to me."

Morgan started to ask a question, then shook her head. With her Celtic blood had come bursts of intuition with no explanation, and she had been wise enough never to ignore them. She would not ignore Caro's intuition now.

"Everything checks out. All the windows are locked and the doors are secured. The cars are fine. The fire is off. No problems that I can see." Morgan took off her coat and slung it over the wing chair that overlooked the bay. "Do you still have that itchy feeling?"

Caro nodded slowly. "But it's different now." Her hands twisted restlessly. "It's almost as if I can't breathe, like a big rock pressing against my chest. Maybe I'm just going crazy, imagining things because of stress."

"Imagination is a good and powerful thing, Caro. Never dismiss it lightly. And now I'm going to call Peter. I want to make sure everything is okay over there."

Peter Lindstrom looked tired and worried when he opened the front door of his house. He was dragging on a robe as he waved Caro and her grandmother inside. "What's wrong? Caro, if it's your hand—"

"No, I'm fine. But…something feels wrong. It could be crazy, but I had to come and check on Gage's pets. And on the clinic, too, to see if everything's okay."

"Bogie and Bacall? I looked in on them just before I went to sleep. They were both fine then. They're sleeping in the back bedroom right now until I can fix up the sunroom for them. Let's go check."

The vet led the way to the rear of the house and flipped on a light.

Caro heard him let out a deep breath of relief. "I'd say there's nothing wrong here."

When she peeked around his shoulder, Caro saw Bogart stretched out on a soft tartan doggie bed. His head was resting on his front paws, and Bacall was sound asleep, curled up on the dog's back, with her tail across Bogie's head. In spite of her uneasiness, Caro had to laugh at the comical picture they made.

"I'm so relieved, Dr. Lindstrom. But…would you mind

if my grandmother and I drove to the clinic? I don't think I'll be able to rest otherwise."

"My dear girl, neither could I. Give me two minutes and I'll drive you there myself."

"Well, that looks like another question answered." Morgan McNeal stood next to Peter Lindstrom, her hands on her hips as she glanced back at the neat cages filled with sleeping animals. "Let sleeping dogs lie," she murmured, turning to rest her hand on Caro's shoulder. "Nothing's amiss here, so why don't we have a last walk around and then go home. I'll make us tea." She glanced at her oldest friend. "Peter, will you join us?"

"I'd love to, Morgan, but I've got two early operations scheduled, so I'd better pass. Why don't you stop by my house instead? Then Caro can say good-night to her two friends before you go home."

As they were leaving, Caro glanced behind the door and then bent down to the floor. "What's this?" She picked up a battered Frisbee and turned it between her fingers. Something about it called to her, holding her attention.

"That's curious. I've been looking for that Frisbee ever since Lieutenant Grayson left. It was the one he brought for Bogie and Bacall to play with. It must have fallen over behind the door and been forgotten." The vet glanced oddly at Caro. "How did you know it was there?"

"I haven't a clue." She kept turning the pitted plastic, feeling a deep thread of connection to Gage, wherever he was. "But you're right. Nothing seems out of place here. Maybe…maybe it's just my imagination, running amok." Yet as she watched Peter Lindstrom lock up, Caro kept one hand across her chest.

The odd, crushing weight was growing worse.

* * *

"Lieutenant, we've got at least twenty men moving in from the east."

"ETA?"

"Fifteen minutes, maybe twenty. That appears to be a major weapons cache that they're protecting up here."

Gage swept the ridge with his night goggles. His orders were to secure any weapons against use by insurgent forces, and he had to act fast, before the full band returned to their mountain camp.

He raised a hand, gesturing to his point man. Silently the squads moved forward into the night. They were crossing the top of the ridge, with the weapons cases in clear sight, when the ground shook and the first earthquake hit.

# *Ten*

After a stop at his house, Peter insisted on escorting the women back home. Caro rode in his car with Bogie and Bacall, who were awake and strangely restless now. One minute they would press against Caro's lap, and the next they would turn to the window, staring out intently into the darkness.

"Something's wrong," she said softly. "Both of them are acting strange."

"It's our job to make them comfortable." The vet turned into the driveway that wound up to Caro's house, then reached back to stroke Bogart's neck. "I'd better go inside with your grandmother and be sure everything is okay. Will you be good out here for a couple of minutes?"

"Of course." Caro held Gage's cat in one arm while Peter walked around to meet her grandmother. Bogart raced ahead of them, then stopped. Suddenly the dog turned away, facing the ocean, growling low in his throat.

Caro rolled down her window. "What's wrong?"

Peter shook his head. "I don't know. I don't see anything here." The vet reached down for Bogart's collar, but the dog refused to budge, his ears angled forward.

"I can't believe I didn't think to tell you before, Caro. About an hour ago I heard something about insurgent forces on the move in Afghanistan. The television said there were clashes predicted near the border. I think we should check for updates." Peter frowned, tugging gently at the big dog's collar. "Come on, boy. There's nothing out there."

Across the grass Morgan took a quick breath. "What kind of clashes?"

"They didn't say. No details available."

*Gage.*

Suddenly cold with worry, Caro held the cat tighter. She saw Bogart strain forward, breaking free of Peter's hold. The big dog banged against the vet's legs, knocked the man sideways, then bolted across the driveway.

Small claws dug at Caro's arms.

A second later Gage's cat tore from her grip and leaped through the open car window, following Bogart off into the darkness.

"I couldn't react fast enough. I'm still too slow, too clumsy. All I got was a handful of cat fur." Caro was breathing hard, her head out the window as Peter steered his SUV slowly through the darkness. "I think they were heading up toward the meadow. After that I lost sight of them."

"Don't worry, we'll find them. Something's got them stirred up, that's all. Maybe coyotes or an owl."

Caro knew coyotes and owls could snatch a small animal like Bacall in seconds. Even the retriever might have to put up a fight against a dozen coyotes working together. "Can't you hurry, Dr. Lindstrom? We have to *find* them."

"I'm driving as fast as is safe, my dear. You know how quickly that big turn comes up on the ridge road. And I don't want to—"

His head angled forward. "There. Did you see that flash of light fur, up the hill to the right?"

Caro had seen it. She could have sworn it was the white cat, scrambling up the overgrown slope. Without a thought she unlocked her door, a flashlight gripped in her hand. "Stop, Dr. Lindstrom. I'm going after them."

"You'll do nothing of the sort. I'll park and come with you." The big wheels had barely come to a halt when Caro was running across the damp grass, heading toward the hillside. She saw another flash of white under a tree where the forest began. The growth was dense here, if she remembered correctly. And the slope stopped abruptly at a big ridge overlooking the coast.

Her heart began to pound. "We have to hurry." Her voice broke. "We can't let them get away."

Peter aimed his light across the ground in front of her. She lost her footing in the wet bushes and fell sideways, biting back a cry of pain as she landed on her right forearm. But she didn't stop, didn't even brush the dirt off her hands and face as she ran headlong up the hill, focused on the spot where she had last seen Bacall.

If only she had been faster. If only she had all her strength and her muscle control back, she could have caught the cat. And with Bacall in her arms, the dog might have returned freely.

*If only.*

*If only.*

Another flash of movement. Caro caught sight of a second shape. At least Bogie and Bacall were together. They would be safer that way.

As the moon broke from behind tattered clouds, she had a sudden glimpse of trees at the top of the ridge. On the far side of the slope, gray boulders gave way abruptly to cliffs above the interstate. Beyond that lay the sea.

Suddenly the clouds parted. Light bathed the trees and Caro saw two animals poised at the very top of the ridge. The big retriever was frozen with tension, staring down at the distant line of the interstate.

Caro had a strange flash of understanding. This had been the way that Gage had left Summer Island. The anxious dog had tracked Gage's faint scent, trying desperately to find him.

Ignoring the ache at her hands where she had fallen, she moved quietly through the high grass and sank down beside Bogart. She opened her hand on the dog's head, trying to offer a measure of comfort, which she needed just as much as Gage's animals did.

"It's okay, honey. We'll get him back. He's going to make it home fine. And so are we. That's not a promise, that's an order." Her voice broke as Gage's cat let out a restless cry and then turned, crawling into her lap.

Wind roared up from the sea, tearing at Caro's face. But they were together now. Caro would fight and defend them, the same way Gage was fighting and defending far away.

*Be careful, my love.*

The words seemed to well up from deep inside her, drawn from emotions that were still too new to name or recognize. She felt Bogie's body strain against her as he pushed at her hand, trying to move closer to the cliff, but she held him firm, speaking quiet words of reassurance. At last the dog seemed to relax.

He lay down beside Caro, his head across her knee

next to Bacall, with the cold wind riffling his thick fur. And that was the way Peter Lindstrom found them a few moments later as he strode up through the trees.

# *Eleven*

The television was filled with news of earthquakes and growing violence in Afghanistan. Caro kept a constant vigil over the next forty-eight hours, manning the news broadcasts while she listened for any emails from Gage. But nothing came.

To distract herself, Caro went to Peter's house to spend extra time with Gage's pets and then she did a double set of hand exercises. When nothing else could calm her, she curled up in a big wing chair overlooking the ocean and sketched from memory.

First she captured Bogart, jumping for Gage's Frisbee. Next came Bacall, golden in a bar of afternoon sunlight, rolling onto her back with her paws in the air as she slept.

Finally Caro sketched the dark image of the two pets huddled on the edge of the cliff, staring down at the road where Gage had left Summer Island.

"That last one is good, Caro. Actually, it's beyond good. I think I may have a buyer for it, if you're interested. She collects animal pieces for her gallery up in Seattle."

"No, Gran. This one's not for sale. None of them are." Caro didn't add that these designs would be for Gage when he came home. *Not if but when,* she thought fiercely. She'd give them to him along with the knitting she'd been working on for him every day.

She put down her pencil and stretched her cramped muscles. "Have there been any updates from Afghanistan?"

"Nothing concrete. There's something big going on, that much is clear. But no one has any details—or if they do they're not broadcasting them over public news channels. For obvious reasons." Caro's grandmother hesitated. "I might as well tell you. I put in a call to an old friend in Washington and asked if he could help find out about Gage's situation. With his connections, I think we may have an answer soon."

Morgan turned as the phone rang in the kitchen. "That's probably Peter. He was worried about us."

When Morgan came back, her face wore a dogged expression. "Let me look at your hands."

"Why? I'm fine, Gran. There were only a few scratches after I tripped in the mud. Maybe one or two bruises."

"Since you're doing fine, you won't mind me having a look." Before Caro could move back, Morgan gently pulled up the sleeves of Caro's robe.

The wild chase to recover Gage's pets had left faint bruises and jagged welts when she had fallen. Peter had bandaged them for her, but Caro had been too worried to pay attention since then.

Sighing irritably, Morgan McNeal took a medicine kit from the counter. "Fine, do you call it?" Shaking her head, Caro's grandmother began to apply a salve that Peter had given them.

"Is that veterinary salve that Peter gave me, Gran?"

"Yes, it is. Peter swears by this stuff. And if it's good enough for million-dollar racehorses cut during a training session, it should be good enough for you. Though frankly, I doubt any horse is as difficult a patient as you are."

They continued to grumble and bicker as Morgan tended to Caro's arm. It was easier that way. Grumbling helped them forget their growing worry about Gage and his men.

When the phone rang, Caro ran to answer. A stranger's voice echoed through faint static. "Is this Ms. McNeal? Caro McNeal?"

"Yes. I'm Caro. Who is this?"

There was a pause. Papers rustled. "I'm a friend. I know that you are looking for news about Lieutenant Grayson, Ms. McNeal."

Caro felt her heart pound. "Yes?" she whispered. "Gage—is he okay?"

"There's not a great deal I can tell you right now. The details are classified. I can tell you that he was involved in hostile action."

"Please tell me how he is. I *have* to *know*."

The man made an irritated sound. "It isn't good over there. Communications are in disarray. The earthquake has left some areas in rubble." Caro heard a chair creak. "I can't give you any more details."

"What are you trying to tell me? Is Gage hurt? Is he—" Caro's hand closed into a fist. *No.* She refused to consider the darkest of possibilities.

"What I am trying to tell you, Ms. McNeal, is that things are…in flux. Now that I have your direct number, I'll update you as much as possible," the man said grimly. "And I don't think I need to tell you that this conversation is highly confidential. Use utmost discretion in sharing what I have told you. Definitely not with members of the press."

"I understand. I'll be here. Please call me at this number anytime, whenever you have news. And thank you—thank you for telling me whatever you can."

Before Caro could ask anything else, the line went dead.

Caro kept her cell phone beside her at all times now. She carried it in her pocket when she took Bacall and Bogart outdoors. She had it beside her when she took her physical therapy. It sat on the sink when she showered. If anyone else called her, Caro cut off the call immediately. Meanwhile, Peter and Morgan helped her screen the news channels, watching for updates.

On the third day after her mystery call, her cell phone rang just as she was settling into sleep.

"H-hello? Yes?"

"Ms. McNeal. I have some news."

Caro struggled upright, hugging her pillow to her chest. Her heart was pounding so loud she heard it above the sound of his voice.

It was him. *Her mystery caller.*

"Yes. I'm—here."

"Your lieutenant is alive."

Caro felt her breath whoosh out in a wave. Her hands clutched at the pillow and she swallowed hard. "Thank you so much," she managed to rasp. "What can I do to help? Tell me. Anything."

A chair creaked, just like before. Caro heard someone talking in the background. Then the talking stopped. "Well, I do have an idea, Ms. McNeal. It's rather unusual.

But perhaps we live in unusual times. How soon can you get ready to travel?"

She started to ask who and where and what for. Then Caro cut off the questions. None of that mattered. Not one single thing. Whatever, wherever, she would go.

"Right now. Ten minutes. I've had a travel bag packed ever since you called. I've been waiting—hoping for news."

The man chuckled. "Smart one, aren't you? He told me that about you." Caro heard papers rustling. "Do you still have those two animals with you? Lieutenant Grayson's pets?"

Caro had expected *any* question but this one. "Yes. They're with our local vet, but he's just across town. It's very close."

"Okay." Papers rustled again. More voices came and then faded. "Well, then, you're on. Here's what I want you to do, Ms. McNeal." The man's voice took on an edge of authority, the sound of someone accustomed to a command position. "You'll need to move quickly, so get yourself a pen and take some notes. Give my regards to your grandmother, too, if you will. We were in college together." He laughed dryly. "About two centuries ago. I was the one in the yellow sweater. She'll remember. Now—do you have that pen ready?"

"Yes." Caro's head was spinning as she grabbed a notebook. "I'm ready."

"Good. First go and get Lieutenant Grayson's animals. Then here's who you need to call."

# Twelve

"What do you mean, go for a trip? Go *where?* Caro, are you feeling okay? I know you're worried about Gage, but—"

"Gran, I can't explain. I just need to go now. *Right now.*" Caro tossed an extra sweater into her suitcase, then zipped it shut. "I can't answer any questions. I'm sorry, Gran. I need you to trust me."

"Of course I trust you, honey. But why—" Morgan's eyes narrowed as she saw Caro carefully check the recent calls on her cell phone. "Someone called you a few minutes ago. You're going because of that, aren't you? Because of something you found out?"

"I—" Caro ran a hand over her eyes. "I can't tell you anything, Gran. That was part of the deal. But he did say to give you his regards."

*"He?"*

"The man who called me said he knew you in college. He said to tell you he was the one with the yellow sweater."

Morgan gave a soft laugh. "It's been years, but that boy was always a mover and a shaker. He had quite a little crush on me, too, back then. *Not* to brag." Morgan squared her shoulders. "If Harris is involved, everything will be fine. I'm going to get packed. I'll be ready to leave in fifteen minutes."

Caro picked up her bag and shook her head. Her grandmother's past was colorful and Caro knew only a small part of it. Clearly Harris, the mystery man, was an important person. Caro wondered what their true connection was.

She would have long hours to ponder that question. Her driving instructions had been very clear. "Sorry, but you can't come, Gran. I'm taking Gage's pets with me. It's part of the deal."

"You're driving?" Morgan crossed her arms, looking worried.

"That's what he told me to do."

"Then I'll fly and meet you there," Morgan said firmly. "Just where are we going?"

Within half an hour Gage's pets were stowed safely and Caro was on the road. Despite her protests, Peter had insisted on following Caro to the state line. After that he was going to drive Morgan to the airport.

Bogart and Bacall knew something important was happening. Once they were inside the car, the big dog kept moving between the seats, licking Caro energetically and whining. Bacall meowed for ten minutes, then curled up on Gage's old T-shirt and went to sleep.

They crossed the mountains and headed south. Caro gave a prayer of thanks that her last cast had finally been removed. After a fair amount of arguing, Peter waved goodbye to her at the Oregon state line, and she drove on into the darkness.

As the miles flowed past, Caro felt her life hurtling

forward, taking new shapes that couldn't be seen clearly yet. But she felt fearless now, welcoming each change, full of joy and a certainty that Gage would be part of that future.

## Southern California

Caro had never seen anything as wonderful as the sunlight gleaming off the Pacific near San Diego. She was restless and full of energy after too many cups of coffee as she studied the tile roofs and palm trees of Balboa Park.

San Diego.

This was the place.

Caro pulled out her cell phone and the name of her contact. She scratched Bogart's head and laughed as the dog tried to wedge his body between her and the side window. "Calm down, honey. We're almost there. You've been a real trooper, and our trip is nearly over."

Her heart hammered. "Let's get ready to see Gage."

Caro took several hours to rest and shower at a hotel near the freeway. Then she gave Bogart a good run and dressed carefully. Suddenly nervous, she paced in front of the mirror.

Was her sweater too tight? Or was it tight enough? And her hair—more tousled? Or less?

She wanted to look nice—but a little sexy. Okay, a lot sexy. Gage had seen her last with a cast. Not very pretty.

Half an hour later Caro's grandmother arrived from the airport, and after a quick hug, she nodded approval at Caro's choice of clothes.

"You look lovely, honey. I love that red sweater, but only leave the top three buttons open. Any more than that, and you'll be a medical hazard."

Clutching her handwritten directions, Caro drove the last mile to the Naval Medical Center, waited for gate security to let her through, and then parked. While Morgan held Gage's cat, Caro leashed the golden retriever for the short walk to the small garden where they had been directed to wait.

Five minutes passed. Nurses and attendants moved by them, smiling and nodding at the animals. Caro tossed Bogart his rope pull toy. "Your friend said someone would meet us here, Gran. I texted him when we got to the gate, the way he said."

"Great dog you have." Two wounded soldiers moved past on crutches, stopping to pet Bogart. Three more appeared. Soon Caro had a noisy group of patients clustered around her.

Bogart was restless, but gloried in all the attention, running through the commands that Peter and Caro had taught him over the past weeks. Caro managed the dog, while Bacall reluctantly accepted a leash, too, which produced even more comments.

"No animals on military grounds, ma'am. Not unless those are officially licensed service animals."

Morgan heard a clipped voice behind her. She cleared her throat. "They were approved."

"By whom?"

As she pulled Bacall away from a rosebush, Morgan had a sideways glimpse of a tall man, white hair, rows of medals against a navy uniform. "You want a name?"

"Yes, ma'am."

As Morgan watched the distinguished officer walk

toward them, recognition hit. "Harris? My heavens, I wouldn't have recognized you. So many medals. And you're just as handsome as ever."

The lean face softened. "And you are just as lethally beautiful, Morgie."

"Morgie. Dear heaven, it's been decades since anyone called me that." Morgan gripped Bacall's leash and watched the circle around Caro grow larger. Someone brought out a camera with a big flash. "You arranged this all very well, Harris. Knowing you, there is an excellent reason. So tell me."

"Morale, maybe. Or doing an old friend a favor. Maybe both."

"Good answer. Is Gage—is he here?"

Her old friend watched a second soldier pull out a camera. "They're enjoying this, I'd say. Your granddaughter looks very good at making strangers feel comfortable."

"Yes, she is. But you didn't answer my question, Harris. *Where* is Gage Grayson?"

The distinguished officer pointed to the far side of the garden. "Several of those men are from his squad. Several others didn't make it back. Things went bad fast, Morgie. Too many casualties. Without First Lieutenant Grayson, the statistics would have been a whole lot worse. We *all* owe him. I don't forget things like that," he said gruffly. His eyes darkened as he looked at her. "In fact, there are a lot of things I don't forget."

Caro felt Bogart tug at his leash, swinging around sharply. The men around her laughed as the dog pranced back and forth, tail wagging furiously.

She didn't see the small crowd behind her part. She didn't see the shadow that fell over her shoulder.

"Bogart, sit. Be good and sit, honey. It shouldn't be long now."

Caro smoothed her sweater nervously while Gage's retriever turned in a frenzied circle, barking and ignoring every command.

"Honey, settle down."

A hand opened on her shoulder.

Startled, Caro looked up. She forgot about her surroundings and the crowd gathered around her.

Her heart twisted in her chest.

He was thinner. Tougher. His face was lined and sunburned. In one glance, Caro felt as if she had come home to a place she had searched for forever, a place where this man waited, with his laugh threading through her dreams and his touch wound right around her heart.

His laugh was hoarse. Its strength filled her, just as the feel of his arms around her waist left her dizzy. In a moment she was caught against his chest while Bogart barked furiously, shoving his way between their bodies.

"I have your pictures," Gage whispered, his face against her hair, his hands locked on her waist. "I had them with me for three days, out on a ridge at the back of nowhere." He held out a crumpled, dusty computer printout. Caro saw that it was her sketch of Bacall, sleeping on her back in the sunlight. "And you told me you couldn't draw," he said in a low, rough voice.

Someone laughed. "Kiss her, Lieutenant. Go on. Stop talking already."

Gage pressed the paper into Caro's hand. "I kept it with me all the time. I could feel you when I touched it. I carried it inside my jacket day and night." His voice tightened and then he reached down, laughing when Bogart licked his hand wildly, with the full measure of a pet's unstinting love. He laughed again when he caught sight of the clumsily knit bandanna tied jauntily around his dog's neck—Caro's gift to him. Bacall was staring up at him, eyes huge.

A video camera whirred, but neither Gage nor Caro cared, oblivious to everything but each other.

Caro held out a navy blue wool hat with a misshapen, irregular brim. She smiled crookedly. "Here's your gift. It's pretty ugly, I'm afraid, but I promise that a lot of work went into it."

"I love it." Gage pulled her closer. "I would have called you, but they wouldn't let me talk. There was an explosion and I got buried. My throat was messed up. And then—well, I didn't want to write down words and have someone else say them to you."

"It sounds very sexy. I like it."

Gage traced her cheek with a bandaged hand. "Strongest woman I ever met," he said huskily.

His mouth skimmed hers and he took another raw breath. "I love you, Caro. Bogart and Bacall—we all love you. I think I loved you from the first second I saw you in that doorway back in Oregon, with dust on your cheek and sunlight in your hair." He kissed her hard. "We all want to make our life part of yours. Now and forever." His eyes were dark, searching her face. "Is that going to be a problem?"

*Now and forever.*

Caro smiled up at him, loving the feel of his hands and the little lines at the corners of his eyes. She felt dizzy and alive in a way she'd never thought was possible. "Now and forever, Lieutenant? That sounds like a good mission plan to me. You'd have to fight hard to get those two guys back now anyway. They walked into my life and charmed me right off my feet. So you've got your now and forever. But…"

Gage didn't move. "But?"

Caro slid her fingers through his hair. She watched his eyes take on depth and emotion. With a deep breath, she leaned closer, her future laid out before her.

Attitude was everything.

"My only problem right now…well, like the man just said, Gage. Why don't you stop talking and kiss me again?"

\* \* \* \* \*

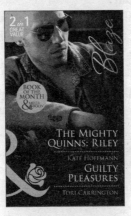

# Laughter, sunshine and love—
## spend summer in Orchard Valley

Falling in love is the last thing on Valerie's mind.
And with Dr Colby Winston, of all people! Her dad's
heart surgeon—they're complete opposites in
every way.

The Bloomfield sisters, Valerie, Stephanie and Norah,
have all returned home to help look after their
father, but romance seems to be blossoming
in Orchard Valley...

*Make time for friends.*
*Make time for Debbie Macomber.*

www.mirabooks.co.uk

M276_SIOV

# Welcome back to Cedar Cove – have you heard the news?

Have you heard? Bruce Peyton's wife has left him. She's pregnant and can't handle the stress in their household any more.

His thirteen-year-old daughter, Jolene, is jealous of Rachel and claims she ruined everything. But of course that's not true.

The real question is: how can Bruce get his wife back? And when will Jolene grow up and stop acting like such a brat?

*Make time for friends.*
*Make time for Debbie Macomber.*

www.mirabooks.co.uk

**Home, heart and family.
Sherryl Woods knows what
truly matters**

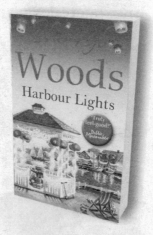

Struggling in his role as a newly single father,
former army medic Kevin O'Brien moves home to
Chesapeake Shores in search of a haven for
himself and his son.

Main Street bookseller Shanna immediately
recognises Kevin as a wounded soul—and,
with his little son in arms, Kevin is almost
impossible to resist.

Confronted with a threat to their hard-won serenity
when someone from Shanna's past appears, Kevin
and Shanna face their toughest challenge—
learning to trust again.

www.mirabooks.co.uk

**Healing families, healing hearts.
In Chesapeake second chances
happen in the most
unexpected ways.**

Bree had dreamt of seeing her name in bright
lights on Broadway, but her dreams are fading.
Going home is the perfect safe haven; she needs
time to wrap herself in her family's love
and forget everything.

But not all is peaceful and serene. Her ex-boyfriend
is demanding answers. Bree had given Jake Collins
plenty of reasons to want her out of his life,
but now she's right back in it. Is she
home for good?

www.mirabooks.co.uk